NO HARM

An absolutely gripping British crime thriller full of twists

JUDITH CUTLER

Fran Harman Mysteries Book 2

Originally published as *Cold Pursuit*

JOFFE BOOKS

Revised edition 2024
Joffe Books, London
www.joffebooks.com

First published as *Cold Pursuit* by Allison & Busby Ltd
in Great Britain in 2007

This paperback edition was first published
in Great Britain in 2024

This book is a work of fiction. Names, characters, businesses, organizations, places and events are either the product of the author's imagination or are used fictitiously. Any resemblance to actual persons, living or dead, events or locales is entirely coincidental. The spelling used is British English except where fidelity to the author's rendering of accent or dialect supersedes this.

Cover art by Nebojša Zorić

ISBN: 978-1-83526-589-5

CHAPTER ONE

'Chief Superintendent Harman! Ms Harman!'

Fran caught the eye of one of the many reporters frantically claiming her attention. The press conference room was packed this Wednesday morning. As you'd expect. Sex crimes always brought reporters out of the woodwork, especially ones they could say had a whiff of the serial rapist about them. Most questions were vacuous, eliciting bland responses, with just a few reporters making acute points she had no intention of responding to. What was this young woman's line? Her face was familiar, but Fran would swear she'd not seen her at a gathering like this before.

'Dilly Pound.'

Of course: Dilly Pound was the reporter who had precipitated the headline-catching enquiry, going first regional and then national with a piece about the rash of so far very minor assaults on teenage girls throughout the Kent area. Definitely no rapes, nor anything approaching rape, or Fran would have been the first asking questions. And not in a news conference. 'You're from TVInvicta?' Fran confirmed.

She got a nod and a rush of words. 'Is it true, Chief Superintendent Harman, that they've brought you back out of retirement to investigate these cases?'

'Golly, did I forget to park my Zimmer frame properly?' She looked about her in comic distress. 'No, Ms Pound, I hadn't retired and have no immediate intention of doing so.'

'But the case is no longer in the hands of Detective Chief Superintendent Henson?' Pound pursued.

'That's absolutely correct. But since poor Mr Henson is currently in Intensive Care following an emergency triple by-pass, I don't think he could be expected to give the problem his full attention, do you?'

In the past she might have added a quip about his heart not being in it. Those she had trained still quoted her awful puns back to her, many on her own name. None had quite got round to risking calling her 'harmless'. Indeed, if someone was in for a dressing-down, it was termed by those who feared her as being put 'in Harm's way'. Which is where she would very much like to put the next reporter who piped up, with the vacuous question, 'Is it true that the stress of the rising crime rate brought on the heart attack?'

'You'd have to ask a medic about that. Next?'

Fran actually had precious little to tell them. Her response to Dilly Pound's first question had been the literal truth. She prided herself on never lying at these events. But someone had leaked a conversation that she had thought only three other people had been privy to — the Chief Constable of Kent Constabulary; Mark Turner, the Assistant Chief Constable (Crime); and Cosmo Dix, the Head of Human Resources. But this was Headquarters, where there were always rumours sprinting round. She wouldn't waste too much time or energy finding the mole, less still whacking it. No harm done, after all.

Pound was on her feet again.

'You have a reputation for being one of the best police officers in the country. Is it true that you were the first officer to take these attacks seriously?'

Best to ignore the compliment, though it brought a surprising glow. 'Every officer takes every incident seriously, from bad Zimmer-parking—' she paused for the predictable groan — 'to murder. When a pattern seems to emerge, then we take them even more seriously.'

'And it's true a pattern is emerging?'

Fran smiled. 'As I saw on the news the other evening, you and your colleagues at TVInvicta have already suggested there might be a pattern. We've already been able to eliminate some of the assaults you've recorded from this possible pattern. But others will be the focus of our on-going investigation. And now, ladies and gentlemen, more talk means less work. So if you'll excuse me . . .'

Pound didn't take the hint. 'Do you agree with the theory that criminals who commit serious sexual offences often begin their careers with petty harassment?'

'That depends on the nature of the harassment. Whatever these episodes may or may not lead to, Ms Pound, they are upsetting to the victims and as such we intend to find the perpetrators.' She overrode a frantic observation that she'd used the plural, not the singular. 'We have a very strong team of detectives, led by DCI Jill Tanner, normally working in Ashford. But for the time being she will be based here at Police Headquarters in Maidstone, where we have all the latest facilities. As you can see', she gestured to Tanner, a woman in her later forties, who responded with a suddenly gamine grin, 'DCI Tanner can hardly be regarded as geriatric either. Ladies and gentlemen, if there's anything to report to you, there will be another conference at this time tomorrow. Meanwhile, if any of your readers, listeners or viewers have any information — and remember, many of these crimes took place in broad daylight — DCI Tanner and I would be more than grateful if they would contact the incident room or Crime Stoppers or their local police station. You'll find all the phone numbers on the reverse of your sheets. Thank you.' She made a great play of struggling to her feet and tottering from the room, earning a smatter of applause.

'There, that wasn't so bad, was it?' she asked Jill, as they got into the corridor.

'Not when you're on top of your brief,' the younger woman agreed. 'But you seem to be able to fence with them in a way I've never managed.'

'*Make 'em laugh, make 'em cry* and above all *make 'em wait* until you're ready to tell them what you want them to know. Come on, Jill, you've given enough press conferences in your time. You've even taught some of our media handling training courses.'

'You make them sound like badly behaved dogs!'

'And the difference is? Now, have you got everything you need? Because I'm going to bollock Personnel or Human Resources or whatever it calls itself today about that sodding leak.'

* * *

'Mole? Absolutely not me, Fran,' Cosmo insisted half an hour later. 'Though I must say the rumours that you'd been plucked from the life of a retired Reilly to rescue the other plods gave a certain dramatic frisson. By the way, we've already fielded a call from Auntie Beeb: they want you to get back to them ASAP. Between you and me,' he whispered, leaning forward confidentially, 'I think they want you for regular appearances on *Crimewatch*.'

At heart not convinced by his denial, Fran nibbled at his bait. 'Regular? Not just this harassment case?'

'Nope. That's a bit trivial as yet, isn't it? It's for when you finally hang up your handcuffs. The camera *lurves* you, no doubt about that. Well, we recorded the whole press conference — you can see for yourself.'

'Cameras always add at least half a stone and ten years in wrinkles, so thanks but no thanks.' She edged to the door.

'That Dilly — another nice-looking woman, if I may say so — she never took her eyes off you.'

'New on the block, isn't she?' Fran had almost escaped but couldn't resist stopping to ask.

'Apparently. According to the gossip column in the local freebie, she's not worked long in the media. Did something else completely different, had some sort of mid-life crisis (well, she was in her thirties, which nearly counts) and then toddled off and got herself a journalism degree. So Bob's your aunt.'

With an amiable wave, Fran swung off enjoying not being retired. This part, at least. She had a fair idea she wouldn't enjoy the rest of it. At her level, it wasn't a detective's job to get out on the mean streets; she paced the rather meaner corridors where back-stabbing was of the verbal, career-impeding sort. No worse, no better than any comparable organisation such as a university, she supposed, two of which had invited her to join their staff as a visiting lecturer. And presumably the other bane of her life, meetings, would be just as prevalent elsewhere too. So perhaps, when she'd shredded her resignation letter in response to yesterday's anguished appeal from the Chief Constable himself, she'd merely declined to jump into the fire of university life, staying in her familiar frying pan.

* * *

Fran had been summoned, at eight-thirty the previous morning, to the Chief Constable's office. Waiting for her were the Chief himself, Cosmo Dix, and Mark Turner.

'Postpone my retirement? But my resignation's been in a week!'

She'd looked from the Chief to Mark, present in his capacity not as her live-in lover but as ACC (Crime) and looking as impassive as he could. Was this his idea? She'd thought he'd been in favour of her taking a career break. They'd chewed it over long enough, goodness knew. Surely he wasn't doing a *volte face* now.

He looked as blank as she did.

If — and it was a big if — she was going to do what the Chief wanted, she wanted Mark's positive agreement.

Acquiescence wasn't enough. Equally she had no intention of appearing before the Chief as anything except her own woman, so she could hardly ask for an adjournment to talk it over.

'Well?' the Chief prompted. 'Come on, Fran. You'd no particular plans, had you? You've been a loyal officer for thirty-odd years: surely you can't let us down now!'

The bugger. He knew she'd respond like one of Pavlov's greedy salivating dogs to the words *loyal* and *can't let us down* and so she bloody did. At least enough to ask, 'You're absolutely sure you can't free up another officer to take on Henson's role?'

'Would I be asking you if I could?' he replied. 'Come on, Fran, just three weeks, four at most, until we can get the proper advertising and interviewing procedures in place.'

She shot a look at Mark.

'The advertising and interviewing procedures you drew up,' he agreed.

So that was the way his vote was going. And there was no doubt who would have to shoulder the extra work if she turned her back on it. The ACC (Crime). He worked a damned sight harder than most his rank. She wouldn't have him risk his health by taking on more.

She agreed slowly, 'Just until you have a proper temporary replacement for Henson. I'm happy to act as his or her mentor, but then I'm off. After all, it's not entirely policy to encourage partners to work together.' She nodded in Mark's direction.

The Chief huffed a bit. 'That mostly applies if they're lower down the ranks and in a . . . transient . . . relationship.'

'And younger than Mark and me?' Her tongue was well concealed in her cheek.

'These days I think most officers are younger than us three.' The Chief sounded like Eeyore, minus his tail, and cast a waspish glance at the absurdly young-looking Dix, hitherto — sensibly — completely mum.

'Come, sir, no clichés about youthful constables! They're for the public to spout,' Dix said, perhaps unwisely.

There was a silence Fran found herself filling. 'OK, if it gets you and Mark out of a hole, I'll stay. So long as I can delegate. And so long as the people I delegate to get appropriate recognition, in terms of rank and pay.'

Mark spoke for the first time. 'So you'll sit back with your feet on the desk while others run themselves ragged? That'll be a first, Fran!'

The Chief was not amused. 'OK, Dix, that's it for now. Get Fran's resignation into the shredder immediately, will you? Now,' he continued, while Cosmo was still picking up his file, 'the first thing will be to set up a team to deal with all these assaults. I want them stopped, now.'

Fran waited till the door was firmly closed. 'With respect, sir, they fall into two quite different types. There's the kids' stuff — this horrible new game some cretin's devised and miscalled "happy-slapping", which I'd have thought best dealt with by local forces and community support officers — and the man-on-woman assaults, which really are alarming.'

'You're telling me that if your son or daughter comes home with a black eye delivered simply to amuse other children filming it on their mobile phones, there's no point in calling us because it's trivial!' he thundered. Of course, he was a parent, wasn't he?

'Of course it should be taken seriously, and of course we should be involved. I'm just saying I think it should be dealt with by people with local knowledge of schools, youth clubs, and places where kids hang out — and not shunted up the food-chain. We have expertise the locals don't have, but not in that area.'

'I can't agree. The public expects something high profile.'

Fran bit back a series of scathing ripostes. He was, after all, the Chief, who must be obeyed. If she argued, it would fall to Mark to back one or other of them, an invidious decision he shouldn't have to make.

'Very well,' she nodded. 'In that case, if it's going to be one big investigation, and with women the victims, I think we should have a woman running it.'

Mark nodded. 'What about that DCI in Ashford?'

'Jill Tanner?' the Chief queried. 'She's very . . . homely.'

Fran chose to ignore the implicit sexism. 'I know. Her office at Ashford nick looks like her sitting room at home: you can't see the dust for family photos.'

'You know her that well? Visiting her at home?'

'We've been mates ever since she joined the force.' All the same, she wasn't a hundred per cent happy with Mark's suggestion. 'Jill's good, all right. But even though she's a friend, I have to ask, do you really think she's good enough?'

Mark might have been about to step down, but the Chief was in there with both feet. 'He wouldn't have suggested her otherwise.'

Mark blinked. 'She was only one name amongst several, sir.'

The phone rang. The Chief took the call, snapped at the caller, and replaced the handset, all in the space of a minute. He looked at his watch. Clearly he didn't have long to resolve the issue.

'Tell me about Tanner.'

Mark wrongfooted her. 'You know she played at Wimbledon as a junior?'

'You're joking!'

'He's not, sir,' Fran said. 'We've played badminton a couple of times, but I only beat her because I'm so much taller and my reach is longer.'

'But you were county champion.' He was stowing items in his briefcase.

'In my youth. Anyway, she zips about the court like a flea on speed. You should see her chasing a suspect. They think they've got some nice mumsy old dear after them and before they know it she's got them in an arm lock that brings tears to their eyes. No villain ever tries to escape her twice. And she's brainy as well as brawny. She's got an OU Master's on top of her original degree. God knows how she does it, with a family to care for too.' Juggling family demands was something Fran had been expert in, even if her family had been at the opposite end of the age-scale. 'Which is why I'm concerned we don't put extra—'

Briefcase now in hand, the Chief said, 'So we'll have a press conference first thing tomorrow, which will give her today to whip together a team and set up her incident room here.'

Mark had picked up on her reservations. 'Well, there are other officers I'd have liked to run past you. But it's your decision, sir.' He sounded as grudging as if he hadn't spoken the literal truth.

'Fran?' the Chief prompted, hand on door.

'As Mark says, it's your decision, sir.'

And they would have to live with it, for better, for worse, because he was no longer in the room to argue with.

* * *

'You are absolutely sure about staying on longer?' Mark had prompted, letting her into his car, at the end of the working day.

'I'm not so much sure as relieved,' she confessed at last, buckling her seat belt. She and Mark had made it a rule to be honest, if humanly possible. Another was that while it was permitted to tie off loose ends on the drive to whoever's house they happened to be living in that week, talking shop once the front door was shut was totally forbidden. 'It puts off the evil day of retirement a little longer.'

'And saves you having to decide which of the tempting job offers — three now? — to accept.' When she said nothing, he added, 'Oh, Fran, why didn't you admit you didn't want to retire? Silly girl.'

A girl. At fifty-five. But she felt like one these days, breathing the heady air of middle-aged love.

'I wasn't sure that I did, much as I've enjoyed the last few months working on that "dead" case.'

'When you were essentially working on your own at your own pace without those banes of your life, working parties and government initiatives. You'll have those aplenty again now.'

'And Jill will be leading the team,' she added, not permitting herself a sigh. 'But the good thing is that since we're mates we can exchange ideas without either of us losing face. Not like Henson and me.' It had been hard for them to exchange the time of day, let alone vital information.

'All the same.'

She touched his hand, which turned to squeeze hers reassuringly. 'And working in the same building with you is very nice.' Sharing a car, managing lunch occasionally: she wanted to snatch every moment of his company that she could. Hell, she was still like a teenager with a giant crush on the captain of cricket.

It might have been the traffic that made him frown. Removing his hand, he said nothing until he'd cut across into the lane he needed. 'It's just that . . . I suppose we couldn't break the rule and talk about it tonight?'

'It'll be a bit late then, surely.'

'It's already a bit late actually.' He managed a rueful grin. 'I can't see you tripping in tomorrow and telling everyone you've changed your mind. Of course, there's no denying it'll get us out of a hole. And no denying you'll do a great job, whether supervising or being hands on. It's just the hours you'll have to work that worry me.'

'Nearly as long as yours? Come on, how many times have I had to kick my heels here while you finished some document the Home Office wanted yesterday? How else do you think I've managed to get my paperwork up to date and my desk so tidy?' she added.

'I'm glad it served some useful purpose, anyway. But now your desk will be cluttered again, and it may be me waiting for you. Maybe we should revert to taking two cars again.' He sounded resigned, gloomy, even, rather than critical.

'Why don't you pull over and we'll talk this through? You're obviously not happy,' she continued, as he took no apparent notice. 'Is it because we shall find ourselves in professional disagreement from time to time? Like this morning, when I could have wrung your neck for banging on about Jill's virtues? Because we've managed before. I'm sure we will again.'

For answer he dropped his hand from the wheel on to hers again, flashing the smile that took ten years off him. 'If you're happy, I'm happy.'

It wasn't quite enough. The old Fran wanted to nag and worry at it, but the new one would try to take everything he'd said at face value, hard though it sometimes was. Now wasn't the moment for a heart-to-heart, anyway. One of their colleagues was giving the blues and twos to all before him as he tried to make the red sea of rush hour tail-lights part. Mark pulled neatly on to the kerb, and then dropped back onto the road.

'At least neither of us has to work shifts,' he said, nodding at the vanishing tail-lights, 'like that poor bugger. Rush hour RTA I suppose. I always hated dealing with crashes after dark — worse than in daylight, with everything rendered ghastly by the emergency vehicles' lights. And the blood a funny colour . . .' He changed tone deliberately and audibly. 'Now, can I pop into my house before we go on to yours?'

'We can stay at yours if needs be. I've got plenty of clothes there.' Not to mention her make-up, laptop and yellow Marigolds, still on his draining board after her determined and possibly vain efforts to clean his oven. During his wife's last illness, though he had mastered the roast — to perfection, Fran was the first to declare — he'd never realised the concomitant part of roasting meat and potatoes, cleaning the oven. Since she had systematically neglected her gutters, and, indeed, much other house maintenance while she made regular dashes to Devon to help keep her aged parents in their own home, he offered reciprocal help.

At least she no longer had to worry about her parents. Her father had died after a fall, and her mother was now in Scotland, ruling the roost in a retirement home and battling daily with her older daughter, an activity both seemed to enjoy, though neither as much as her brother-in-law, who might have set the whole thing up simply for his entertainment.

For the first time in twenty years, she was free — to do anything she wanted.

Except now her cottage had decided to interfere. On the outskirts of the picture postcard village of Lenham, it was absorbing effort like three-dimensional blotting paper, and she found herself rationing the time they spent there. Mark's work life was as exhausting as hers, and he needed to relax as much as she did.

'Let's eat and then decide where we stay,' he suggested.

In other words, yes. It made sense. So he turned off to Loose, the village — more like a suburb of Maidstone — where he lived in an Edwardian house she always found forbidding. Loose, home to a Thomas Telford bridge, was correctly pronounced to rhyme with *whose*, but provided them with endless opportunities to pun. She rather thought the pretty Victorian ring she sported on her engagement finger might be a response to jocular colleagues' suggestions she was a Loose Woman, since neither she nor Mark had ever mentioned marriage.

If, in the kitchen, he was a roast man, she — since their thirty years of friendship had blossomed into love a couple of months ago — was a quick and speedy woman. She had graduated from supermarket-prepared stir-fries with the aid of a pile of books. Jill Dupleix, Nigel Slater, and Jamie Oliver were all her heroes now. Some lodged in her kitchen, some in his, friends supporting her when occasionally she was all too aware of the ghost of Tina, Mark's late wife, hovering over her shoulder to offer intimidating advice. The shelves of jams, pickles and chutneys testified to her industry. Or perhaps the poor woman had just wanted to leave something behind when she'd gone. Was that how Mark saw them, as a culinary memorial? Certainly she'd never seen him eat any preserve from their ranks.

'Do we need a supermarket run?' he asked.

'Not after last night's! There's plenty in the fridge.'

'Champagne to celebrate your decision?'

'Probably some of that, too.'

'I can think of another way to celebrate, too.'

'So can I!' And the jars in the kitchen paled into insignificance.

CHAPTER TWO

I've been searching for you, my darling, so very long, and now I've found you at last. I can't wait to see you again.

* * *

Jill Tanner was looking around her new base with less than enthusiasm, though Cosmo had installed her in the quite palatial surroundings of Henson's office. 'If this is Henson's room, shouldn't you have moved in here?'

Hierarchically, Fran should have done. 'I'm happy where I am,' she said, offhand.

It was one thing to admit to Jill as a friend the reason she wanted to stay put, but quite another to admit it to Jill as an officer working under her. Mark had allocated her office to her when she was at a particularly low point in her personal life. He had also organised its redecoration and had it furnished, and she liked to think of it as his first love token.

'I suppose it's very chic,' Tanner said doubtfully, touching the blond wood desk. 'But I hate to think how much of the budget this has consumed. And it's a bit . . . sort of male, isn't it?'

Fran grinned. 'I'm sure you'll get rid of any nasty vibes Henson's left lying around — they'll be black and spiky, should you come across them.'

'And I bin them? Or try to recycle them?'

'Definitely don't put them in the green bin, or they'll contaminate everything. That yellow medical sharps bucket in the FME's room should do the job. Now, you know where everything is, you've met the team, and you're ready to go. And you promise to let me have any tiny tasks no one else wants — just so I keep my hand in.'

'On those days when you don't have wall-to-wall meetings?'

It should have sounded like a joke, but didn't. It didn't sound like matey sarcasm, either. It sounded more like an anxious plea for professional hand-holding, as it were, as if the room blurred her confidence, even though only a moment ago she'd been joking with Fran as an equal.

'I'd welcome anything to provide an excuse to keep the meetings short. Some of those Home Office guys think all we have to do is formulate impossible policies. They forget we have to implement them.'

At least that provoked a laugh. 'And you want to come to our briefings?'

'Whenever I can. So long as no one thinks it's to check up on you. That stint working on my own to sort out that Persistent Vegetative State victim case was an eye-opener: I'd forgotten the adrenaline rush that comes when you're on the chase.' She smiled reminiscently. She checked her watch. 'Hell, is there such a thing as an adrenaline drain?'

* * *

Jill must have seen her sneak into the back of the Major Incident Room as she was in mid-spiel but she didn't so much as falter. '. . . So I want us to interview every single young woman who has reported an assault, however trivial it may seem. Even if it doesn't appear to be part of our pattern, log it. I'm sure the government would be delighted if we introduced a zero-tolerance policy on violence towards women.'

'Does that include domestic violence?' came a male voice from the front, the groan implicit.

'Under Chief Superintendent Harman's regime it always has, or so I understood.' Jill strained to see. 'Has anything changed, guv?'

Fran stood up. 'Not that I know of. Now, I should imagine we'll pick up some girl-on-girl violence. Policy is to treat that seriously, whether it's casual bullying or happy-slapping. Hell, what's happened to a society where kids gratuitously assault an innocent victim purely for the pleasure of showing as many people as possible what they've done?' There was a murmur of agreement, not altogether to do with her rank, she hoped. 'Now, I want to stress, everyone, that I'm part of this team, neither more nor less. My obvious role will be backstage, to expedite any equipment or back-up you need. But I'm also here as another pair of hands should you need them.' She waved them, palms out, fingers straight, like a stiff puppet. 'Part of the team,' she repeated. 'Not its leader. That's DCI Tanner. Is that clear? Great.' Suppressing an urge to ask what they'd found so far, sitting down firmly, she looked back at Jill. It was her call.

Accepting it, Jill pointed to the map affixed to the whiteboard. 'You can see these clusters are similar to those originally shown on TVInvicta's piece.'

A correspondent from Tunbridge Wells could now quite legitimately sign himself 'Disgusted' — a couple of girls from a quite exclusive seminary had been goosed in the Great Hall Arcade, and another young woman complained of similar treatment in Royal Victoria Arcade. All three assaults had taken place in broad daylight within about three hours of each other the previous Saturday. The MacArthur Glen Outlet, a shopping mall near Ashford, reported a man hanging round near one set of ladies loos, but the CCTV had failed to pick him up. In Canterbury things were rather more serious, with flashing involved. The same in Dover and Folkestone. The series — if series it was — had sprung up quite suddenly, as if someone had flicked a switch.

A hand went up. It was Tom Arkwright's. Fran had worked closely with him before, and had him down as a bright and enthusiastic lad who was more sensitive than would be comfortable for him if he wanted to stay in the force. 'Guv, is there anything to link all these other than the TV news? They don't seem to have any connection at all — not from what I can see, like,' he added, as if he'd gone too far.

'One peculiarity in the MO for one thing — at least in the flashing incidents,' Jill responded. 'It seems that when he's finished wanking, Chummie likes to wipe what his willy's produced on to the victim's clothes. And seminal fluid has been found on the clothing of the girls who complain of being groped.'

It wouldn't have been Fran's choice or words, but she couldn't deny that Jill had everyone's interest.

'And one child — thirteen — had it wiped on her face.'

'God, that's sick! They didn't mention it on the news, though,' Tom reflected. 'I suppose they wouldn't, not before the watershed, like, would they?'

'You never know with the media,' someone observed darkly. 'I suppose it's the same DNA, guv?'

'It is. But we have no other record of it on file. The guy's a first offender.'

'Then the attacks really are getting more overtly sexual?' Tom again, surprising Fran with his change of tone and vocabulary. Well, that was what graduate entrants were supposed to do.

'Not as far as we know, that face stuff apart. But kinky is as kinky does, and I don't want him to get the chance of being any weirder. Nor — and I stress this absolutely — do we want this information to go beyond the team. Imagine what the media would make of it, especially the red tops. OK, to work, everyone. Get those computers sparking with information.'

But a hand went up. 'Any chance of anyone acting as bait? You know, a young PC?'

Jill's face didn't so much as crack. 'Chummie prefers thirteen-year-olds, DS Swann. Anything else?'

* * *

'This is what you get when you're media-driven, not crime-driven,' Fran said, jabbing a canteen lunch cherry tomato with unnecessary violence. It responded by bursting all over her shirt. She tipped her bottle of water on to a tissue and scrubbed furiously.

'For which that poor innocent tomato has just provided a perfect image,' Mark suggested. 'You poke away at something long and hard enough and you get a big mess. I think you've got rid of the stain now, but you've got tissue-fluff everywhere.'

She had. She picked off individual shreds. 'Loves me, loves me not . . .' When she concluded on 'loves me not', in a rare public declaration, he replaced a speck. 'Loves me!' she beamed.

He gave a furtive left-right check.

In response, she put a finger to her lips, shrugging extravagantly. Didn't everyone know, for goodness' sake? But it was his whim to pretend their relationship was covered by the Official Secrets Act. In any case, did it still qualify as simply a relationship after all this time? Surely it would be more properly described as a partnership? But she still couldn't refer to him as her partner without producing a mental image of herself and a spotty youth in a patrol car.

She retrieved the conversation. 'So you think we should press on the search for the phantom fingerer?'

'It's like the man says, you've started so you'll have to finish.'

'At least until the media simmer down,' she agreed, pragmatically. 'Or Henson returns and squashes everything.' Their eyes met, and dropped to the tomato. The canteen rang with their laughter. 'I did think,' she added seriously, 'of suggesting a profiler.'

'But you know what the Chief thinks of them. And truly, it's still pretty low level.'

'Until it gets higher. And by then, if we're not careful, he'll have twigged we've got our eyes open and use a condom, which he'll carefully remove from the scene.'

* * *

Though a budget meeting kept her occupied all afternoon, the implications putting a huge question mark over the expense of a profiler before she'd even mooted the idea, she made a point of dropping in on Jill before she left.

'I've just fielded my sixth phone call from a head teacher wanting one of us to talk to their girls,' she wailed. 'Sixth different head, I mean. How not to get groped. And I can see the point—'

'You need someone to intercept your calls,' Fran said, making a note to contact the switchboard and talk to Cosmo about finding a temporary secretary for her. 'And you really don't have to do all the talks yourself. How about Crime Prevention?'

'They want positive female role models. Top brass.'

Fran interrupted the hopeful glance with a basilisk stare. 'And they all want the same thing?' She frowned. 'Are they some sort of educational mafia?'

'They must have had some meeting or other — all posh girls' schools.'

'And you said?'

Jill stuck out a lip, like a child caught in a fib. 'See what I can do. Made no promises. But they'll be back, I know they will.' She stared at the handset with something like terror.

'How about a female Crime Prevention team now and something like a tour of selected parts of the place when everything's sorted? Nothing like a trip around HQ with all the sexy lads in uniform to help recruitment. Photo opportunities too.'

Jill looked mulish. 'For a load of posh girls who won't ever have to work? Bugger that for a game of soldiers!' So the class war wasn't dead. 'Are we going to turn out to every bog-standard comp?' Bitter quotation marks inserted themselves almost visibly. 'Every bog-standard secondary modern, this county being what it is? They'll probably ask for crime prevention for just the grammar school kids, not the others, if I know them!'

What could one say to a tirade like that? Nothing. But suddenly Fran's brain fired in a quite different direction. 'Is there, as a matter of interest, any breakdown of the educational background of the girls who've been groped? It might just be worth checking, Jill.'

* * *

'Terminal neglect,' Fran wailed, as Mark knelt with a pair of inadequate pliers trying to fix a loose toilet seat — loose as in not safely secured, and in Lenham. 'What this place needs is a team of maintenance men devoting themselves to it for a clear two weeks. And another couple of minions for the garden, full-time, in perpetuity.'

'First find your maintenance men,' he groaned. 'That's the best I can do, I'm afraid.' He scrabbled to his feet. 'How about that for your post-retirement career? A job in plumbing?'

'First find your course. Last I heard, post-graduate scientists were queuing round the block for a college place. And I don't so much need a plumber as a whole new bathroom and kitchen. Avocado: who'd imagine that it was the colour to die for once? Brand new when I bought the place — that's why I've put up with it so long.'

'That, and never being in the place to see it. How many years were you constantly careering down to Devon to your parents? On top of the sort of hours you always worked? Well, then. But there's no reason not to change it now. You could move into my place full time, for as long as it takes. In fact,' he continued, perching beside her on the edge of the bath, 'I was — Drat!' He fished for his phone.

Simultaneously she fished for hers. The message was the same. Another flashing incident, this time in Whitstable.

'Gets around, doesn't he?' Mark observed. 'No reason for either of us to dash to the seaside, is there? Not in the dark, at this time of night? Come on, Fran — this is a CID job, true, but you've got to let others do the legwork. You know that.'

'So I do. And you. All we've got to do is pity the poor buggers out there and toast them with a single malt.'

'All the same . . .'

* * *

The police station in Whitstable was a part-time office, only open in shop-hours, and not even all of them. The policy always made Fran fume, as did the closure of local A and E units — in the interests, management inevitably asserted, of helping the public. As if a closed door with an inadequate answerphone link to the nearest nick was any substitute for a live bobby. So they headed to Canterbury, simply to assure, in Fran's case, the parents that a senior woman officer was taking the child's allegations seriously, and in Mark's to appear to be showing a decent interest in the drones.

Fran's task was the more traumatic. A child of twelve had had her first contact with semen when a handful of the stuff had been wiped across her mouth and nose. She was still shuddering, still retching. Fran took her by the hands, and then responded as she wanted, by taking her in her arms and letting her cry.

'I'll get the bastard,' she said, making a personal promise.

* * *

On the grounds that they were in the city anyway, they headed off to a Vietnamese restaurant. Halfway through their main courses, Mark let slip that it was his late wife's favourite.

Had someone sucked all the nam pla from her curry? But she mustn't get twitchy. She'd known and liked Tina, after all, and done all she could at work to take on Mark's workload so he could spend time either at home or latterly at the hospice. Mark's house wasn't a shrine, any more than hers was to her fiancé, Ian, who'd died of a brain haemorrhage. But she'd never have told Mark about Ian's favourite eateries. Tact or timidity? Was she afraid of upsetting him or irritating him?

'You're very quiet,' he prompted her.

'Long day.'

'I know. But you were perky enough until we came here. I thought you liked Vietnamese.' He sounded pained.

'I do. I love it. And this is a brilliant restaurant. I once won a free meal here, in some church raffle.'

He eyed her. 'So you brought Ian.'

So it was all right for him, but not for her? At least he'd had long loving years with Tina, whereas she and Ian weren't even living together when one of her colleagues had brought the news of his death. She swallowed, trying very hard. 'We both cart our ghosts round with us, don't we? Ian only came here on sufferance, him being a fierce Indian curry man. He never found the same pleasure in other cuisines, no matter how spicy. But it was Tina's favourite place.' Her face was so taut it was hard to make the smile genuine.

'Heavens, we can't wipe out our histories! Even assuming we want to!' He pushed away his bowl.

'Of course we can't. But we need to establish a mutual history, not exclusive ones.'

He stared. 'You're not jealous of the dead!'

'No. Yes. I probably am. Not jealous, but aware that there are great chunks of your life where I was just someone from work, just as you were simply the boss for me. Aren't you aware of missing out on my life?'

'I don't understand.' At least he pulled his bowl back and started to eat again.

She took a deep breath. 'I just wish you'd known my body when I was young and slim and didn't have saggy breasts and hair that needed help from a bottle of colour.'

'I love you just as you are.' For a declaration of love it sounded remarkably edgy.

'And I you.' But in a cubbyhole of her heart, one that must clearly remain firmly locked, she admitted that he might have been even sexier in his footballing and cricketing days, when he carried if possible less spare flesh than he did now. Only she'd never realised it, had she, and must just count herself extraordinarily lucky now. Many another man would have simply disciplined her for failing to do her job properly — she was sure that was what the Chief had told him to do. Instead he had found an imaginative way round her problems, and at some point had fallen in love with her. And she with him, quite painfully.

Was there some rulebook for the mature lovers attempting to blend quite different lives? If not, there ought to be — and the first copy would leap into her hands. Teenage love was supposed to be the worst, wasn't it, all acne and hormones. But no one could tell her that middle-aged hormones weren't just as vicious, either when they were absent or when they came surging in almost uninvited, crowding an already overfull life and landing you with two houses neither of which you both liked, both demanding attention with the insistence of an incontinent geriatric.

'In fact,' she said, dabbing her lips and smiling, 'I'm not sure I want to bother with a dessert. What about you?' At least bed — or the living room floor — was one place they could always resolve their problems.

* * *

'Does watching the late news count as work?' she asked later over a Glenfiddich. 'Come on, yes or no?'

'Well,' he considered, pulling her feet on to his lap, and massaging away the day's cares, 'it all depends. Yes and no, I'd say. Depending on whether you want to watch it or ought to watch it.'

'If I don't it's work?'

'You might want to pick up the football results in which case it's not work.'

The work story was actually the main one after the break. 'Parents all over Kent are threatening to keep their daughters at home after the latest attack on a teenage girl in Whitstable. This attack, worse than the others which have shocked parents and terrified young girls throughout the county and led to threats to boycott schools, is number twenty-three overall, and the seventh this month.' The reporter was Dilly Pound, the woman who had been so pressing at Wednesday's press conference. She reminded Fran of a schoolteacher, in her calm delivery — somewhat at odds with the emotive language of the report. A familiar computer graphic obligingly showed each cluster of offences.

'Is that true?' Mark asked, dropping her foot abruptly. 'Is there really a school boycott?'

'I'd certainly want to know if there was — and not via TV!'

Suddenly Jill Tanner's face was on the screen, her hair blown into a frenzied halo.

'That can't be Tanner!' Mark dropped Fran's feet. 'She looks more like a bag lady than the senior officer in charge of a sensitive case,' he added, strongly disapproving.

'Blame the lighting,' Fran agreed. 'We've got a perfectly good room for interviews like this, so why have they dragged her outside? Why go for that ghoulish shadowing? And why let the wind blow away all her carefully prepared words? Who could ever trust a spokesperson like that? What with that and their allegations, I think I may get on the phone to TVInvicta tomorrow and have a word. I don't like it when the media try to undercut an investigation. Not when we do all in our power to feed them stories and cooperate with them.'

'I suppose we can't blame the TV people if she doesn't comb her hair.'

'Just watch me.' She squeezed his hand. 'You protected me when I needed it; I must do the best I can for her. Mustn't I?'

CHAPTER THREE

It won't be long now, I promise. And then I shall never leave you. Wherever you go, I shall go too.

* * *

It was possible for someone of Fran's rank to summon the TVInvicta News editor to her office, but since she had a morning dental appointment in Canterbury she decided to pay him the apparent courtesy of visiting him in his office in the new Whitefriars complex.

If Jill Tanner had found Henson's office overly masculine and unwelcoming, goodness knew what she'd have made of this. The view might have been to die for — at night the floodlit tower of the Cathedral would dominate it — but there seemed a distinct whiff of MFI about the executive furniture, and the room itself was rather smaller than her own. But there was nothing to relieve the white walls or the laminate floor, and she suspected the blinds had never been used in anger. Someone was making a statement, even if he didn't quite know what it was.

'Clearly you're here over something more than an unpaid speeding fine,' Huw Venn stood to greet her, possibly wondering whether to emerge from behind his desk to shake her hand but deciding better of it.

'Do you have any outstanding?' Fran inquired, eyes wide open. 'I'm afraid I don't do American Express.'

'So what brings such a senior officer in the flesh?' In his pink and white baby-face, his eyes, dark as his carefully tousled hair, narrowed perceptibly. He might have been in his late thirties, or well-preserved forties.

Uninvited, she sat. Perhaps he was grateful — their difference in height was less obvious, and not every male ego liked being seven or eight inches shorter than his interlocutor. 'The excellent research your people have been doing on the sex assault cases.'

'Doing your job for you, eh?' He sat too, spreading his pudgy hands over an incipient paunch, as if he were a provincial Citizen Kane.

'Absolutely.' She kept her face straight. 'That sort of coverage really reaches the public consciousness in a way we couldn't hope to do.'

He was too bright to smirk. 'But?' he demanded.

'But that sort of power carries responsibilities, Mr Venn. All that stuff last night about people keeping their teenagers at home, not letting their children go to school — tell me, do you know something we don't, or are you making a story where there isn't one?'

'We only report the story as it comes to us, Chief Superintendent. If we hear mothers crying because their daughters have been raped—'

'My God, it's come to that, has it?' she asked seriously. 'Where's the victim been taken?'

'You know what I mean,' he said pettishly.

'What's your background, Mr Venn?' She continued calmly, 'You see, I've never met a TV journalist who invented stories to raise his profile. The red tops, yes. But I can't see how spreading needless alarm throughout Kent is going to do anyone any good. It certainly won't help us stop these crimes, and may make our job of finding the perpetrator more difficult.'

Damn it, he pounced. 'You think it's just one man, do you?'

'Whatever I may think is currently immaterial. What my colleagues and I need is evidence we can — and will — work on. I'm not a woman for theories, Mr Venn. I like facts.'

He produced a sudden impish smile, not wholly attractive. 'Detective Chief Superintendent Gradgrind!'

Touché! She would have loved to ask if his Hardyesque name was genuine, but preferred to seize the moment. 'I'm afraid the majority of your viewers wouldn't recognise your allusion — even if it went national. But only TVInvicta carried last night's story: the national network wouldn't touch it. Why do you think that was, Mr Venn?' she asked, her voice still eminently reasonable.

He shrugged. 'They had another story! It's not every day you get a cabinet minister caught with his trousers down. They spent a lot of time on that.'

'So they did. It's a good job really — we wouldn't want the good burghers of Bridgewater, Bolton and Birmingham getting the impression that we've got Jack the Ripper cavorting round Kent, would we? To be serious, Mr Venn, what you did last night was dangerous. You created a whole fabric of non-information and made one of our most capable officers look a fool because she could say nothing new or useful. Come on, if you were a concerned parent would you believe that a distressed scarecrow, badly lit and with a poor mike, could trace your child's assailant?'

'I'm not responsible for some woman's bad hair day.'

'Of course not. But when Detective Chief Inspector Tanner offered your colleagues the use of a perfectly good room, they insisted on the outside location. And lit her so that she looked like a Hallowe'en pumpkin and fastened her mike the far side of a wind farm. I presume,' she prompted him, 'that that was an editorial decision, not just some artistic whim on the part of a cub reporter?'

'I rely absolutely on the discretion of the reporter,' he said.

'Just as I rely absolutely on the ability of my DCI. How nice our views of our junior colleagues coincide. Now, Mr Venn, we're clear about this, aren't we? We've always done all we can to provide TVInvicta with good local stories, and you've supported us in return. It would be nice to return to this — symbiotic — relationship, wouldn't it?' Not waiting for a reply, which could hardly be in the negative, she stood. 'It's a magnificent view, isn't it?'

He stood too, magnanimous in defeat. 'I like the way they're developing the city, I must say.'

She patted back the conversational ball. 'But it's a pity that we've got no concert hall or proper theatre and that plans for a new library were axed.'

'Imagine the City Fathers putting themselves up as contenders for European City of Culture indeed!' he snorted. 'Pathetic, wasn't it, to think they could lift that sort of honour!'

'I suppose you couldn't do a bit of campaigning to improve facilities for music — I love the Cathedral, but not as a concert venue, and now we've got a link with the Philharmonia . . .'

* * *

All sweetness and light to end the discussion, then. And he ushered her down the stairs in person.

On impulse, she didn't go straight back to the car but to Castle Street to one of her favourite shoe shops. Succumbing to one temptation, in the form of evening shoes that positively caressed the feet, she found herself ready for another, a proper breath of fresh air. It wouldn't take much longer to walk back via the Dane John Mound, or at least in the grounds in which it stood. As a Roman burial ground, it wasn't of any particular interest, as far as she knew, since it had been remodelled to suit eighteenth-century sensibilities. Now the area hosted occasional food and other fairs, and, even on a winter's day, provided pleasant walking away from the crowds of shoppers. Today only a couple of pairs of pensioners were taking the air, trying pointedly to ignore the jeers and catcalls of a group of schoolkids.

Cheek their elders, would they? She strode closer. They were mostly girls but a couple of lads were larking around on one of the benches. She'd rather not know what was so amusing them. But that was what she should, as a cop, be doing: she should be keeping an eye on kids of just that age — the younger teens. They might not all be happy-slappers but she for one treated the by-laws with respect and expected others to do so as well — so if they were carving their initials or daubing the seats with magic markers, they'd hear a few words. Evidence? Better get some of that too before she waded in. She slowed to a halt some fifty yards short of them. If they took any notice all they'd see was a lady of a certain age making a phone call. What they might not notice was that she was using a pretty up-to-date, and certainly desirable, bit of mobile technology and also photographing their activities. There'd be a dozen or so, maybe fifteen.

She could always delete the results later.

They'd clocked her. Delete, hell! Despite their youth, they exuded menace. She sent the images to Mark's phone, and switched on her police radio, calling in urgently. There was no time for any more. Like starlings, they wheeled and swooped. In seconds she was surrounded, and she couldn't imagine it was to admire the carrier with her new shoes. The very situation when you want both hands free and she'd got this encumbrance! Plus a damned handbag.

She left the radio open. The switchboard would be able to locate her and pick up what was going on.

Which was, for the moment, just a confrontation. Perhaps her height fazed them. Or the fact she looked more like a headmistress than they'd expected, and some residual respect still operated.

Meanwhile, they must not see fear in her face. Or shock, if they hit her. That was the idea, wasn't it? And what should she do if she were attacked? Grab the would-be assailant? Good publicity that would be. She could see the headlines now: *Top Cop floors City Tot.* Maybe better than *City Tot floors Top Cop*!

Unhurriedly, she flashed her ID and gave her name and rank. No clever lawyer could say she hadn't warned any potential assailant.

A couple of the younger girls slouched away. The rest closed ranks.

She waited, face carefully blank, with just a hint of inquiry, perhaps. Then she saw the craft knife. 'Drop that knife please. Come on. Drop the knife.' She held the child's gaze, though it meant reducing the others to no more than movements at the edge of her vision.

Transferring her bag to share her left hand with the carrier, casually, she hoped, as if she were waiting for change at the checkout, she pointed. 'Drop the knife. Drop it there.'

The girl swung her arm not down, but up, in a slicing movement.

Instinct took over. She grabbed the girl's wrist, and twisted it hard. The knife fell. Arm-locking the girl, she stamped on the sets of fingers reaching for it. So far so good. But there were still a dozen kids to deal with. If they simply closed in and kicked her she'd be powerless.

'Back-up urgently required!' she told her radio. Didn't raise her voice. Tried to sound efficient — menacing, even.

And, propelled by hands in the small of her back and a vicious kick to her shin, she fell flat. The girl in the armlock screamed as Fran's weight came down on her, forcing her to the ground, too.

Would they stab her? Even a blade as short as that could kill.

And then came the blessed sound of a siren — two, three sirens. But someone grabbed her hair, jerked her head back, and slammed it forward.

* * *

The call came through while Mark was between meetings, or he might not have picked it up. She was right to describe the bunch of kids as threatening: he could see that from the images she sent. The very way they stood spelt danger, superior, impregnable smiles on their vicious little faces. Weasels. The sort that took over Toad Hall.

Why did the brain always throw up such irrelevancies when every cell, every synapse, should be dedicated to solving a problem?

At least his fingers were working. Canterbury. That meant his old mate Colin, who could be guaranteed to mobilise their colleagues the moment his shout went up. Favours! Hell, you didn't need favours when the safety of a Chief Super was at stake.

Safety. Mark found he couldn't frame the word *life*. She was less than two hundred yards from Canterbury nick, for God's sake, two hundred yards — two hundred yards that included a busy dual carriageway ring road and a twenty-five-foot defensive town wall that had been impregnable for Christ knew how long. Sorry, God. Please, let her be all right, my lovely Fran.

He took the stairs to the control room two, three at a time.

'Canterbury are on to it, guv. Sir,' the woman monitoring the incident corrected herself.

'Guv'll do. Can you put me through to their ops room?'

She passed a headset — must have had it ready. He barked his name.

'CCTV located the assailants, sir and Canterbury nick is tracking them. There's a big warm welcome waiting for them — arms outstretched, you might say.'

Bugger catching the kids! He yelled, 'What about Harman?'

'Flat on her face, guv. Lying still. Seems to be on top of a body. No sign of any blood, but an ambulance has been summoned all the same.'

'I should bloody think so.'

'Was she wearing body armour at all, guv?'

'For a visit to the dentist? No, of course she bloody wasn't. Sorry.'

'She's moving now, sir. Pushing herself up as if she's doing a press-up. Ah! The first constable's reached her now. Yes, she's bleeding from her nose. And someone's attending to — yes, a child, still floored.'

'Call me back the minute you know something.'

He slumped on to a chair someone had found for him, discovered he was sipping water. Where had that come from?

This was worse, far worse, than being injured yourself. He was supposed to be discussing the use of taser guns with other senior officers any moment now. OK, ten minutes ago. Even if he wanted to go, he didn't think his feet would carry him. He had another swig of water. No wonder the police service in general preferred officers not to be in relationships with other serving officers. If he'd been out on a shout himself, how could he have performed, knowing his woman was in danger? There should be some news, for Christ's sake! Hauling himself to his feet, he started to pace.

No, he mustn't let himself down in front of his colleagues, however sympathetic they might be. Thanking them for their trouble, he stomped back to his office, but dawdled over finding the paperwork he was supposed to be collecting. What the hell! The meeting could wait a bit longer.

At long last his mobile rang. Fran.

'I'm fine.'

'They said there was blood on your face . . .'

'I banged my nose on something as I fell — had a bit of a nosebleed. Nothing serious. Though it'll look good in the log — stiletto injury! Stiletto as in strappy sandals, Mark! I couldn't phone earlier. One of the kids had nicked my mobile then slung it in a bin. The fall made a bit of a mess of my knees, and the paramedics want me to have an anti-tetanus booster. You couldn't fish a pair of trousers from the wardrobe in my office and get someone to drop them into the William Harvey, could you?'

'William Harvey, as in the hospital in Ashford?'

'Nearest A and E, of course.'

Some fourteen miles from Canterbury. What if she'd been severely injured? Sod the meeting; his secretary could explain. 'I'm on my way myself,' he snapped so fiercely he found himself phoning back to apologise.

* * *

'So there you are,' he greeted her, trying to sound mild and amused. It was all he could do not to scoop her into his arms, but a self-conscious WPC in her twenties looked all too interested in the proceedings.

Fran's squiffy smile suggested she might not have objected to the passionate treatment. 'Look, Constable Daws, I'm in good hands now. Thanks for giving me a lift,' she smiled.

'Couldn't have let you share an ambulance with that animal, ma'am,' the constable said, still hovering. 'Imagine that, sir, that's what the paramedics wanted! About a witness statement, ma'am—'

'I'll get Mr Turner to run me back to Canterbury to pick up my car — I could drop by then. OK?' And Fran smiled so sweetly that the woman probably didn't realise she was being shoved out.

'You're going to have a lovely pair of black eyes,' he began, half-sitting on the bed beside her. A light blanket covered her legs.

'I could have had a lot worse,' she admitted. 'One of the girls had a Stanley knife. If I'd been your average middle-aged woman, she might well have got me. Just a slash on the face — enough to scar the victim for life, of course — so you can show it to all your mates. Happy-slapping? Happy-slashing! As it is, I got her first — she'll probably be suing me for assault. I fell right on top of her. I think I dislocated her shoulder. She was certainly in a great deal of pain, poor kid.'

'Poor kid my arse! For God's sake, Fran!'

She shrugged. 'I'm no lightweight. A good ten inches taller than her. And I didn't release my grip as I went down.' She pulled a face. 'I know I ought to have done, but that shove in the back caught me completely unawares. I didn't even relax.

That's why I've got ruined trousers and playground knees. I'm getting too old for this job, Mark. At least for confronting little savages,' she added, as if prompting him.

For answer, he bundled up her discarded torn trousers and put them in an evidence bag. 'You'd better let me have your jacket too. And you needn't pull that face: you know we always look after our own. And if that pack of hyenas have been after other folk, they have to be stopped.'

Behind her panda eyes, she looked quite shocked at his abruptness, but she didn't argue.

'You will press charges?' he insisted. 'Fran?'

'I don't think I have a choice,' she continued, swinging her legs off the bed and opening the bag of clothes he'd brought.

'You haven't,' he said. Why did he sound so grim, when what he ought to be doing was holding her tightly and whispering comforting words? Because he was angry, that was why. Angry with the kids, but angry with Fran for being there, and angry because she was hurt and she could have been killed and he could not, simply could not, have lost her.

In turn, she avoided his eye as she zipped the trousers and eased a jumper over her head, wincing as it brushed her face.

Damn it, did she have to look so martyred?

Why not, with him so firmly in the wrong?

He took her in his arms. 'Fran, Fran — I was so worried. You know what? I pulled rank and got a driver. A hundred and ten we did, down the M20. And I had to bite my lip to stop myself telling him to go faster. And all the time I was thinking you could be safe on some university campus, strolling round the groves of Academe with a host of adoring students drinking in your every word.'

'A nice safe civilian. Just what I thought I was this morning. A lady capable of lunching, a pair of posh shoes in my bag, going for a stroll in the park.'

'Come on. I can't promise we'll do a hundred and ten, though.'

'I think we ought to make it a hundred and twenty: I left the car in the short stay car park. We shall need a bank loan to retrieve it.'

CHAPTER FOUR

Delay upon delay! How can I bear to wait any longer, knowing where you are? Does your heart beat faster too? It must!

* * *

In Fran's more comfortable visitor's chair, Jill Tanner regarded her boss over the rim of the coffee mug, her eyes clearly appraising the damage. 'Are you sure you're well enough to be at work this morning, Fran? I mean, it was only yesterday. You're entitled to be . . .' But she broke off, rubbing her chin as if in speculation.

'Well?' Fran prompted, mixing amusement and irritation in almost equal measures. She was only at her desk because she'd promised Mark she would do no more than sort out the papers for a committee Henson sat on, but seemed to have paid scant attention to. If she was going to delegate, as she most certainly was, at least the legatee would now have some idea what the whole operation was about. It was only when she found that her reading glasses sat on the exact centre of her bruise that she realised she wasn't being totally sensible. But she was too much of an old soldier to give up now and have to submit to even the most kindly of *told-you-sos*. Especially the most kindly. Mark had been through too much with Tina's suffering to have anyone else's inflicted on him. She would be brave to the point of heroic if necessary. With him, but not necessarily with her colleagues, especially when they were pussy-footing around as Jill was now. 'Come on, spit it out.'

'It's just a thought . . . You know how we never show a victim's face in a TV appeal . . . because of their privacy. I was wondering — but maybe it's not such a good idea . . .'

Fran found that rubbing the heels of her hands over her eyes, a habit she'd never been aware of until now, was too painful. Raising an eyebrow in interrogation wasn't very sensible, either. 'Spit it out. You want me to go on TV as a victim and show what happens when gangs of kids indulge in so-called happy-slapping. The trouble is, this isn't a result of the slapping. It's a result of my falling over — OK, being pushed — and landing on my lovely new shoes.'

'How are they?' Jill sounded as concerned for their safety as she was for Fran's.

'Tougher than me, thank goodness. And they were beautifully wrapped; you know how they do it there.' A glance at Jill's face suggested that expensive shoes were not a weakness she comprehended. 'I just caught the heel.'

'But you wouldn't have fallen over if you hadn't been assaulted — isn't that the correct term for being surrounded and jostled, not to mention being attacked with a knife, guv?'

'And if I had let the child go, I wouldn't have dislocated her shoulder so badly it might need surgery.'

'But you wouldn't have had her in an armlock if she hadn't tried to slash your face. You may not know that there was blood on the Stanley knife: the gang have already used it on someone else. We're checking hospital records right now.'

'You've located their schools?'

'Yesterday, guv. Thanks to your photos and the CCTV we've located every last one of the little runts. Good schools, too, and they all seem to have decent middle-class parents.' She put her mug down. 'So I'm afraid the whole thing'll probably be your fault by the time the expensive lawyers have chewed it over and spat it out.'

'I'm sure you're right.' Thank God for evidence in her favour. 'The rats! The kids, I mean. Compensation lawyers are far nastier than rats. OK, Jill. I'll think about it. And quickly — I know you'll want the full panoply of bruises still at their best. But I think you should run it past the Chief first. You, not me. Your case. I'm just the victim, remember.' Had she heard herself saying that? That she was a victim?

'You couldn't just talk to Mark about it?' Jill didn't often wheedle, but there was a distinct plea in her voice now.

'Absolutely not. You can, if you want. He's more approachable than the boss. Normally. But he'll respect you far more for doing it yourself than for relying on me, especially if you point out that TVInvicta would probably give it real sob-story coverage.' Jill still didn't move. Fran patted the bulging file. 'Sorry, Jill. "Light duties," indeed!'

* * *

How many women in Fran's situation would expose themselves to that sort of publicity, with the mixture of pity and derision it might incur? Mark shook his head slowly in admiration.

Jill Tanner clearly took it as a negative — hardly surprising, since it almost was one. 'I mean — I can quite see . . . I don't know why I ever thought of it.' She blushed, the rush of blood making her look angry, however, not embarrassed. Although she was probably ten years younger than his Fran, she looked more middle-aged. Perhaps it was the weathered skin and the deep wrinkles — an outdoors face. And the vicious TV interview had done no more than exaggerate hair that had been confined in, but not controlled by, a collection of combs.

'I do.' He let himself smile. 'Because it's a good idea. It may get TVInvicta on our side rather than baying for our collective blood, and it may get some parents checking up on what their kids are really up to. After all, that craft knife must have come out of someone's toolkit.'

'We're on to DIY stores just in case a child managed to buy it, despite the legislation.'

'Good. I'd like to think seeing the results of violence might spark contrition in some pubescent consciences. Or perhaps that's being overly optimistic.' He straightened. 'OK, Jill, I'll take this to the Chief. If he doesn't actually squash the idea flat, we'll run with it. But I think we'd have to stipulate that the interview was recorded, not live, and that we'd have power of veto.'

'I should think for an exclusive they'd agree to anything.' Her colour had subsided now. She produced an engaging, complicitous grin.

'Possibly.' He stroked his chin. 'And if they didn't — how would you run with it then?'

'A standard press conference, with Fran — with Chief Superintendent Harman — chairing it as usual. A really nice shock tactic, we thought.'

'Shock indeed. What effect do you think it'll have on our morale?' He leaned back in his chair, and was amused that she mirrored his movement.

'Good, I should think. It lets everyone know that it's not just front-line officers who are suffering.'

Or would it carry the opposite message, that top brass were weak and effete? 'You know, I might just run it by Personnel, too. Well done, Jill. We'll get back to you and the team as soon as we can. Before the bruises have a chance to fade, definitely.'

Jill stood but made no attempt to leave his office. 'I know you'll want to talk to Fran first. But take my word for it, sir — she's keen.'

'She always is.' So what was she waiting for? He raised an eyebrow.

She flushed, but only retreated when the phone rang. He'd better ask Fran if she knew what was wrong.

* * *

Fran was just considering the matter of another painkiller, to benefit not just her face but also every single joint in her body. But she was glad the tablets were still in her bag, not lying temptingly on the table, because Tom Arkwright tapped on her door, putting his head round it with his usual favourite nephew to indulgent aunt grin, and she didn't want to worry him.

'I've just heard from my mum. Dad's had another cancer check-up and another all-clear.'

She clapped her hands, but wished she hadn't and hoped the sudden cessation wouldn't alarm him. 'I couldn't be more pleased. So how are you all going to celebrate?'

'I've got them tickets for the Old Trafford Test this summer. Honestly! Yes, Mum likes cricket as much as Dad. Anyway, thought I'd just let you know.'

And, knowing Tom, to let her know something else, something just dropped out in the course of a natter.

'Are you going up this weekend with a bottle of bubbly? Go on, take a seat. And lean forward earnestly, as if we're discussing some major policy decision.'

'Oh, she's not bad, that DCI Tanner. She won't miss me for two minutes.'

She rounded her eyes in mock-amazement. At least opened them as wide as was comfortable. 'She isn't working your socks off, then?'

'She is and she isn't. She's just decided we should separate out the two lines of inquiry, one into happy-slapping and the other into groping and what have you.'

'The "what have you" involving Masturbation Man.' So why hadn't Jill told her this? Not that it wasn't what she'd have done from the start. Perhaps she'd allowed Tom to come in knowing he'd deliver the message.

'Quite. I'm on that team.'

'Happy with that?'

Tom wriggled. 'It's not for me to be happy or unhappy, is it, like? She's the boss. It's the job.'

'You're not grassing her up, Tom, if you tell me your feelings. I shall almost certainly send you away with a flea in your ear, and tell you not to be a wuss, if that's the current term. But I should like to know why you'd rather be involved with happy-slapping, which seems to me to be insoluble. You know, like that many-headed monster.'

'Hydra?'

'That's the chap. You cut off one head, and another appears.'

He nodded. 'Websites. That's why. Ever since you got me on that forensic IT course I've been looking for an opportunity to use my skills. And I reckon I could get into most of the little scrotes' websites. Half an hour. That's all. Well, maybe longer.'

'Why not do it anyway? Just out of interest. An hour's neither here nor there, is it? Unless you are going up North for the weekend?'

'Well, a bit of a family party, like . . . Did you want me to do anything?'

She might have done. But he was young, his father was in remission, and what the hell.

* * *

'If TVInvicta won't play, and the Chief isn't happy with thrusting Fran into the limelight of the regular press conference, we've still got another card up our sleeves,' Cosmo reminded them.

Four forty-five on Friday wasn't the most popular time for meetings, so by common — if professionally tacit — consent they would try to keep it short. They'd gathered in Cosmo's office, a humdrum room Fran would have eyed up for instant refurbishment. Cosmo's immaculate shirt and suit made it look even shabbier, even though he certainly wasn't trying to peacock.

He leaned forward over the coffee table around which they were seated. 'You remember I told you *Crimewatch* were after you, Fran? They go out this coming Monday and would be as deferential as you like.'

Mark looked at her enquiringly. But he spoke to Cosmo. 'Are TVInvicta adamant about having complete control?'

'I don't think they would be if we floated the BBC as an alternative.'

Fran nodded. Much as she hated the renaming of dear old unpretentious Personnel as Human Resources, with a manager rather than an officer at its head, she was finding her respect for Cosmo was less grudging by the day.

'The trouble, as I told him, is, of course, that if Fran does either programme, and doesn't appear at the press conference, there'll be just as many questions about her,' Mark said.

'And I'm inclined to think speed is of the essence,' Fran said. 'If we're trying to shock people into grassing up their neighbours' kids, then the more spectacular my bruises the better.'

'Darling, d'you think they won't be able to fix that in make-up?' Cosmo tutted.

Fran avoided Mark's eye. Modern and reconstructed man as he was, he tended to regard the celebration of things gay or merely camp without particular favour. Perhaps he'd long ago been on the receiving end of a bravura embrace when policing a Gay Pride march. She'd ask him on the way home.

The phone rang. Cosmo was clearly tempted to ignore it, but eventually stood up and reached across. 'TVInvicta!' he mouthed, and held up his index finger warningly. It was beautifully manicured.

Fran and Mark exchanged glances. Cosmo's share of the conversation was mostly confined to affirmative little grunts, but at last he said, 'To sum up, we'll be shown the script before the programme, and the reporter will guarantee not to ask unscripted questions? Live. And not exclusive. OK.' He winked hugely while the person at the other end spoke. 'Six-thirty at the studio. One moment. I shall put you on hold.' He pressed a button on his console. 'There, endless loops of soothing Chopin, poor bugger. OK, Fran — you heard enough of that? You're on tonight, girl. The only problem is getting you to Canterbury in time. On the other hand, we've got an awful lot of highly qualified drivers in the building. Shall I tell her yes, if only to spare the poor dear any more of *Les Sylphides*?'

* * *

'In conclusion, Chief Superintendent Harman, what advice would you give to young people tempted to happy-slap?' Dilly Pound asked, leaning forward deferentially, as she had throughout the interview. Either she was a very good interviewer or she really wanted to hear everything Fran had to say.

Fran smiled. 'Don't. Even touching someone without permission is an offence. So-called happy-slapping is a criminal assault, and my officers will treat it as such. An attack with a weapon is a much more serious affair, and incurs a heavier penalty. I'm sure your viewers know that. But what they may not know is that to publish photos of the victims on websites or anywhere else may well constitute harassment, another crime that Kent Constabulary views very seriously.'

'Thank you, Detective Chief Superintendent Frances Harman. And we hope you soon recover completely from your injuries. And now for those numbers we promised you. Crimestoppers is . . .'

* * *

'Do you have time to join us for a quick drink?' Dilly enquired, as they unhitched their microphones. 'You're not on duty, are you?' She flashed a smile.

'Indeed not. And my partner's driving me home.' She had never hated the term more than now. But — as her eyes dropped to her ring — at her age fiancé sounded precious and possessive. 'I'm sure he'd like a bitter lemon, however.' She certainly didn't want to leave Mark cooling his heels in the rather comfortless waiting area. It was packed with photos of past TVInvicta personalities, and images of current ones, as the next programme appeared silently on a huge monitor dominating the whole space. If you turned in the opposite direction, there was another, smaller screen, the colours subtly different. If you tried to ignore both, and picked up one of the complimentary newspapers, the tail of both eyes picked up irritating flickering images. How did the security guard and receptionist stay sane?

A minion despatched to rescue Mark, Dilly ushered Fran through to the bar, a room more spacious and a tad less pretentious than Venn's.

'You treat harassment seriously?' Dilly continued in the same voice as in the studio.

'Very seriously indeed.'

'And stalking?'

'Anything that threatens your life or comfort is potentially a crime. There's legislation called The Protection from Harassment Act, 1997. You can actually be convicted of GBH for psychological harm.' Fran dropped her voice, looking intently at Pound. 'Are you a victim, Dilly?'

CHAPTER FIVE

Soon, very soon. I won't be denied.

* * *

'"I don't think so." What kind of answer is that? Either a woman's being stalked or she's not, surely?' Fran asked Mark, as they joined the tail of cars snaking down Canterbury's Whitefriars car park ramp to street level.

'Why didn't you ask the woman herself? Pound? Whatever sort of name is Dilly, anyway? Sounds like a toy duck.'

She flicked a glance at him. He wasn't usually this tetchy, even at the end of a long, hard week. He'd been a bit grim and gruff ever since the assault, come to think of it. Since he knew exactly why she hadn't been able to question Pound herself, Venn having swept effusively up to her and elbowing the reporter out of the conversation, she responded to his third question. 'Short for Delilah?'

'Would any parents actually inflict a name like that on a sweet, innocent child in its cradle?' He glared at the tail-lights ahead. 'My God, look at this lot. This time of night at least you'd expect the roads to be quiet.' A curt radio enquiry to HQ elicited the information that a serious accident had closed the A2 northbound: all the diverted traffic was being funnelled through Canterbury's already inadequate system, now in danger of becoming grid-locked.

'Wonderful. Do we go back up and park and eat in the city? Or fight our way through to whichever route is the most promising?'

'Ask the oracle.' The satellite navigation system had been his Christmas present from Fran. Not very romantic, but then, what could you give to a man who had everything except time to enjoy it?

The A28 seemed the best bet.

'Straight to yours?' he sighed. 'Or shall we press on to Maidstone?'

'The central heating will be on at both,' she said. 'And there's plenty in both our freezers. Or we could stop and pick up a meal. Whatever you want. You're driving, after all.' And she was so tired and in so much pain — she never had got round to taking those pain killers — all she wanted was a long bath with scented oils and no decision-making. She wouldn't admit it, not even to Mark, maybe especially not to Mark, but she couldn't even choose between an Indian and a Chinese.

'I've an idea the oracle's got it wrong. We've hardly moved in the last ten minutes,' he said.

It was true. They might be within sight of the poached egg island at the foot of the car park ramp, but the A28 was as unattainable as Everest.

'What we'll do, then,' he said, a hint of amusement suddenly threading through his grimness, 'is head straight back up the ramp. We'll park and find somewhere to eat.' At last he could inch on to the poached egg. It took several manoeuvres to get back up again, but once he'd set the trend several others followed. 'We'll then dawdle back past all those estate agents and look in their windows for a dream house. We'll take a note of all the details and then we'll go to your cottage. Tomorrow we'll go and check the places out.' He got out of the car.

It would be *lèse majesté* to query any part of the diktat. But she had to pick up on three words, as she slowly heaved herself out. 'A dream house?'

'Yes,' he agreed, holding out his hands for her to grip. At least he didn't try to lever her himself. 'For us. What about it?'

Aware that momentous things were happening, all she could say was, 'For us? But we've got two houses.'

'Neither of which is ideal. For some reason mine oppresses you — no, don't argue — you always put on a bathrobe before you leave the bedroom, while at your place you pad round mother-naked. I'm sick of banging my head on the beam in your bathroom. And I don't know why you don't, because you're only an inch shorter than me. Let's throw some money at both places and sell them or rent them out. And we'll move into a new one. Then at least we'll know which washing machine our clothes are in.'

As if they needed such an excuse. She turned to say something warm and romantic — one of them ought! — but was shouted down by a load of strangers patting Mark on the back. Where on earth had they sprung from? She turned round. It seemed they'd all completed the same manoeuvre and come back up to the car park. And no, they weren't congratulating him on his sudden commitment to Fran, but on his brilliant idea in giving up the unequal struggle with the traffic. Next they bombarded him with questions.

'Any idea what time this place closes? Don't want to be stranded overnight. Can you recommend a good eatery?'

Mentally Fran ran over the places she'd like to eat and sent their fellow refugees in the opposite direction.

At last she had him to herself, as they linked arms and headed slowly towards the exit. The thudding in her chest was almost painful, but her voice came out as flatly mundane as if he'd asked for change for a *Big Issue* seller. 'Mark, are you suggesting we live together? In one house? Properly?'

His own voice wasn't much warmer. 'You make it sound like living in sin. Come on, we're adults, and have been consenting ever since we got together. Neither of us bothers God all that much. Or would you want a white wedding and a coy honeymoon?' Now he was almost jeering.

What on earth made him so damned joyless? She would never have expected the one-knee treatment, but this seemed so offhand.

'Yes, actually, I would. Eventually,' she conceded. 'I might not qualify for a white wedding and I might not demand the Cathedral as a venue, or three weeks in the Caribbean to round it off, but yes, I'd like to be married.' The silence deepened. 'I'd like to be married to you, at least.'

'But not yet.' It was a statement, not a question. 'It wouldn't have to be part of the house deal. Would it? We can think about it. Later — when we've got our heads round the idea.'

For 'we' read 'Mark'.

'I'd like — yes, the house—'

He jumped in. 'So you think it's a good idea. The house.'

'I do.' So long as they both said the words in a more formal setting later, she added under her breath.

What was going on between his ears? It clearly wasn't very comfortable. Half her brain told her she was being supine and should have held out for what in her heart she wanted. The other half told her that sooner or later Mark would come round, but that life was too short to shilly-shally over fine-tuning. How many police fiancés had she seen killed before their Big Day? *Carpe diem*, that was what any serving officer should do. Hell, she was so tired.

* * *

He'd nearly blown it, hadn't he? Not exactly a suggestion to remember! More a grudging business offer, with a waspish allusion to missing shirts. The timing, too — she looked as if she'd gone a round with Amir Khan, and from the way she moved he judged her joints were sore as well. Plying her with the mandatory champagne — they had to celebrate commitment somehow although he suspected neither of them truly liked it — prevented her from taking painkillers, too.

And here he was, turning a bad scenario into an even worse one, telling her over their starter that he couldn't face marriage, not yet. It was tempting providence, for God's sake. Cocking a snook at fate. If they didn't make any grand gestures, perhaps fate wouldn't notice, perhaps it'd just let them get on with everything. But as soon as they popped their heads above the parapet, he was terrified that something, some indefinable thing, would get one of them. Both of them. If only he could have explained all this without sounding crazy. So all he managed was, 'Later on. When things are settled. How about that?' Not enough. 'I'm just so afraid . . . that something'll go wrong. Like yesterday.'

Was she hurt? Puzzled. Too tired to argue? She managed a confiding smile. 'Not with you to watch over me.' She covered his hand with hers. The one with the less badly grazed and bruised palm. 'Not to mention the rest of the Kent Constabulary,' she chuckled.

'Look at tonight! A motorway pile-up!' Less and less celebratory. Some people said champagne made you melancholy and then maudlin. Not that he'd had enough for either, surely.

'But we were in the traffic jam, not the pile-up,' she objected, 'and now we're here. And I don't see why we shouldn't grab us a room in a hotel here in Canterbury so we can enjoy all this without having to worry about being a millilitre over the limit. Mark, sweetheart, we're supposed to be celebrating quite a momentous event, not worrying about tenancy in common and power of attorney and wills and next-of-kin. Aren't we?' She tried to raise her eyebrow, one of her most endearing gestures, but winced. 'I suppose,' she added wistfully, 'it's a bit hard to feel romantic about a panda. Unless you're another panda.'

'I could go and head butt a wall so I got eyes to match? I ought to anyway. Blurting it all out like that. It was supposed to be roses and bended knees and everything.'

She hesitated. What had she meant to say? She ended up mocking. 'With all that CCTV around? You'd have been a laughing stock — and me, too. So long as you carry me over the threshold of our new home, that's fine by me. But not by fate, in the form of our colleagues,' she added, fielding her phone. 'From Jill Tanner. Shall I take it?'

He shrugged, eyes heavenward.

'I could tell her I'm on my sick bed?' Getting up painfully slowly, she left him and went to take the call in the lobby.

He had a feeling a nearby hotel room wouldn't be on the agenda tonight.

* * *

Fran wouldn't limp. She wouldn't let herself. Not for anything would she let him down when he had made such a huge effort. She'd no idea why he'd found it so hard, and was sure all those excuses about fate really masked something else. But he'd done it, and there was only one way to celebrate a decision with such implications, such repercussions, even one that seemed to have left them both flat and exhausted, not fizzing like kids on speed. She'd never yet admitted to being too tired for sex, and she wouldn't begin tonight, headache, face ache or any other ache. Lying still and thinking of England wasn't an option either. He'd given love freely and without demands: she would always do the same.

So when she made her way back to the table, she tried to give the impression of a languorous dawdle. It turned into something perilously like a waddle. Or even a drunken roll. He caught her eye. They were gasping with laughter by the time she'd reached their table.

But he sobered quickly enough to pull back her chair for her and to ease it forward again. And his face was straight when he asked, 'What did she want?'

'Her hand holding. Can't think why. She's an experienced officer and usually a capable administrator.'

'Why tonight?'

'Not enough bodies to staff the switchboard. I told her to check her budget and press gang more.'

'Couldn't she have done that without your say-so?'

'Of course she could. But there was one thing her budget certainly wouldn't stretch to. My co-option on to the team.'

'Yours! Someone your rank on the switchboard!'

'Well, think of all the celebs answering phones on Children in Need. And I've an idea we both rolled up our sleeves and took calls when that child went missing.' She smiled, squeezing his hand, again with her better one. 'Neither ACCs nor chief supers make a habit of that.'

'That was because you were there. I couldn't have gone home and left you toiling.' His eyes said far more, a more open declaration of love than he'd made all evening.

'Any more than I could go over there now and leave you to twiddle your thumbs at home. Whichever home.'

'So what did you say? That you were having a champagne meal with your lover?'

'Not exactly. I said all the pills—'

'Which you haven't actually taken!'

'—have left me light-headed and woozy, and you wouldn't let me drive. There's no point in working in a hierarchical organisation if you can't blame the senior officer sometimes, is there?'

* * *

'Are you sure you want to go into work?' Mark demanded, watching her dress on Monday morning. 'Absolutely sure?'

'I've dossed around doing nothing all weekend, so I should be all right.' If only fastening her bra didn't mean compressing her palms.

It was true she'd had a restful couple of days, starting with the night at the Canterbury hotel she'd suggested. Impulses: it was so good to be able to act on them for once. Especially when he'd signed them in as Mr and Mrs Turner, reducing her to secret hysterics.

'Those bruises—'

'Just coming out nicely — they shouldn't hurt so much now. It's not as if I were on the beat. Just a meeting: quite a big one in Folkestone. Customs and immigration officers and me all discussing the latest breaches of the Tunnel's security.'

'Really exciting,' he said sardonically.

'Exactly. Just the sort of thing I should despatch a deputy to if I had one.'

'Get on to Dix about it. You're sure you can't get out of it? It'll be little more than a photoshoot, to convince the denizens of Kent that Something is Being Done.'

'It won't work, then — not since half the people I come across never seem to use the words "asylum seeker" without prefacing them with the adjective "bogus".'

'But given the colour of your face this morning it'll at least be colourful. Oh, Fran, why not give yourself a break?'

'And look at more houses?' After wading through dozens of sheets of estate agents' particulars, they'd driven past some of the most promising to see whether it was worth making appointments to view them. In the vast majority of cases it hadn't been. But they were still optimistic. 'Get thee behind me! Anyway, you can give me a lift into work first, if you wouldn't mind. I want to slip into Jill's briefing before I go. Then I'll take a car from the pound.'

* * *

The curious looks she got as she strode through the corridor to Jill's meeting amused and irritated her in equal measure. Didn't people know what a black eye was? Her dad used to sing a song about two of them! But she couldn't imagine anyone making up a ditty like that these days — or one about a railroad running through the middle of a house.

As for the top brass she was due to meet, it wouldn't do them any harm to be reminded what their jobs were really about — fighting crime. And her eyes in their now purple and yellow sockets could look as shrewdly as theirs down the railway line and at plans; her knees were decently hidden by the trouser suit she always wore to such jollies.

'. . . CCTV cameras,' Jill said, and stopped, looking about her expectantly.

God, she'd heard none of it, had she? Not a word! She scanned other faces, most of which seemed to be looking serious.

'Everyone clear? All right, we'll move on to the happy-slapping incidents. Nice to have you with us, ma'am. Glad you're feeling better.'

Damn it, was the woman trying to be sarcastic? To her boss's boss, a woman who'd given her support and encouragement from day one?

'So we know from Ms Harman's injuries that happy-slapping has serious results, as the TVInvicta interview confirmed. The good news is that we have a number of leads, but we agreed to wait till today, when the possible offenders will be in school, to follow them up.'

Who agreed? And why? Fran would talk about that decision later, too. Before she knew it, she was asking, 'Has anyone asked schools to confiscate mobile phones as the kids go in? If the slappers can't communicate immediately perhaps that will tone down its charm.'

'Websites and blogs, ma'am,' Jill said, as if that answered everything.

A young man Fran only knew by sight drawled, 'I had a go at one or two of those on Saturday, ma'am. I'll drop the results on your desk, shall I?'

And thus neatly told everyone, including Fran, that Jill hadn't been at her desk over the weekend. It was a good job for Jill that Fran didn't have time to speak to her.

CHAPTER SIX

And what will you be wearing, Dilly, to greet me? That stern suit of yours? Or black lace, altogether more welcoming?

* * *

Normally she'd have headed back relentlessly to work by the quickest route, in this case the M20. But she was suddenly tempted on to the A20, a nice ordinary road winding through villages, altogether more homely, less minatory about missing minutes at her desk, than the motorway. At the first lay-by she phoned Mark, who had thrown himself with amazing gusto into their house-search, and brightened their weekend with breathtaking spontaneous gestures — flowers, earrings to die for, and a huge coffee-table book on garden design. Guilt? Possibly. But for a man not given to grand gestures or making easy apologies, pretty impressive.

'I'm taking the long way back,' she informed him, 'and keeping my eyes open for dream cottages as I go.'

'Do they exist? After this weekend, I've lost hope.'

'That's because you wouldn't repeat after me, "I believe in fairies!"'

'Sweetheart, to please you, I believe in the Sacred Heart and the Banshee and any other phenomenon, just like who-ever it was in *Dubliners*.'

'Fairies?'

'Fairies. A whole Midsummer Night's Dreamful.' And he started to hum the Mendelssohn overture down the phone to her, cutting the call on a particularly off-key donkey-like bray.

Suddenly the sun was breaking through, and who knew what the fairies might bring.

In the event they'd brought no more than the promise of spring and a general feeling of benevolence, which lingered even as she eventually sauntered into work, thinking of a cup of green tea, to which Mark had converted her. But even dear old builder's brew was off the menu for the time being, it seemed. An artistically arranged pile of Post-its greeted her, someone apparently having used a ruler to give exactly the same distance between the top of each one and its predecessor. Dumping her case and shrugging off her coat, she peered at the top one. Jill; Jill; Jill; Dilly Pound; Tom. And Jill. All needed her urgently, it seemed.

It was probably safe to assume that Pound was merely making a courtesy call to thank her for her appearance. But there was a number, which meant she ought to return the favour. Jill. Was she trying to pre-empt the bollocking Fran had mentally promised her and which she must know she deserved? And Tom — well, he was the one she was hap-piest to share a tea bag with. She was torn between a duty she'd never enjoyed, carpeting a colleague who was also a friend, and asking a junior officer for information. Hoping fate would decide, she strolled along to the incident room. There should be an air of purpose, eyes glued to screens or ears clamped to phones. There might also be knots of officers clearly discussing an issue. Or even joking — she didn't ban joking. A bit of hilarity meant pressure was being relieved. But she didn't like to see a lot of people standing in close knots, surreptitiously checking no one was listening in, and scurrying back to their desks when she hove into view. It smacked of the schoolroom, when the teacher had been called away and the head had suddenly appeared. There was no immediate sign of Jill in Henson's office, either. If Tom had been anywhere in sight she'd have invited him to share his auntie's bikkies and the latest news.

But there was no excuse for it: she would have to spend the afternoon fulfilling her promises to her coastal colleagues this morning, and sulking and kicking the desk wouldn't help either. Administration! Bah, humbug! Oh, for a bit of decent, honest detection. She knew in her heart that prevention was better than cure, of course. But there was a man out there who was busily committing dirty little crimes and there was nothing she could do about it.

* * *

Cosmo Dix rolled into her office just as, conscience squeaky-clean after a whole afternoon's administrative efforts, she'd thought it might be safe to phone Mark and discuss what time they could reasonably leave. Cosmo returned her smile with a charming one of his own, sitting on her more comfortable visitor's chair and generally looking as if he had all the time in the world. 'I am the bearer of good news and I hear your coffee is excellent.'

'Is it too late in the day for the real stuff, or would you prefer decaffeinated?'

'Whichever is easier — oh, what an irritating thing to say. As bad as, "whichever you're having". Fran, pour me something which involves no decisions, preferably a tot of under the desk whisky. No? OK. Now, I've drawn up a long list of possible temporary replacements for our friend Henson. Any chance of an hour of your time to reduce it to a short list?'

'An hour? At this time of day? Tomorrow, maybe.' She popped a hand over her mouth, rounding her eyes like a toddler caught with its hand in the biscuit tin.

'We could get the invitations to interview out tomorrow if you did them now. And, before you ask, you know you're not allowed to take them home with you. Highly confidential.'

'OK. You make whatever beverage takes your fancy and hand them over. You don't need Mark's input too, do you?'

'He'll have to ratify our selection.'

'Fill the kettle, then. He might as well come and ratify as we go.'

* * *

Mark could hardly contain his laughter till they got to his car. 'Perfunctory or what! Fran, I'm ashamed of you.'

'It's called being demob happy. It's only a temporary appointment, for goodness' sake! We don't need a conclave of cardinals and white smoke.'

'My darling, you're being remarkably cavalier over the guidelines you yourself drew up.'

'Who better to be cavalier than me then? No, I'm bored with all this administration already, Mark. I want to be out there doing a job, not sitting behind a desk. Hell, how do prisoners out in the community on licence force themselves to go back to prison at the end of each day? Knowing what it's like?'

'It's called deferred gratification, I believe,' he said, still laughing at her over the top of the car. 'Plus if they don't go back they get banged up even longer when we catch up with them.'

She slid into the car more easily than over the weekend.

'Eat at mine, sleep at yours?' he asked.

'Eat at yours, stay at yours. And spend an evening in front of the computer trawling for possible houses. I just want to be up and doing!'

'You always want to be busy-busy when something's on your mind.' He shot her a sideways look. 'So what's worrying you?'

'Jill Tanner.'

'Want to tell me about it?' He cut the engine, turning to face her more fully. 'I can tell you she's dropped in on me a couple of times and didn't seem to know when to go, if you see what I mean. The first time was at your behest, mind, to ask how I'd feel about your going on TV. The second — and third, come to think of it — she was on about quite trivial procedural issues.'

'Maybe she fancies you.'

'She can fancy away to her heart's content.' He patted the back of her hand to reassure her.

'Or maybe she's finding this job too much for her. I don't know why. I've seen her tackle far worse cases before and not turn a hair.'

'And I thought that was how she fixed her coiffure!'

'But clearly the troops aren't happy — she's made a couple of weird judgements and doesn't seem to be throwing herself into it. I'll have to talk to her in the morning.'

'Poor you. I never like having to chew someone's ears off.'

She turned her hand to squeeze his, but then realised that that wasn't a good idea. 'When I was in a mess, you didn't chew my ears off. You changed things. That's what I might have to do. But how to do it without her losing face I don't know. OK, guv, let's hit the road. The sooner we're in a work-free zone the better.'

* * *

And so they would have been had it not been for the news, which carried reports of two more sexual assaults, this time right in the middle of Jill's own manor, Ashford. TVInvicta News's tone nicely balanced restraint and triumphalism. Mark didn't argue when she picked up her car keys; he might have done had he known she was going to walk round Ashford's streets herself.

It was a long time since she'd been on night patrol, and then of course she'd been with a colleague and the full issue of equipment. Now she was a lone woman, middle-aged and not at her fleetest. She was being bloody stupid, but she had to get the feel of what was going on. She checked for CCTV cameras, peered into corners, disturbing not masturbators or potential rapists but a prostitute and her client and a kid sleeping rough. The first two got an earful, backed by her ID — at least she'd had the sense to bring that. The latter got the Sally Army's address. Suddenly she realised she had to walk down that nasty little alleyway linking the high street via the public car park to the police station car park, and she strongly wished she hadn't. Not a flasher. A group of kids. All with mobile phones. For two pins she'd have turned tail and gone the long way round. That was what violence did to you, wasn't it? Even the fear of violence? She'd been reduced to being Ms Average.

Well, she'd better reclaim the streets for Ms Average. Head held high, she plunged out of the light into the darkness.

The kids swore a lot, but not necessarily, she supposed, at her. If she assumed it was, she'd be lost.

* * *

'Ashford's was a much more serious attack,' Jill admitted to a feverish incident room the next morning. 'Contact was made — enough to constitute indecent assault. But we have no DNA, because this time the scrote wore surgical gloves. And a condom.'

Tom asked, 'Does this mean it's the same scrote that got wiser or that it's a different one? After all, previous attacks have involved him smearing semen on his victims.'

'A fact that has never been revealed to the public,' Jill emphasised.

'Has anyone thought of the effect all this must be having on the ordinary woman in the street?' Fran asked. No one knew of her little adventure, and she'd prefer to keep it that way. All the Ashford team knew was that their governor had joined them in a cuppa and asked about their kids.

'Since when did the ordinary woman last feel able to walk round towns at night?' Jill countered. 'There's the perennial problem of streetlights and CCTV and nimbyism: I had a bloke complain yesterday that some streetlights I pressed to have installed in a village that's been in darkness till now are messing up his stargazing! Karate lessons for all girls? Curfew for all men? Come on, guv, you're the one in charge of policy decisions!' She got the laugh she'd set up.

Jill was doing quite well this morning, Fran thought, but that didn't mean she could let her off the hook. Any more than TVInvicta were letting Fran off the hook. There was another Post-it waiting on her desk when she arrived shortly after seven-thirty. Mark had grumbled at the earliness of the hour, but since he had to spend the day at the Home Office and needed an early train she had felt able to ignore his protests, especially as she'd dropped him off at the station and promised to collect him that evening.

She made a point of merely falling into step with Jill as she terminated the briefing. 'I'm sorry I wasn't available yesterday when you needed me,' she began, turning towards her office, not Jill's, 'but I had a meeting down in Folkestone that took for ever.' She closed the door behind them before she continued, 'That's the problem when the boss isn't on the premises.'

'Tell me about it. It seems I no sooner leave for a school visit than there's another crisis in the Incident Room.'

'You're doing all those yourself? My goodness, Jill, that's spreading yourself a bit thin! I thought we'd agreed to bring Crime Prevention in on those, by the way.'

'This wasn't to warn about gropers and flashers! This was to talk about happy-slapping!' Jill flared. 'Part of the on-going investigation into the sort of incident that left you looking like this!'

'Tea or coffee? Do sit down. And try one of those biscuits — they're homemade,' she said proudly. 'This weekend I tried my hand at baking for the first time for years.' She had — when it became quite clear that the perfect house wasn't going to drop immediately on to their laps. But for the time being she didn't need Mark to ask her to keep their decision under wraps. 'I was inspired by Tom Arkwright's auntie who, I have to admit, does a far better job than I.'

Jill looked, but didn't quite dare say, 'Lucky you to have time even to try.' She took a biscuit anyway.

'This case getting on top of you? No, no — let me finish, please. How many cases would you say we've got here?'

'Two, possibly three.' She sounded as if she were on solid ground at last. 'The happy-slapping is a dangerous fad. We'll identify the perpetrators and charge them, but then what? Criminalise them by asking for a custodial sentence? Tag them? What about a few hours' community service?' she demanded ironically. 'And the problem is, they're decent kids at heart. Just kids.'

Fran pricked her ears, but said nothing, nodding sagely as if there were indeed nothing to be said. 'What about the sex crimes?'

'We've got a highly mobile perpetrator of minor ones. Masturbation Man keeps popping up all over the place. But he's never behaved in a truly physically threatening way like he did last night — which is why I wondered if it was really him, or some other bastard jumping on the bandwagon.'

'Nothing on CCTV?'

'It's as if he knows the locations of all the cameras and waits till he's out of range. We've been able to identify the young women who became his victims, but never him.'

'OK, let's storm our poor old brains. He fitted the cameras? Or operates them? Or he's a transvestite?' At last her teetering walk from the kettle to her desk with two mugs of coffee made Jill laugh. She even made a note on a scrap of paper she stuck into her pocket. 'You know what I'd want to do in your case?'

'Concentrate on the sex crimes, just in case they escalate. Get all the local heads in at once and talk mobile phones and happy-slapping. Leave investigating your assault to Canterbury. That's what you'd do.'

'Well, why not do just that? We'll get brickbats whatever we do, especially from TVInvicta and the red tops. But the real sex attacker's got to be the main brunt of the investigation, surely. Even if — especially if — it's a different suspect.'

'These biscuits are very good,' Jill said, with a distinct sigh. 'God knows when I last did anything in the kitchen. It was all right when the kids were small — I could get them to help. Now all I get is "whatever" and they're not hungry. But they're good kids really.'

Who was she telling, Fran or herself?

'Brian OK with them?'

'He's got a shed.' The sentence seemed to say far more than the four words justified.

Fran rested her bum on the desk. 'And you're trying to juggle everything.'

'You did! You were always buzzing around like a blue-arsed fly. Ask any of the older ones.'

'In that case I was a very bad boss.' She shook her head at the recollection. 'And I didn't have a family.'

'You had your parents.'

'Who were safely down in Devon, manageable most of the time. Until they became very old,' she conceded.

'And all those responsibilities!'

'At which point I nearly lost it. Everything. That's what happens when you take on too much. Blokes like Henson have heart attacks. Women, I gather, tend to have breakdowns. Neither's a good option. But while people know about heart attacks and treat them with some sort of macho respect—'

'"There but for the grace of God"—'

'Exactly! People don't seem so sympathetic to nervous illness.'

'Despite your efforts — all that debriefing, that business about avoiding post-traumatic stress.'

Fran wrinkled her nose. 'That's almost become macho, hasn't it? But no one appreciates that someone subject to sheer every day intolerable grind can be just as ill as the next bloke.' She made a point of slipping off the desk. 'There! I'm off my high horse. So that's what you'll do, then — pull all the stops out on the sex crimes case? Cases?'

'If it's OK by you.'

Fran spread her arms in exasperation. 'Since when did you have to ask permission? You're *in charge*. All I'm in charge of is making sure you've got enough paperclips. You wouldn't have asked Henson for his permission.'

'Because he wouldn't have put me in charge. He'd have had some young snappy-suited bloke, all degree and iPod.'

Fran choked on her biscuit. 'So he would. But I put you in charge because you've got the brains and the experience. Go on, Jill — you can do it.'

The phone rang. It was the secretary Fran shared with other senior officers. An urgent outside call, she said.

'I'm sorry, Jill — I'm going to have to take this.' Nonetheless she switched to hold. 'Remember what I said — and remember what you said. You can do it.' Provided Fran could stop standing between her and the light.

CHAPTER SEVEN

Black lace, I think. A basque. And stockings. Definitely stockings, showing off your lovely thighs. Dilly, my beautiful Dilly. Your love is better than wine.

* * *

'Ms Pound,' Fran greeted her surprise visitor, wondering if the dirty mugs, both with lipstick round the rim, would improve her image or otherwise. At least they were tucked away by the coffee machine.

'Chief Superintendent Harman.'

'Such a mouthful! Call me Fran, please.' They exchanged smiles as they shook hands. In daylight — it was with something of a shock that Fran realised she was once again spending so much of her time in artificial light — Pound looked slightly older and rather less poised than on television.

'I really don't think we're ready to do a follow-up story on the sex cases,' Fran began, gesturing the reporter to her better visitor's chair. 'It was very good coverage on Friday and stirred up an excellent response. Thank you.'

Pound's smile was perfunctory. But she said nothing. She looked around the office, and would surely have prowled, picking up personal items and examining them, if it had been that sort of room.

At last she said with a surprising rush: 'I was wondering about a full-length feature on you yourself, Chief — Fran.'

Fran asked the obvious but not the most polite question. 'Why me?'

'Because you're such a role model for our young women viewers.'

'With my face looking like this?' Fran demanded dryly.

'Well, not in the immediate future,' the younger woman conceded.

But Pound had known about her face all along. What else did she have on her agenda? 'Quite.'

It took a moment for Pound to respond. 'I understand you're due to retire.'

Fran tried hard not to sound sarcastic. 'A point you made yourself at the press conference when we talked about the assaults.'

'Exactly.' For the first time her face relaxed and Fran could see how attractive she was, even without TV make-up. 'And I still don't see your Zimmer parked anywhere, Fran.'

'Today's one of my good days,' Fran cackled, hunching like a cartoon crone.

'The programme would make a good valediction for you.'

'So long as it didn't turn into an obituary! Come on, Dilly — I'm an administrator. I don't leap around doing good deeds, not these days anyway.'

'But you used to until very recently. You solved that child abduction case.'

'I was involved. But it wasn't "my" case and I didn't solve it. I was part of a team. And I don't think it would do anyone's morale any good if you were to focus on one old bat.'

Dilly nodded at least temporary defeat. 'After a life as busy as yours, what will you do when you retire?' She sounded genuinely interested. 'Will you be hanging up your handcuffs for good?'

'I could take them home to use in the bedroom?' Fran grinned.

But the joke fell terribly flat. Pound looked puzzled, shocked even, as the penny dropped. She rallied swiftly. 'Have you had any job offers?'

'One or two. Since I'm still pondering the implications I can't tell you what.' This must be the tail end of the conversation they'd started after her TV interview.

'There are rumours that you've been approached by universities to lecture in criminology. Wouldn't you find that a bit dull after a life pursuing criminals? Have you ever thought of becoming a private detective?'

It was best to put her out of her misery. 'Come on, Dilly. You'll have to tell me sooner or later. You're being stalked, aren't you?'

Was she shocked at the direct question or relieved the problem was again being vented, this time without her boss's interruption? 'I don't know. I really don't!'

Fran got up and switched on the kettle. 'Let's have a nice cup of tea.' While she waited, she returned to her desk, diverted her calls and reached out for her notepad, something Dilly had conspicuously lacked. 'Now you can tell me all about it. When did it start?'

'The day after that TVInvicta piece I did went national. A letter care of the office.' Pound fished in her bag, producing a blank envelope crammed with A4 sheets, computer printed, of course.

Fran's heart sank. No original envelopes. 'I don't suppose you remember the postmarks?'

A shake of the head. Funny, it was the first thing Fran always looked at when an unexpected letter arrived.

Taking the bundle still in its envelope she said firmly, 'If you get what you suspect may be another communication, use rubber gloves when you open it and stow it straight into a freezer bag. Better still, resist the temptation to open it and put it straight into the bag.'

'Evidence?'

'Exactly. We may get some DNA from it. It's a pain the Post Office use adhesive stamps these days — a single lick of a stamp used to provide a big enough sample to send down a criminal. That's what stalking is, Dilly. A crime. So you're not being weak or foolish in showing me this. You're stopping an offence. Now, tea or coffee? I've got green tea if you prefer.'

The domesticity over, Fran donned latex gloves and turned her attention to the letters. They were short, most of them no more than a couple of lines, and seemed tender rather than threatening — the sort Mark might have sent her during an enforced absence. She could see why Dilly had hesitated to admit they were a threat. 'The first question, of course, is obvious: do you have any idea who might have sent these?'

The younger woman blushed deeply. 'I did. I thought I did. But now — the latest one — I'm not so sure. In fact, I don't think I do anymore.'

'So while they were just romantic, you thought you knew the sender and were happy to have them, in fact?'

Pound licked her lips. 'Reasonably happy.'

'But not entirely? Dilly, I can see there's a back-story here. Nothing that isn't strictly relevant will ever get beyond these four walls. It's OK. Take your time.'

This interview might have been better in the comfortable surroundings of a rape suite, but she could hardly move her now. At least there was always a box of tissues in her top drawer. She fished it out and pushed it across. 'Come on — you've been brave enough to get this far.'

Although she tried to appear neutral, impassive even, Fran found Dilly's story moving. She had been the librarian at a Birmingham college where people were trained for the priesthood — Church of England, Methodists, United Reform Church. For three years she'd been in love with one of the students, a mature man with a family. She referred to him only as Steve. Even speaking his name made her blush and brought a flash of tears to her eyes. An affair was out of the question, even though she suspected he returned her feelings. It was only when he came to say goodbye at the end of his course that they declared their love for each other.

'No more than declared? It was no more than heightened emotion?'

'Even looking at a woman with lust in your heart is as bad as adultery.'

Fran frowned. 'Are you sure? So you didn't think you might as well be hanged for a sheep as for a lamb?'

Pound stared at her mug. 'We had the briefest of physical relationships.'

'I'm not judging you, Dilly. I'm just trying to work out if someone who was just a platonic friend might have written these notes.'

'We only slept with each other three times!' Dilly wailed. 'But a man with a vocation doesn't pick and choose bits of the church's teaching. What he was doing was sinning. Committing adultery. Breaking the commandments. So he broke it off. But he promised, if he were ever free, he'd contact me, no matter how many years down the line.'

'Free?' Was he planning to bump off his wife?

'If his wife — er — predeceased him.'

'Was she likely to?'

'She was a few years older than him.'

'And he was — when you knew him?'

'About forty.'

'So he'd be nearly fifty now. And his wife?'

'About fifty-six.'

Fran did a lot of sums in her head but none of them added up to anything sensible on Dilly's part. At last, with some relief, she asked, 'But you didn't wait for him?'

'What was the point? It was impossible to keep seeing each other when . . . You see, he still needed to use the college library — he became a curate in a parish in the Black Country.'

'That's that industrial area near Birmingham?'

'At one time it was far more important than Birmingham — it was the cradle of the Industrial Revolution,' she added, with a sudden surge of pride.

'You've got rid of your accent,' Fran observed.

'One does if one wants to work in the media,' was the dry response.

'And you've moved on a long way from being a librarian.'

'Why not? When I was a kid, I was too shy to become a journalist, but I asked God if he wanted me to remove temptation from Steve's way to give me some courage. So I did a degree course at Kent University—'

'Can you give me the details?' She jotted them down. 'Did you have a boyfriend there?'

'I didn't want one. And no one ever approached me. And they all know I've got a job with the TVInvicta News team; we have reunions every so often and share updates. So they wouldn't have to *find* me.'

Fran's eyes shot up. 'Some people might be jealous of your landing such a good post?'

She shook her head. 'I was a just backroom girl for a couple of years and then got a break reporting. Just low level stuff. Then this happy-slapping and the assault cases came up and I went national — first time ever! They're promoting me — I'm going to be their crime correspondent.' Her face glowed. But her mouth suddenly turned down, almost comically, but not quite.

'Which was when you had the first letter?'

'I thought it was from Steve. That his wife had died and he was free. And this was his way of contacting me.'

'You didn't wonder why he'd not given an address?'

'I thought it was just a lovely — yes, titillating — joke.' Pound made a visible effort. 'But then all I got were more notes. Then the one about black lace. I knew that wouldn't be from him.'

'Because?' Fran prompted.

Pound looked genuinely shocked. 'Steve wouldn't be into that sort of thing!'

Fran suppressed two thoughts: that sex with Steve might not be as exciting as Dilly hoped, and that as a crime reporter Dilly would have to come across far more than black lace.

'If it isn't Steve, do you have any other ideas?'

She shook her head. 'I'm just afraid that my fiancé will get to hear.'

Fiancé? What was she doing getting engaged when news from her erstwhile lover made her heart beat so much faster?

'So you're going to be married?'

'Yes.'

'And why don't you want your fiancé to hear about the letters?'

'Because he wouldn't like them.'

'In what way?'

'Well, people thinking those thoughts about his girlfriend.'

'Even though his girlfriend had no idea who was thinking them?'

Dilly looked shocked. 'But I must have done something — dressed some way—'

'Nonsense!' Fran used her most headmistressy voice. 'You'll be telling me next that it's a rape victim's fault if her vagina's penetrated with a broken bottle and she's left to bleed to death!' she continued brutally.

Perhaps deep down that was exactly what Dilly wanted to tell her.

'Let's talk about your fiancé. What does he do for a living?'

'He's a teacher. Well, a deputy headmaster. He's been sent in to save a failing school in Ramsgate,' she added, with a touch of pride.

So where would that put him in the sense of humour stakes? Discipline, yes. But would that extend to his private life?

Fran smiled, as if set for a sisterly gossip. 'What's his name?'

'Daniel.'

Daniel what, for God's sake? But she didn't want Dilly to think she might be ready to grill him. And the number of deputy head teachers in Ramsgate called Daniel was probably pretty low. 'Where did you meet?'

'At a church meeting — an Alpha course.'

'And where do you live?'

'Chartham.'

'Then that's quite a commute for him, isn't it? From Chartham to Margate?'

Dilly looked shocked. 'But we don't live together. I told you — we're engaged.'

Best make sure she said nothing of her own situation, then. 'Do you see much of each other?'

'At weekends, of course. Not much during the week — I work funny hours and his job demands he work incredibly hard.'

'So he might have sent you these little notes just to remind you he was there?'

'Heavens, no! He's a good man, Chief Superintendent.'

'But you thought your ex might have done, and you can't get much more virtuous than a parish priest.' One who sleeps with a young woman with a crush on him and only then conveniently remembers the rules about adultery. She was beginning to think poor Dilly could do with some relationship therapy. Not getting a bite, she went on, 'Is there anyone else you can think of — any other boyfriend from your Midlands days?' The sooner she got hold of a franked envelope the better. In fact, getting the post office to intercept them and redirect them here might be the best idea.

'I didn't have many boyfriends. None that would send notes like that.'

'But you're sure the first didn't arrive until the day after you went national?'

'I'd have remembered something like that.'

'Did your mates at work take you out for a drink to celebrate?'

'Why should they?'

'Quite a milestone, I should have thought.'

'I suppose I'm not particularly close to any of them, not really.'

Why not? Lack of self-confidence on her part, or resentment on theirs that a newcomer should have had a good break? Enough resentment to build up a hoax involving letters like this?

'Might one of them want to get close? Might he think it a good anonymous chat up line?'

'I wouldn't have thought so.'

'Have you been followed?'

There was a distinct hesitation before Dilly said, 'I don't think so.'

'Are you sure?'

'Sometimes — but I'm sure it was only my imagination. No, I haven't. Definitely.'

Fran didn't think she was going to get any further with that line, not yet. 'Have you had any anonymous phone calls?'

'The switchboard would filter them.'

'But you've had no one breathing heavily down the line and then cutting the call?'

'I don't think so.'

Fran managed not to swear. 'Let's make sure. Ask the switchboard not to put calls through directly to you. The caller can leave their details and you'll call back.'

'It's not how it works.'

'All right — so long as you promise me that if you do get an anonymous call you'll tell me and I'll think of some security excuse so everyone's calls are filtered. Your mobile provider can do the same if you ask them. Trust me, Dilly, if we can get to the bottom of this we will.'

'I do trust you. As soon as I saw you at the press conference I knew I could trust you.'

A tiny but insistent alarm bell rang. 'You realise that I won't be dealing personally with the case, don't you? I'm just an administrator these days. I'm sorry.' She broke off, ready to snarl at the idiot walking in with no more than a perfunctory knock. But the idiot was the Chief Constable.

* * *

'I might have known he would have got in on the act,' Fran laughed, as she backed neatly into Mark's drive. 'He can't resist a luvvie, can he? He was all over the poor woman like a rash.'

He retrieved his coat and case. 'We'll suspend our ban on talking shop, just for tonight, won't we? Just so that you can fill me in?'

'Just this once. Go and run us a bath. I'll bring up some wine and I'll tell you all about it.'

* * *

'So he wants you to drop everything and investigate this sad woman's only bit of excitement?' Mark sat up in disbelief.

She blew some foam at him.

'Not everything. And not immediately. Not until we've got in place a proper acting DCS. He's already told Cosmo that the interviews must be this week, which won't please the Superintendents' Association.'

'It's certainly very short notice. And he'd want whoever it is in post when?'

'Middle of next week.'

'Bloody hell. What's this bird got over him?'

'You saw her on Friday. An air of vulnerability. She's brought out his protective instincts. And she is very pretty.'

'Much too bland for my tastes,' he assured her, blowing foam back. 'I like a woman with some spirit! Hey! No! I surrender . . .'

CHAPTER EIGHT

Come back, come back, to our screens, so I may look on you again. I want to see your beautiful feet, your knees, your thighs.

* * *

'London postmarks,' Fran said, flipping a week's worth of still sealed envelopes addressed to Dilly on to the desk of Mike Dalton, her tame forensic scientist. 'That's a big help, isn't it? You might as well have these too, just in case.'

He eyed the sheaf, but donned gloves and picked up that morning's delivery, which had been intercepted by the Royal Mail and diverted to Maidstone, as Fran had requested anything addressed to Dilly at work should be. Until an anonymous note arrived at Dilly's home address, she'd reluctantly acceded to Dilly's pleas that her ordinary mail should continue as usual.

Mike popped it into an evidence bag. 'Quite a lot of people in London. Commuters. Not just Kent. Sussex is in TVInvicta's catchment area too. And you said this woman went national? Northerners come to London too.' Mike dropped the fact as if it were a leaden weight.

'And so do Brummies. And that's our only, very tiny, lead so far.'

'Come on, Fran, what am I supposed to be looking for? It's a big place!'

'What do they make in the Midlands these days? Not cars any more.'

'Chocolate. They still make chocolate. Yes, someone working for Cadbury's would be nice and obvious.'

'Wouldn't it just? Just give it your bog-standard going over, Mike — bearing in mind it was the Chief himself who dropped this on to me.'

'I thought you were retiring? Funny, you spend forty years longing to do all the things you didn't have time to do when you were crawling up the promotion ladder and when you know you're going to have hours and hours to do just what you want it's dead scary and you can't think of anything you really want to do. They're so short of experienced forensic scientists . . .'

'I thought the universities were snowed under by applicants!'

'You missed an essential adjective, Fran. Experienced. They want me to carry on working part-time. On the face if it that sounds brilliant. But I don't know I could do the job if I didn't put my heart and soul into it.' He touched the evidence bag. 'OK, then. If I can't get anything from this, do you want me to pass it on to Guy the Graphologist, let him see if he can find any word patterns?'

'That'll come expensive. Just hunt for chocolate. Yes, and anything else the Black Country makes these days,' she joked.

He lifted a minatory finger. 'For a start, Cadbury's is in Birmingham, not the Black Country. For seconds, half the Black Country industrial output has disappeared. Have you looked at the figures for our manufacturing base?'

Fran couldn't say she had, but knowing Mike they were serious. He had the sort of flesh free face that would have made him the perfect extra in a Dickens TV adaptation and had once famously said he didn't do joy. But he brought to his job an imagination that some of his colleagues declared was unscientific — his response being that all the great scientists had made leaps of the imagination that ordinary mortals couldn't even guess at.

He'd picked up and was reading a random page from Fran's sheaf. 'Quite poetic, isn't he? Biblical even. Are any of the others?'

Biblical! But, not wanting to give him any pointers that might be quite spurious, she said flatly, 'Not as far as I know. What she hadn't opened I left sealed. I thought my loss might be your gain.'

'Well, at last I've got you trained,' he observed with what in anyone else might have been a smile.

* * *

Strolling back to her office — these days she consciously tried to resist the fashion of clutching a file and striding, grim-faced, as if late for an appointment with her doom — Fran popped her head into the Incident Room, its walls now papered with notices, photos, diagrams and maps. With the arrival of the new acting Chief Superintendent, Jill had been moved, not altogether tactfully, as Fran had already told Cosmo, to a goldfish bowl at the far end of the room, leaving Henson's office to Joe Farmer. The newcomer was a youthful forty-minus and shy-looking but no doubt fearsomely competent. Another white male middle-class face, of course: she kicked herself for having been so slipshod in helping select the short list. Positive discrimination wasn't an option, but keeping an eye open and encouraging certainly was. At the interviews Fran had really wanted a Sikh — minus a turban, it had to be said — but the majority supported Farmer, and she had to acquiesce. His CV glowed in the dark; she just hoped his spiral up through the ranks hadn't been at the expense of getting proper experience.

She flapped a casual hand; with a fleeting, possibly respectful smile, he responded in kind. Jill, on the other hand, did a fair imitation of a rabbit caught in the headlights. At last she overcame her paralysis to lurch from behind her desk, bumping her thigh hard on the corner as she did so.

Fran winced for her. The two women laughed, and Fran settled on a singularly uncomfortable visitor's chair, Jill retreating to her own side of the desk.

'I want to pick your brain,' Fran said. 'Girls' talk sort of thing.' She didn't particularly want to discuss the Dilly Pound case with anyone, but hoped it would get Jill to open up a little. 'The Chief's got a pet stalking case.'

'That's not a job for you, Fran, and so you should have told him!'

'Funnily enough, it probably is, you know — at the moment it's manageable enough for one person and goodness knows you've got enough with all these assaults to keep twice as many people busy. How are things going, by the way?'

Jill gave an embarrassed smile. 'I took your advice. I've got a team of bright young things who might talk the lingo dealing with the happy-slappers, and the rest of us are doing everything we can to trace the sex offender. Whoever it is — they are! — there's no record on the sex offenders' register. And as you know, there's no DNA match. The bugger's now heavily into sexual assaults. I'm afraid any day now we'll have our first rape. Quite,' she acknowledged Fran's grim expression. 'He's like the damned Scarlet Pimpernel. We seek him here, we seek him there — we seek him bloody everywhere.'

'Still no decent description to go on?'

'Half the girls were so traumatised they didn't — maybe couldn't — recall any details. The others just said he was "ordinary" — and no two e-fits match! Some said he wore specs. Others were equally convinced that he didn't. So we're checking couriers, taxi-drivers, train drivers: if it's male and it moves we're on to it.'

'And you're managing it all without frightening the horses. Well done. CCTV installers?' she added, as she stood up. She could have sworn she'd suggested them before, but — no, she couldn't swear to it. Just to thinking about it? Senior moments . . .

'Shit! I knew there was something . . . I wrote it down and put the note somewhere. I'll get on to it.' As Jill looked frantically for another piece of paper, the phone rang. She took the call, but promised to phone back. As she replaced the handset she said, 'Guv? You wanted to talk to me about Pound?'

'So I did!' At least wrinkling her nose in irritation hardly hurt any more. 'She really doesn't want to give me the name of the only suspect. He's a family man, very respectable.'

'Just the sort of man you'd expect to be stalking,' Jill said cheerfully but not entirely accurately. 'Did they have a red-hot affair or something?'

'Pretty lukewarm from what I can gather. Which is what worries me. It's too pat. But I'd like to eliminate him from the enquiry.'

'Not like you to use cop-talk, guv.'

'No, indeed. I think my subconscious has just given me my answer, don't you? Thanks for the natter, Jill. It really cleared my brain. Look, don't beat yourself up over these cases. If you need more resources, more personnel, you know I'll always . . . be your advocate,' she finished tamely. With the advent of Joe Farmer, she'd relinquished control of the purse strings. They exchanged rueful grins of acknowledgement. 'And my door's always open too, remember. Any time I need to make a decision, please drop in!'

* * *

'You don't suppose I'm going to march up the vicarage path and demand to speak to Steve in front of his wife and kids, do you? Or stand up while he's giving Communion and denounce him as a sinner? For goodness' sake, Dilly, do you think I came down in the last shower?' Fran kept her voice low: she wanted them to seem like just another couple of women drinking coffee in a popular Canterbury teashop. Aunt and niece, maybe.

Pound shook her head. She was letting her hair grow, and one strand was the perfect length for her to chew, like a troubled teenager. 'He may not be there anymore!'

'You mean he may have another curacy? Or have been promoted?'

'May have been. Though his wife—'

'Yes?'

'She worked full time, as I recall.' She blushed so deeply it must have hurt. 'It would have been difficult for them to move unless she could get another job. A senior teacher. Earned about five times what he was getting. And, of course, she was never going to be there to help about the parish.'

Well no, not with a couple of kids to worry about on top of the hours teachers were supposed to work these days.

'Would you remember their address? And the name of his church? Holy Trinity? Let me write it down. Right, now we're getting somewhere.'

The younger woman's jaw jutted. 'I really do not want some plod kicking down his front door. I want to withdraw the charges.'

'You haven't made any yet. As for a plod, the investigator will be a woman in her fifties, one you trusted enough to ask to help you in the first place.'

Dilly looked up, eyes round. 'You'll do it yourself?'

'Something as delicate as this we don't send in police cadets with no GCSEs, Dilly. One thing you can do, however: tell me where I would find information on Church of England clergy. I want to make sure he's still in the Black Country before I try my luck with the M25.'

'Something called Crockford's Directory. There should be one in the public library.'

Fran took a deep breath, regarding her steadily. 'You're telling me you've never been tempted to look him up? To see what he's doing?'

Dilly's voice was firm. 'Tempted, Chief Superintendent? I've been tempted every moment of every day. But I've never, ever fallen.'

* * *

The interview with Dilly completed rather more quickly than Fran had dared to hope, she had time to kill before her next meeting with Joe Farmer. The obvious port of call was the city library. Externally it was a magnificent Victorian Gothic affair; inside it was cramped and dingy. A shiny new one in the Whitefriars development should have replaced it. However, the Powers-that-Be had claimed they couldn't afford to improve the lot of readers, so the historical premises remained. Whether Fran was pleased or otherwise she couldn't say. If Birmingham's Central Library was an example of what librarians thought their clients preferred, she was glad to stay old and cosy. At least she knew where everything was, even if there wasn't much of it. The volume of Crockford's was only a couple of years old. By that time the Reverend Stephen Hardy was no longer a curate. He was now priest in charge at St Philip's, Moat Road, Warley. So he was still in the Black Country. And his address? Another road in Warley, she'd no idea how far from the church. A quick call to one of her Midlands colleagues would confirm he hadn't moved to a new parish recently.

She dawdled back to the Castle Street car park past another batch of estate agents' windows and collected more handfuls of particulars and thus over-ran the time on her ticket. But she was there before the parking attendant, and hightailed it out before she could be humbled.

Should she take to the lanes again? Why not? She could keep an eye peeled for estate agents' signs. She might fancy a home in Pluckley, especially as there was a station on the outskirts, but Smarden never. The very name suggested a down-turned mouth. Boughton Malherbe, now — would that give humans hay fever or cows bellyache? Further south was Cuckold's Corner: it would take a man with a fine sense of humour to want to put that on application forms or letter headings. Boldshaves, on the other hand — would Mark like that? What about Hunger Hatch? One day maybe she'd take a course in local history and find the origin of some of these place names.

Meanwhile, she drove gently on, keeping parallel, she hoped, with the motorway. What would it be like to live in that gatehouse over there, guardian to what seemed to be some great estate? To her astonishment, a discreet for sale sign jostled the garden gate. She was certain she'd never seen the place during her Internet searches.

She pulled over — plenty of hard-standing opposite the front gate, but none within.

In the thin February sun, the place seemed perfection itself, pretty curtains flapping through the open diamond paned windows in the roof. Exactly what she and Mark had at the top of their wish list: an old cottage, on a road but not a main one, with no close neighbours to disturb them.

In a rosy mist of dreams, she stared on, repainting, replacing — who on earth had planted Leylandii quite so close? — and, wearing an apron because she'd been cooking Mark scones for his tea, standing on the front-door step to welcome him home.

Someone was trying to get into the car!

Adrenaline a-pump, she nearly cried out. But the face at the driver's door was canine, if no more attractive for that. At last someone pulled the baying brute away.

She switched the ignition back on and opened the window.

'Are you interested in the house?' a woman at the far end of the dog's lead shouted. She wore a folded headscarf, just like the queen. 'Sit, Toby. Sit!'

'Yes, I suppose I might be.'

'Want to look round?'

'But I don't have an appointment.'

'That doesn't matter. You can come in now if you want.' There was such desperation in the woman's voice and face that Fran almost agreed.

Eyeing the dog, she got out slowly. She was greeted by a roar. Not the dog, or any other resentful pet. Traffic. The M20.

She was torn. They couldn't possibly live with such a constant din. Clutching at straws, she turned to the woman. 'Is there always so much noise?'

'What noise?'

'The motorway?'

'Never notice it,' came the prompt reply. And maybe it was even truthful.

Perhaps she should just take the offered tour? But that would be to raise the woman's hopes in vain. And now she thought about it, the place was more likely to be poky than bijou, the ceilings too low for two tall people. If only her phone would ring.

At last she spoke the honest truth. 'I really don't have time today. But I'll phone your agent for particulars. Thanks.'

She slipped back into the car. But, as she noticed when she'd driven a further mile, the dog had had its silent and not very subtle revenge. She slung the mat and offending shoe into the boot and drove back in bare feet.

CHAPTER NINE

My love is as strong as death, but my jealousy is burning me, a great fire I couldn't put out, even if I wanted to.

* * *

'So while you two enjoy your jolly, I intend to do Selfridges and any other palaces of conspicuous consumption I can find,' Fran blithely informed the two heavily braided men, as she nosed the unmarked police car through the centre of Birmingham. Mark and the Chief Constable were joining other senior officers from across the country in a discussion of matters of national security, a response to the Home Secretary's latest diktat. Officially, of course, she was in the Midlands to interview the Reverend Stephen Hardy, whom she had phoned to arrange a meeting. Since she needed transport to reach him, car-sharing had been the obvious option.

Her declaration had a resonance only Mark picked up. The last time Fran had been to Birmingham on police business, she'd immediately been summoned down to Devon to her dying father's bedside.

She was still speaking. '. . . the moment I've checked out that theological college.' She pulled up outside Lloyd

House, the administrative HQ of the West Midlands Police. Grabbing his briefcase, Mark came round to her window, his face furrowed with anxiety. 'Are you sure you can fight your way back into the city? God knows why they don't have a park and ride scheme or two.'

There were days when she wanted to point out that she had even more police driving qualifications than he did, but they both had enough stress in their lives not to want to add to it by petty arguments, and, truth be told, she enjoyed being worried about.

'I shall be all right. I can always ask a policeman. One of which is looking at me very hard even as we speak. Let's shock him to the core.' She leaned out and, pulling Mark closer, kissed him on the lips, enjoying the poor constable's patent embarrassment, and the Chief's extreme amusement. He had done at least his share in bringing the two together, so she blew him a twiddle-finger kiss too. Or was that going too far? Whatever his reaction, she was too busy dealing with traffic and getting into the right lane to notice.

She'd worked out a plan of campaign. Should anyone ask, she wanted to discuss with Steve Hardy the situation of one of his ex-parishioners. With luck the question wouldn't arise. She always preferred the straight truth to even a half lie.

The main Hagley Road, now an arterial link between Birmingham and the M5, must have been full of gracious houses once, she mused. Now it was a mixture of mega-pubs and budget hotels, plus offices of various ages.

Bearwood, in what must be a fringe of the Black Country, was on a smaller scale altogether. It took her several changes of lights to cross what was presumably the main street. Then she found herself driving past lots of Thirties houses; a promising-looking park; some pubs which might have been grand drinking-palaces when they were built in the Twenties or Thirties, but would have been dwarfed by the ones she'd passed earlier. What clientele would they attract? Kids getting bladdered on alcopops or, complete with their cloth-caps and whippets, thin-faced men favouring mild?

What she hadn't bargained for was the hills. Not just the one she was halfway down, but those on the horizon. It must have been a fearsome place when poor old Queen Vic demanded the curtains on her train be drawn against the ugliness of the industrial landscape.

Moat Road at last. It was full of houses of all eras crammed together, none very big, some pretty small. What would they cost? Had London prices oozed this far north?

Ah. There on her right were school playing fields. And a school that might have had the words Thirties Grammar blazoned across it, though the name on its notice board was more prosaic. So that poor specimen next door must be the church. St Philip's. Brick-built, it sat round-shouldered with hardly even a token tower to give it dignity. It couldn't have been much fun being a pre-war Anglican church growing up alongside the historic non-conformist chapels for which she dimly recalled the area was famous.

There, another topic for post-retirement study. Not just local history, industrial history too.

So what made a man give up his career to dedicate his life to running a sad, graffiti-covered place like this? His career, and an attractive, adoring young woman.

Assuming, of course, that he had.

* * *

Stephen Hardy — it seemed he preferred the full version of his Christian name these days — sat her in a chilly office at the back of his church. He explained at some length that the four-bedroom detached house that he gave as his address was really his wife's, and with two children it was hard to find a spare room for confidential business — which she'd stressed this was. To save the parish money, they'd rented out the proper vicarage.

'Of course, the children are at college and university these days,' he said, biting his lip, as if catching himself out in a lie. Or was it simply worry about the expense? He seemed the sort to worry. Slender to the point of thinness, he hunched his shoulders not so much against the cold as against life itself. Could Dilly really have fallen passionately in love with this man, painted in watercolours, not oils? Had the head she loved already been half-bald, the skin pale, the mouth girlishly pink? Had he already worn spectacles, the sort that darkened against the light?

Sipping from a thick mug, the sort that always seemed to retain someone else's lipstick round the rim, she said, 'It's about someone from your college days I want to talk.' She shifted slightly in her chair so she could get the best view of his face as he reacted, which was with predictable horror and disbelief in face and voice alike.

'Surely no one I knew there would be in any trouble! Ordained priests!'

'Oh, Mr Hardy, you'd be surprised,' she countered, with a lopsided grin that could have been cynical or sad. 'Think Catholic priests and choirboys. But at least the dear old C of E doesn't demand celibacy of its clergy.'

'No,' he agreed. He looked more puzzled than alarmed. 'Look, is this one of those standard police enquiries into someone's possible criminal records? Because I'd have thought your computer files might be more reliable and less time-consuming.' Now there was distinct resentment in his voice.

She shook her head. 'They wouldn't ask a Chief Superintendent to do that.' She flipped her ID again. 'I'm speaking to you because, as I said when I phoned, we have a very confidential case in train at the moment. As far as I'm concerned, if I'm satisfied by your answers to some of my questions, this conversation will never go beyond these four walls, apart from a report to my superior officers — in this case, the Chief Constable himself and an Assistant Chief Constable.'

'What about my wife?'

She asked as smoothly as she could, 'Aren't there some conversations here that share the secrecy of the confessional?'

'Apart from those, I tell her everything.'

'Everything?' she asked gently. 'You don't belong to the school of thought that says that some personal secrets are best kept to save hurting your partner?'

'Partner! My *wife*, Chief Superintendent.'

In most circumstances she wouldn't have bitten. No doubt it was because part of her still smarted because of Mark's decision, however much she might try to sympathise with his reasons. As it was, she snapped, 'And would you tell your *wife* if you were stalking your former mistress?'

Those pretty rosebud lips went white. 'I beg your pardon?' he demanded furiously, slamming down his mug and standing up. 'How dare you!'

'Please sit down. If it's not you, someone else is. Someone is stalking a Ms Dilly Pound. You do know her, don't you?'

'Delia Pound?'

She nodded. Delia, not Dilly. At least it was more appropriate than the Delilah they'd speculated it might be. When had the change happened?

'Know her? *Knew* her. Once. A long time ago.' He turned in apparent fury. 'Why does she say I'm harassing her now?' But he wilted under her gaze and resumed his seat.

'She doesn't. Not specifically. But someone is. And it's standard practice to talk to people with whom the victim may have had a romantic entanglement.'

He stood again, pointing backwards. 'She is in my past, Chief Superintendent. And may God forgive me for having let her into my life at all.' He was either totally sincere or a very fine actor.

Fran might have been inclined to believe the former. But she had seen so many of the latter she had to press him further. 'Do you ever visit London in the course of your work, Mr Hardy?'

His colour came and went. 'I've been on a course recently, as it happens. But what that has to do with poor little Delia Pound I've no idea.'

'Could you give me details, please? Just the dates and where you stayed. Oh, and the name of the person running the course.'

'This is beyond belief! How dare you come in here and — and imply—'

'Sit down. Please. Look, Stephen, someone is committing an offence. Stalking, alas, as I'm sure you're aware, all too often leads to other, more serious crimes against the victim. Physical as well as psychological harm. If it's not you, and I'm quite prepared to believe that—'

'Dashing up here to check up on me! Why not accuse me outright?'

What had happened to the quiet, reasonable middle-aged man she'd pitied?

'Because I'm quite literally trying to eliminate you from my enquiries. Please believe me.'

'And Delia—' He clamped his lips shut.

She relented. '—Is almost certain the criminal isn't you.'

He pulled off his spectacles and opened his eyes wide. They were an amazing blue. Was it they that had first attracted Dilly? And then he smiled, the sort of pure tenderness that turned her heart over. The poor man still loved Dilly. As much as she loved Mark, and he her, marriage or no marriage. Surely he'd want to know about Dilly's feelings, what she was doing, if she was married? Knowledge in this case might be power, but it was certainly pain. Unless asked direct, she would say nothing.

'Thank God,' he said. He rummaged furiously on his desk, then through the baskets of an old wire filing stalk, the likes of which she hadn't seen since she was at college. 'Here.' He thrust a crumpled A5 brochure at her. 'All the details: subjects, course tutors, everything. Two weeks' residential.'

'And when did you come back?'

'Last weekend. You're looking very serious. Is that when the stalking started? When I went on the course? No wonder you wanted to talk to me. Don't you want me to do a DNA test, too?'

'At this stage that's hardly necessary.'

He was on his feet again, only the smallness of the office preventing him from pacing. He turned. 'What's the bastard doing to her?'

She'd not expected such a term from a clergyman but didn't remark on it. 'You know how it is with stalkers — they move on from one thing to another,' she said, knowing he'd spot the evasion.

'What got him on to her, do you think?'

Poor man, he was fishing for news of Dilly without daring to ask. 'I think he saw her on the TV news. Usually she reports for a local channel, but a piece she did went national.'

He sat down heavily. 'TV! Are you sure we're talking about the same Delia Pound here?'

She wanted to give him something to comfort him. 'She said she needed strength to move on from the theological college, and found it. She took a degree in journalism and fetched up in front of the camera.'

'Which region?' he breathed. 'No, I — but you said you were from Kent, didn't you?'

'I think I need to ask her permission before I pass on any details. Any at all,' she said, trying to forestall the inevitable enquiry. She didn't want to be the one to tell him that Dilly was teetering on the edge of marriage, if scarcely diving into it. She got to her feet. 'Very well, Mr Hardy. I promise I shall only contact you again if I really need to, and only here, not at home. And I repeat my undertaking to tell no one except my superior officers.'

'What about Delia? Will you tell her I'm in the clear?'

She picked up the leaflet. 'As soon as we know you are.'

* * *

The theological college where Stephen and Dilly had met was housed in an elegant Georgian building in Edgbaston, a suburb oozing money and status. At least part of it was housed there. Other, less lovely buildings had been tacked on to the back and sides, presumably in pre-town planning days.

She handed over her card to a warmly efficient receptionist. With the minimum of fuss and wait, she was shown straight into the principal's room, lit by a sudden burst of watery sunlight, unkind to the furniture and fittings but generous to the very handsome occupant's patrician features and silver hair. It couldn't have been stage-managed better.

'Delia Pound?' Dr Barlow's eyes widened. 'I'd have thought she was the last woman on God's earth to be stalked. *Wee tim'rous cowering creature*: that was our Delia.'

'So you can't think of any student or member of staff who might have carried a torch for her?'

He shook his head emphatically. 'This college isn't like a university full of testosterone-fuelled young men—' he dropped his eyes to look at her card '—Dr Harman. Most of our students are mature men or women; many have families. All are called by God.'

She nodded. To object would be to compromise the sad lovers' confidentiality. 'It was a very long shot. Thank you for your time.' He kept her card, but she found herself hoping that later he would shake his head at it and flip it into the bin.

* * *

Several hours later, she was back at Lloyd House, in the foyer meeting Mark and the Chief again. At the Chief's suggestion, she had stowed the car in an official parking slot, on the principle that if you had rank you might as well pull it occasionally. All three set off on foot through the rush hour to find something to eat before they ventured south.

Mark turned back. 'Hang on. Have you left everything out of sight?'

'What everything?' Fran didn't move.

'The goodies you've bought. I thought you were going to hit Selfridges!' He looked at her face. 'Fran, what's the problem?' he asked so that only she could hear.

'No problem,' she responded. 'While we're talking about concealing items, why don't you both sling those clothes carriers in the boot? There's no point in carting all those silver buttons around. And since we're in the UK's curry capital, perhaps we should go and try the local cuisine?'

If he'd hoped the Chief wouldn't notice her over-bright tone, he was disappointed. He wasn't a man to miss much, was he?

But Fran was deep in conversation with a youthful passing constable. Was he one of her protégés? He couldn't remember very many Asian officers passing through Kent. All the same, they were clearly getting on like a house on fire — he could hear the lad's rather high-pitched giggle as he pointed into some vague distance. Soon, waving at each other in half-salutes, they parted company, and Fran returned briskly to the two men. 'According to Constable Nazir there, we can't get any decent curry in the city centre. Ladypool Road, that's where we need to go. But he says we need to kill at least an hour before we set out.'

'In that case,' the Chief said, looking at his watch, 'I suggest a quiet drink for the three of us, and a snack and a taxi for me. I hear there's a talk this evening at the Barber Institute, out at the university, about the Florentine School and perspective. Unless you two would like to come too? The galleries themselves are worth a visit.'

Much as he'd have liked to get Fran to himself, Mark supposed polite acquiescence in an evening neither would have dreamed of undertaking for their own pleasure seemed called for.

* * *

The galleries were indeed wonderful, deserving far more than the sprint round that was all they had time for before the illustrated lecture, which lasted a couple of hours. The snack was now more than a distant memory, and Mark's stomach had offered a tentative rumble, but the Chief was keen that they head straight for the motorway and home, rather than return to the Ladypool Road.

It was Fran who stood her ground. 'I wouldn't be able to look PC Nazir in the eye again if I had to confess we'd never tried his cousin's restaurant, sir. He promised the biggest, fluffiest naans in town. And a doggie bag for everything we couldn't eat.'

So it would be after two in the morning before they could speak privately. During the meal, the Chief talked, more interestingly than the lecturer, about Renaissance art.

It wasn't until they'd regained the car, still safe after a bit of *ad hoc* valet-parking by Nazir's cousin's son, that Fran could update them about Stephen Hardy. She took the wheel, maintaining, once they'd reached the M40, an absolutely legal and equally irritating seventy every inch of the stint she'd volunteered for. Mark felt honour-bound to take the next stretch, which he suspected would take them mysteriously to the Chief's front door.

At the change-over, at Oxford services, the Chief asked, 'Will you be checking this course of Hardy's?'

'Low key, not terribly high priority,' she replied, retiring to the back seat. Mark hoped she'd manage to doze. Instead, she was going to have to lean forward to hear and reply to the Chief's questions.

At last she reprised the case to everyone's satisfaction. He hoped. As an act of conversational vandalism, he switched on the radio. Let Classic FM do its bit and soothe them.

* * *

'So why no mounds of goodies from the Birmingham shops?' he asked quietly, fishing out his garment carrier.

'Didn't buy anything.' Fran's voice was still brittle. Was it this case that was upsetting her so much? She seemed to have forgotten the first rule of crime-fighting, never to get personally involved. Were Hardy — they'd all diligently refrained from making wisecracks about kissing — and Dilly really a pair of star-crossed lovers? Or was Fran allowing their own amazing relationship to colour her judgement?

He took her hand and set them gently in motion. 'Why ever not?'

'I was too old. Old, Mark. I'm old.'

'Don't be ridiculous.' When she said nothing, he asked, 'Who says you're old?'

'No one. Not in as many words. But I was looking at all these things — shoes, undies, dresses — and I couldn't find anything I wanted to even try on, just in case. Nothing. Nothing. And then this beautiful young man swanned over and asked if he could help, as if I were some sort of imbecile unable to navigate my way round the store. And like a fool I asked if there were any clothes for someone my age. And very, very seriously, he led me over to one rail — one rail! — of knitwear.'

Anger at the slight surged on her behalf. 'And you let him get away with it?'

She shook her head, the security light peering pitilessly at her features. 'It wasn't his fault. The stuff he'd pointed out was good but I just couldn't face it. So I hitched up my skirt and legged it. Metaphorically.'

'And that's all?' He laughed with affectionate derision.

'It's quite a big all,' she corrected him sharply. 'It's being middle-aged, at the very least. It's being a step nearer my mother.' This time there was a definite catch in her voice.

Even as he responded bracingly, he knew he was missing something, but he couldn't for the life of him have said what. 'You've got thirty years to go before you'll get anything like your mother. Nor will you, if I have anything to do with it. Ever.'

CHAPTER TEN

Every night I watch for you, my beloved. I watch, but I don't see you. Where are you? Where are you hiding yourself? Must I come and find you?

* * *

'He's got to make a mistake, soon,' Jill declared, apparently ready to smash her open hand though the top of Fran's embarrassingly tidy desk. 'Got to. Hasn't he?'

It took Fran a hard blink and conscious effort to wrench her still sleep-ridden thoughts from her middle-aged Eloise and Abelard back to the sex attacker who had in the last twenty-four hours pestered — this time not much more than that — no fewer than three young women, all in the Hythe area this time. All out of CCTV range.

'Absolutely. If only he was concentrating on a particular area, we could put in a few WPC decoys,' she added, hoping to show she was up to speed. 'Or is he still obsessed with teenagers Natasha's age?'

'He went for a fifty-year-old the other day. So apparently not.'

Fran suppressed a shudder. In her bravado the other evening she might have put herself at risk. Had she?

Mentally she squared her shoulders. If some runt of a flasher had come her way, she knew who'd have regretted it more. But she did not wish to allude to her little adventure. 'Do you think it's time for a profiler? If you want, I can bend the Chief's ear.'

'What about the temporary Chief Super? Oughtn't the idea come from him?'

Fran tugged her hair. 'Of course it ought. At very least I should put it to him first before I even breathed a word to you. Or you could put it to him without having consulted me? Which would give you Brownie points.'

'The way he looks down his nose at me I could do with fully-fledged Girl Guide points!'

'Which reminds me, how is Tash?'

'She's given up Guiding. All sorts of issues.'

'But she's still got her cricket?'

For some reason Jill didn't sound enthusiastic. 'And not much else. They want her to have special coaching at Lord's. God knows how we'll fit that in.'

'But what an honour! She must be very good, very good indeed.'

Jill nodded, but the worry didn't leave her face.

'And how's Rob these days? Still into the bass guitar?'

Jill opened her mouth, only to snap it shut again. After a moment she said, 'Actually, he's moved on to the drums. For some GCSE coursework.'

So what else was going on? When Rob was twelve and she'd let him beat her at badminton, he'd been a charming kid. Now he was presumably into mid-teens blues, more likely to yawn at her and adjust his headphones than to pick up a racquet.

'You will tell me if there's anything I can do? Take the kids out for the day?' It sounded painfully inadequate even as she said it.

She was rewarded with a look of contemptuous disbelief. 'Thanks, I'll remember that, Fran.' With that Jill got up quietly and let herself out.

And Chief Superintendent Joe Farmer let himself in, ducking his head shyly as she gestured him to the still warm chair.

'Ms Harman,' he said, clearing his throat and swallowing hard, as if they were teenagers at a long-ago hop and he was about to ask her to dance, 'I do wish you wouldn't undermine my efforts to build a team.'

It was a very good opening. For one thing, she'd been poised to offer maternal congratulations on doing such a good job; for another the attack was so unexpected she couldn't think of a rebuttal. So she said nothing, merely raising an eyebrow to signify puzzlement and disdain and any other challenge he might wish to read into it.

'DCI Tanner is forever running to you for advice. I'm her line manager: it should be me she talks to.'

'Absolutely. I thought she did. No?'

'All I get out of her is that things are progressing or that she needs more resources. Not exactly consistent.'

She grunted in sympathy. 'Take her out for a drink and tell her. Ask her what the problem is.'

'I was hoping—'

'That I would? But that would be to do exactly what you don't want me to. So let's forget that option.' She rubbed her face, clamping down a yawn. 'Sorry. We didn't get back from Birmingham till three this morning.'

'But you were at your desk before I was!'

'My car might have been in the car park, but I was in the canteen having breakfast. I dare say you were slaving away before I'd had my second coffee.' Had that built a little bridge? 'Now, this Jill business. She's a highly competent DCI, but for some reason she seems overawed by this case — which isn't surprising, since Chummie's leaping from location to location like a jumping bean. What's your take on it? Were you thinking about a profiler? Fancy a cuppa while we talk about it?' She gestured to her machine.

'I . . . er . . . black coffee, please. Fran, how well do you know Tanner?'

This was one of those questions that required a far from straight answer. 'I was her first sergeant. When we were both younger, we played badminton against each other. Her kids call me "auntie". Used to. Probably refer to me as the Old Bat these days.'

'So you'd know if anything was wrong?'

'I'd want to know. That doesn't mean she'd tell me. There are times when even the best of mates are aware of the hierarchies. Certainly in this building. The rate you've progressed through the ranks you must have noticed.'

His turn to nod.

But he said nothing, so she asked, 'What do you think she ought to tell me?'

'What's her husband like?'

She suppressed the temptation to goggle. 'Brian? Why?'

'I just wondered.'

An officer at that level never just wondered. Until she worked out what he was after, she would pretend the questions were just social. 'He's very quiet. Works in local government. Good with the kids — he's had to be mother and father to them, of course, with Jill's shifts. He's a brilliant cook, as I recall — you want to get yourself invited.'

He ignored the quip. 'So what are you going to do?'

'Do? Me? Look, Joe, I thought we'd—'

'She's your friend!'

'Us, then. Because as you said, much as I'm her buddy when we're off duty, you're her line manager. We'll need to tackle any problems together. You see, I'm horribly out of touch even with my close friends: until my father died in the autumn I was commuting to Devon every weekend, a real downer socially. But as you've no doubt heard on the jungle drums, I'm now in a new relationship, which also means I neglect my friends.'

'And when did any copper at our level have a proper social life anyway?' he asked bitterly.

'Or a family one?' There was a clear waist on his wedding finger, as if a ring had recently been removed.

'Don't we have the highest divorce rates of all professional groups in the country?' he countered.

Oh, dear. Did she know him well enough to pursue that? On the whole she thought not. She waited, hoping her very silence might be useful, tipping her head on one side in the way that always amused Mark. And reflecting that if his marriage was a mess, then that might be why he'd thought a marital breakdown the reason for Jill's poor performance.

'OK, if you can't think of anything, I suppose we'd better bring in Human Resources,' he said at last.

'Are you sure?' She was damned sure she wasn't. 'That makes it all a bit official. And it might make Jill feel you didn't trust her with this case.'

'I don't.' It was a very bald statement. 'To be honest, I think you made a bad mistake appointing her. But we've clearly got to live with it.'

She'd had the same reservations herself, but wasn't about to pass the blame on to Mark. 'Which means supporting her through whatever her problems might be. Both professional and personal. Tell you what, Joe, why don't we both keep our eyes and ears open for a couple of days? Maybe I'll get a chance to talk to her Ashford colleagues. And I'll certainly make a point of drifting into her office, if you're sure it won't undermine you further.' She stood to end the meeting. 'Thanks for telling me all this. And if you think a profiler's called for, I'll certainly back you.'

Farmer pursed his lips. 'But . . .'

Her phone rang. Feeling they'd made as much progress as they could, she took the call. Dilly Pound was in Reception.

* * *

'I couldn't resist opening today's note,' Dilly said, spreading the by now familiar sheet of A4 paper with its few laser-printed lines between them on Fran's desk. 'Knowing that you'd seen . . . him.' There was a catch in her voice, as if she'd wanted to say his name but had stopped herself in time. But even the little pronoun sounded breathlessly tender.

Ignoring the emotion as best she could, Fran checked the postmark. 'Ashford!' This was a change of gear. She hoped her voice didn't betray how serious a change. 'Look, you should never have received this: I've asked the Post Office to reroute all your TVInvicta mail to me.' She made a note; she doubted they'd let anything further through.

'I didn't notice. I just wondered . . . But it sounds as if whoever it is is going to come and get me!'

So she'd hoped that it might have been Stephen who had sent an explicit message this time. And she'd had a nasty surprise.

Had Mr X literally come looking, or had he simply stopped commuting to London? What if — she had a frisson of irritation — Stephen had got on a train and come down himself? It wasn't impossible. And she'd blithely assured the Chief that checking his London alibi was low priority. But surely he'd have done more than post a letter. He'd have presented himself at TVInvicta's premises. And they were in Canterbury, not Ashford.

If only she'd had a decent night's sleep!

'Excuse me just one minute, Dilly.' She rerouted her phone calls, and set off in search of Tom. If he weren't up to his ears, he could phone the conference centre for her. But she couldn't just dive into the incident room and purloin him — not with Jill's sensibilities being what they were. In any case she might just see or smell for herself the things that had so alarmed Joe Farmer. However good her intentions, however, Jill's goldfish bowl was empty.

'Happy to oblige, guv,' Tom responded, as if she'd just offered him a fistful of fivers, not a battered brochure.

'And come straight back to me, the moment you know something. Knock on the door but wait outside. I don't want the person in my office to hear what you're saying.' Or Tom to see Dilly, of course. Though she'd swear on her father's grave he'd be totally discreet.

Dilly was standing looking out of the window when she got back.

'Is he still at Holy Trinity?' she asked without turning round.

'You don't need me to answer that. You can simply look in Crockford's,' Fran countered.

'How is he?'

She replied as kindly as she could. 'Dilly, I can't answer any questions about yesterday's interview, can I? If I can break his confidences, I could do the same for yours. But I do want to pursue other lines of enquiry too.'

The woman's face fell. 'It wasn't him. Who is it then, Fran?' The question ended on a note of terror.

Fran countered it with mundane information delivered as prosaically as she could. 'The trouble with your being in the public domain is that we need to sort out people who might genuinely have known you and now wish to renew a relationship and those who truly believe you know them but are deluding themselves.'

'I don't want to end up like Jill Dando, dead on my own doorstep!' Dilly's voice rose and cracked.

'Of course you don't. And we won't let anything like that happen,' Fran declared with a confidence she wasn't sure she felt. 'Now, is there any chance you could go and stay with a friend for a bit? Someone you really trust?' She didn't suggest Dilly's fiancé. What would be interesting was if Dilly herself did. 'No one from work?' A series of headshakes. 'OK, then — I'd like one of my crime prevention colleagues to check over your home, just to make sure it's got maximum security.'

'You mean he might try and break in? And rape me? Kill me?' Her voice rose towards hysteria.

Fran might have been Dixon of Dock Green. 'We haven't got that far, Dilly, not by any means. None of his letters has contained anything like a threat, and this one merely hints at him making an effort to see you. But I'd rather we didn't take any risks. Come on, there must be someone you could stay with?' In desperation she continued, 'Your fiancé? You have told him about all this?'

'He's at work all day.'

In other words, no. 'So are you. Though it might be safer if you stayed in the TVInvicta offices and didn't go out to cover stories. That way you're always with colleagues, and security seems pretty tight. So long as someone always walks you to your car.'

Dilly opened her mouth to object, to point out her professional obligations, just as Fran herself would have done.

'And if you do have to do an outside broadcast, at least you'll have a cameraman with you.' Fran took a deep breath. 'You're going to have to talk to Daniel about this, Dilly. He's your fiancé: he'd want to know, and probably deserves to.'

'No. I'd rather deal with this on my own. Without bothering him.' Terror had given way to mulishness. What on earth drove this woman?

'Love brings responsibilities as well as rights, you know. Wouldn't you want to know if anything was troubling him? Would it help if I were with you?'

'I don't want him involved. He's a very busy man. Very pressured.'

'How pressured?'

Dilly narrowed her eyes. 'You're not suspecting him, now, are you?' she demanded.

'Whom would you prefer me to suspect? Have you forgotten to tell me about any short-term relationships that went sour? You need to trust me. You really do. I'll be totally discreet.'

Pound shook her head.

'Flirtations? I know we've been through this before, but what about young men at Kent University? Fellow students? Tutors? Any young man you might have lost touch with.'

Dilly got up with something approaching a flounce. 'You're trying to get me to do your work for you. I thought detectives were supposed to do the detecting!'

Fran spread her hands. 'All I have is computer-generated letters printed by laser-printer, inserted into self-seal envelopes with lick-free stamps. London postmarks. One Ashford postmark. I don't have an awful lot to start detecting with.

Do I?' She ended with a friendly, supportive smile that might just soften her exasperation.

'I'll forget the whole thing then.'

'That's like telling a burglar to carry on helping himself. Stalking is as much a violation of your privacy as a teenager helping himself to your jewellery.'

'And you're violating it more. A friend of mine was raped. She said telling the police about it over and over again was as bad as the rape.'

'Did she go ahead with the prosecution?'

'Why?'

'Just interested. Did she?'

'He got life.'

'So he won't be raping any other women for a bit. Does that make her feel more or less safe?'

For answer Dilly sat down again.

And as if on cue Tom returned.

Dilly, not expecting the knock, might have been shot. Fran laid a calming hand on her shoulder and popped out.

'It all hangs together, like, guv,' he reported, very obviously not peering round the door. 'Except he seems to have forgotten a few days' leave before the course started. He spent a long weekend with the course tutor and his wife, just a holiday like, then a couple of days working, they said, at the British Library.'

'Oh.' Try how she might, she couldn't keep the monosyllable neutral.

'Do you want me to sniff around any more? Only DCI Tanner's back.'

'Leave it for now. And say nowt to no one, eh?'

She schooled her face back into what she hoped was an expression of quiet confidence and returned to her office. Dilly was leaning against the window, as if the view of the car park might inspire her. Perhaps it did. 'Do you really insist on talking to Daniel?'

'Not "talking" as in "interrogating". And you could be there, if you wanted.'

Dilly's nod was surprisingly firm. 'I do want,' she said.

CHAPTER ELEVEN

Closer, closer. Love is as strong as death; jealousy is as cruel as the grave.

* * *

Daniel McDine, thickset, with a shaven head, designer spectacles and a strong Estuary accent, was not Fran's idea of how a deputy head should look or sound, but then, she'd been educated in days before senior teachers were jetted from one establishment to another in search of general educational — and personal financial — success. His government spokesman-like air of controlled truculence in a very pricey suit put her off immediately. Dilly had certainly chosen a different type of man to love this time, even though he was probably the same age as Stephen, possibly even older. Ever since they'd been introduced he'd been chuntering about being made to leave work early. He'd promised to arrive no later than three-thirty but it had been four-fifteen when he'd finally arrived. Since then, he'd taken three or four calls on his mobile; in exasperation, she'd told him to turn it off.

Now they were all sitting together in Dilly's late Victorian cottage, which would probably be described by an agent as bijou, with its downstairs bathroom and low ceilings, but to Fran's mind was poky, more probably built for labourers rather than artisans. The front garden was long, with a parking space large enough for two cars just off the road. The back was more of a yard, but protected by a blessedly high wall, which some previous owner, uninhibited by today's laws against hurting people trying to intrude into your property, had garnished with a liberal dressing of broken glass. A few tips from Crime Prevention, and Dilly's little castle would have an adequate moat and drawbridge.

But not a Lord of the Demesne. Not until that vague wedding sometime in the future. For his visit, Dilly had donned a solitaire engagement ring. Now why didn't she usually wear it? The diamond certainly wouldn't weigh her down. There was also less make-up in evidence and, knees bolted together as she perched on the edge of her own tiny sofa, she was as subdued as she'd been after Fran's verbal assault back in Maidstone.

McDine himself passed round coffee and biscuits, neither very good. Then he sank heavily on the sofa beside his intended, leaning back against the squabs and picking up her left hand and turning the ring repeatedly. It might have been the mute switch for all she joined in the subsequent conversation.

'What I can't understand is someone at your level bothering with something as trivial as this,' he told Fran.

'Firstly, I don't view stalking as trivial. Secondly, it's up to my senior officers who is allocated to which case.' She thought the idea of a hierarchy might appeal to him.

'Even so — surely there's some unit or other devoted to women's problems.'

'Like menstruation or the menopause?' she flashed back. 'Ah, you mean rape!' She leaned forward, just controlling the urge to jab a finger at him in emphasis. 'Believe you me, Mr McDine, rape can affect male victims even more deeply than it does female. As for stalkers, we get our fair share of women illegally pursuing men.'

To her surprise, he came back for more. 'Jactitation of marriage?'

She burst out laughing. 'I don't think I've heard that term since my college days.'

He stared. 'Which college?'

'Oh, Bramshill, I dare say. It certainly wouldn't have been part of my OU doctorate.' Let him stuff those facts up his academic backside and spin on them. Her title was something she very rarely used, except, as in the present circumstances, to inhibit someone wishing to patronise her.

Dilly sat observing the exchange open-mouthed: apparently verbal jousting was something Daniel discouraged.

He might have been bloodied, but he was unbowed. 'You're not some run-of-the-mill bobby, then.' He flicked immaculate trouser legs. She reckoned his suit must have cost at least as much as Mark's, but his search for fashion had put him into a high-chested Italian jacket that made him look like a pouter pigeon.

'On the contrary, I believe the police recruit the highest proportion of graduates of any major employer. So you'll find a whole swathe of Inspector Doctor Dixons of Dock Green. Or you would if we used all our titles as the Germans do. Now, Mr McDine, we're here not to expound on the academic abilities of my colleagues but to discuss how we can improve your fiancée's personal safety: she was very keen to have your input.' Damn, she'd gone too far.

Abruptly, he stopped twiddling Dilly's ring and dropped her hand. 'I don't know why she should be. I'm a deputy head, *Dr* Harman, not a detective.'

She ignored the bitching and grinned. 'You're a senior manager of a school of some thousand pupils. Don't tell me you haven't acquired a few detective skills yourself!'

He didn't know whether to be flattered or irritated, did he? Poor Dilly, she'd have been much better off with the parson. What a pity they were unlikely ever to be reunited.

'If Dilly had been one of those tarty presenters who dress as if they're off to a disco I might have understood. But she's always very professionally turned out.' For the first time he smiled. 'I'm so proud when I see her on TV.' To

Fran's amazement, he patted Dilly's left hand, in the sort of proprietorial gesture Mark sometimes made.

She would have turned her hand to complete the clasp; Dilly's lay passive.

What could be making this couple click? A brilliant sex life sometimes united the most unlikely pairs. But she'd seen not so much as a spark of electricity between these two: it was if Dilly had opted for another older man, in the hope that he'd replace Stephen in her affections, while he — had he simply wanted the smartly dressed trophy of a TV reporter wife?

'I'm sure you're proud of Dilly,' Fran said, smiling at them both in turn. 'But seeing her on TV is giving someone else less laudable emotions, emotions he's expressing with anonymous notes.'

'How long has this been going on?' Daniel asked not Dilly but Fran, who responded by looking at Dilly, eyebrow raised.

'A few weeks. That's all,' the young woman managed.

'But you've not said anything to me — about a matter that now has a very senior policewoman working on it?' he asked sternly, as if he'd caught her out failing to hand in coursework.

'I . . . no, I—'

Fran jumped in. 'Many victims feel it's such a trivial thing they don't care to report it. But Dilly and I happened to be talking about another matter and it came up.'

'What other matter?'

Fran looked suitably, if spuriously, demure. 'Apparently TVInvicta are thinking of making a programme to celebrate my retirement,' she said smoothly. 'The Chief Constable is considering the proposal.'

'Whose idea?'

Fran looked straight at Dilly, who admitted, when she should have boasted, 'Mine, actually.'

'You didn't invent this programme just so you could talk to Dr Harman about your stalker, I presume?'

The bastard. Why the hell didn't Dilly tell him where to go? At least she didn't hang her head. 'Chief Superintendent Harman has such a distinguished record,' she said, but without force, as if she'd prepared a response for just such an eventuality, 'that the BBC have also thrown their hat into the ring. Diggory Venn wants us to get in first. Huw Venn,' she corrected herself. 'But you can imagine with a surname like that we'd have to give him the Hardy nickname.' There was the tiniest brush of hesitation when she said 'Hardy'. Was she putting a tongue against a damaged tooth to see if the filling held? Or did she still love the very sound of his name? If Fran had had a fiver for every time she'd dragged Mark's name into conversations at the start of their relationship — even now she had to stop herself — she'd have been able to make a cracking donation to the Police Benevolent Fund.

McDine nodded, looking at Fran quizzically. 'I'm sorry, I didn't realise you had such a reputation. What's your speciality?'

'Solving crime, Mr McDine. Which is why I wanted Dilly to tell you about her stalker. And why I want to talk to you about possible suspects. When would it be convenient for you to come across to my office at Police Headquarters in Maidstone?'

Dilly's eyes widened as if in terror. McDine's narrowed. 'I don't see any reason why we can't talk here.'

Neither could Fran. Occasionally, however, it felt good to control a control-freak. She fished out her diary. 'Tomorrow? After work again? About five-thirty?' She knew what the response would be even as she goaded him.

'You may finish work at five, Dr Harman, but I assure you our school day doesn't. I'd have thought you'd know better than to swallow the old cliché about teachers' long holidays and short working hours. Let me tell you I'm usually the last to leave, rarely before seven.'

'You'll just have to make an exception for one day, won't you? Unless it would be more convenient at seven-thirty in the morning? My meetings don't start till eight.'

* * *

'Just because you happen to be a morning woman, Fran, doesn't mean everyone else is. What if the poor guy's eyes don't open till nine?'

'It would be even more fun, then wouldn't it? Yes, please, just there!'

Mark applied a vicious thumb: the pain in her shoulder became exquisite. 'What's stressed you out?' he grunted. 'Keep talking. Let the pain happen. Don't fight it!'

'I'm stressed because I'm worried about Jill Tanner.' She explained the problem through gritted teeth. 'And furthermore I don't like this Daniel McDine character.'

'Why don't you get one of our less mentionable lifer acquaintances to do a contract killing? Him or the vicar's wife? Or even both?'

She felt his laughter through his probing digits, but replied, as meditatively as if they were both serious. 'Actually, if we got rid of the wife, Dilly would ditch Daniel herself . . . No, you mustn't tempt me! But,' she added gleefully, 'since I have the power to inconvenience McDine, I shall use it.'

He rested his hands. 'That's not like you.' Then he applied them with renewed vigour.

'Argh! Oh, yes it is. I might be sweetness and light with you, my loved one, but I still have it in me to be a bitter old cow. And he was very nasty to his poor little fiancée, who doesn't have the nous to be nasty back. You can come and sit in on the interview if you like. Oh, yes, not my cosy office, but a proper interview room. It'd add credibility to an otherwise bald and unconvincing narrative. Who was it that said that first? Wow, that's better.'

'It occurs to me,' he said slowly, finishing off the hard work with the most gentle of strokes, 'that for once you've missed a trick. Wouldn't you learn more by seeing him in his home? And such a concession might make him more forthcoming, especially if you made it at eight over there.'

'Shit. You're absolutely right. What about that other eight o'clock meeting I told him about?'

'You invented it! Invent a reason to cancel it. Chief Constable suddenly called away, that sort of thing?'

She nodded. 'You're right, of course. But you could still sit in if you wanted.'

'I might just, you know. Hey, where do you think you're going?'

'To get some supper. I thought you'd finished.'

'When God gave us shoulders, he tended to give us a pair. And I reckon this one hurts just here.'

It did.

But he had ways of making her feel much better.

As they showered afterwards, her thoughts strayed to Dilly and Daniel. No, try how she might, she couldn't image them generating the passion that bound Mark and her — with or without marriage.

* * *

'This is Assistant Chief Constable Mark Turner,' Fran told Daniel, as he stepped aside to let her into his home.

Mark flashed his ID.

Daniel's face tightened visibly, but he was swiftly into bluster mode, glaring at first one then the other, with meaningful glances at his watch — a very chic Dunhill — to get his own back.

It wasn't just the watch that was chic. His house, south of Canterbury and remarkably inconvenient for a daily commute to Ramsgate, was a barn conversion. It shared a private courtyard with other conversions such as, presumably, the former byre. Each had an expensive-looking security system, with enough lights to be seen from outer space.

Inside, it was decorated with a minimalism that was clearly very expensive. The sitting room was a cube. What effect this would have on the acoustics she didn't know, but nothing too detrimental — he had one of the more expensive Bang and Olufsen systems. His CDs must be in that built-in unit. The height certainly gobbled up heat: she was too chilly to surrender her coat.

As he made coffee, she let her eyes roam, Mark padding after him to talk boys' talk about the previous evening's footie. The fact that Mark had been otherwise engaged and had simply seen highlight snippets didn't seem to matter. Yes, he was a good cop.

No books. How could you be a man in such a position and have no books? She got up to prowl. As she reached the hall, she heard chairs scrape. Mark had got him to sit down, as he'd promised he would, so she could check out the study he must have. A sample of his computer printer's work would be useful. Just in case. There was a discarded sheet of paper in the bin. Pocketing it, she looked around. Floor to ceiling bookshelves, the expensive sort that were custom made to fit unusual spaces, were occupied with a collection of books ranging from what looked like textbooks from his youth, surely something best given to a charity, to thick tomes dealing with the latest educational trends. No fiction, light or otherwise, apart from a uniform edition of the classics tucked away by the window. Next to them — yes, now she was getting to the man — was a set of highly explicit erotica. Well, well, well.

She was back in the living room by the time the men drifted back, still into some offside decision.

'How long have you known Dilly?' she asked, with a social smile as they sat down.

'About a year. We met at an Alpha course in Canterbury.'

'That's—?'

'A course to introduce people to Christianity and confirm practising Christians in their belief.'

'And you've been engaged how long?'

'About six months.'

'Have you set the date yet?' she asked, with a girly coyness.

He shook his head.

'You don't live together?'

'You know that.'

'Any reason why?' She looked about her, wide-eyed. 'There's more than enough room for two, surely.'

'If there is a reason it's none of your business, Dr Harman. Upstairs on your right,' he added irritably to Mark, who'd made a silent enquiry for the loo.

Why not a downstairs cloakroom? There must be one, surely, in a house as spacious and expensive as this.

'Of course not. It's just that so many people live together these days before they marry.' Talk about stating the obvious.

'That's one of the problems with today's society, if I may say so. And I have to pick up the pieces, Dr Harman. Two-thirds of my pupils come from single-parent homes. Maybe more. Seventy-five per cent are entitled to free school lunches, they're so poor. I'm trying to bring down the rates of pregnancy amongst our girls, without, I may add, having the school nurse dish out morning after pills like so many Smarties.' For the first time he sounded passionate. 'I work twelve-hour days. At weekends I supervise games. Now do you understand why I don't get married? And until I move to another school, I don't see how I can.'

'How does Dilly feel about this?'

'She's very understanding. At one point she suggested simply nipping into a register office, just the two of us, but I don't see why the girl should be denied her big meringue day, do you?'

'Absolutely not,' Fran agreed, with more emphasis than was necessary as she suppressed fleeting, wistful thoughts of her own, non-existent, one. 'But I was wondering — until you told me about your working week — if it might not be sensible for her to move in with you for protection from her stalker.'

'I can't see how being in an empty house is going to offer more protection than her own. Can you?'

'Chummie is more likely to find her address than yours — especially if she's been a good citizen and put herself on the electoral roll. Tell me, Daniel,' she continued, leaning forward confidentially, 'have you any idea who it might be? I know you wouldn't say anything in front of Dilly lest you alarm her, but I'm sure you must have a theory. Have you met her colleagues, for instance? Might any of them be besotted? Enough to send anonymous notes?'

He shook his head. He clearly hadn't much time for any of them, and Fran suspected only a rigorous application of the equal opportunity laws prevented him making a scathing remark about their sexuality.

'What about other friends and acquaintances? Yours, for instance. Sometimes church groups attract one or two people who are socially inadequate. Would there have been anyone on this Alpha course who might have developed a crush on her?'

He shrugged.

'No, don't dismiss this out of hand. Give it some active thought. And some inactive! I reckon I get most of my best insights when I'm at the gym.'

He sighed. 'Your best bet would be the course leader, I suppose. The Vicar of St Jude's.'

St Jude. According to Hardy, if she remembered her A level days aright, the patron saint of lost causes. Much more appropriate a parish for poor Stephen Hardy, come to think of it. She smiled to herself, saying aloud, 'Thanks. That's a big help.'

He didn't respond. 'I still don't know why you made me take time off work to discuss Dilly's problems. She's a grown woman, for goodness' sake. Getting het up over some quite nice notes.'

She pounced. 'Quite nice? You've seen them then?'

'No. But she tells me they're romantic. Nothing threatening.'

'Not yet,' she conceded. 'Tell me, have you ever been aware of being followed, when you're together?'

'Followed?'

'Followed.'

'She did come to me a few weeks back with a story about hearing footsteps behind her, but never seeing anyone when she turned round.'

'When?'

'You'd have to ask her.'

'Anything else? However trivial?'

'She had a couple of nightmares — she'd fallen asleep on the sofa and woken to imagine men looking through the window, that sort of thing. But it turned out she thought she'd seen President Bush, who was, as I was able to demonstrate, engaged elsewhere at the time. And she promised not to be so silly.'

And now too scared of him to contradict him.

But he hadn't finished yet. 'What I still can't understand is police involvement at any level, especially the highest.'

She suppressed an irritated sigh. 'What happens if a pupil starts tormenting another? If you don't stop it quickly? You see? Only when someone escalates violence against a woman, we don't call it bullying. We call it sexual assault. The next escalation is rape. And you don't need a degree in criminology to work out what the stalker might do next.'

CHAPTER TWELVE

I will come now, and find you, wherever you are, whichever town, whichever street, whichever house, whichever room. I will find you whom I love with all my heart and all my soul.

* * *

'Of course, I haven't seen it,' Mark said, as he started the car, 'not officially, but there was a Bible beside his bed. With the marker ribbon at the Song of Songs. Have you ever read it? It's remarkably erotic stuff. It's supposed to be about God's relationship with the Church, isn't it? But it looked remarkably like human love to me.'

She scratched her head. 'The Bible! Mike the Miserable said the language of those notes was very biblical.'

'Mike Dalton! Is he still working? He's as old as Methuselah!'

'Retiring shortly — may go part-time. Anyway, he said the language reminded him of the Bible.'

'Did he now? And all I was interested in was McDine's reading matter . . . I wonder . . .'

'Deskbound you might be most of the time, but there are still glimmers of the detective in you,' she said, patting the hand on the gear-lever.

'Gee, thanks.'

'You don't want to turn back and challenge him?'

'And stand there like a rookie cadet as he explained it away?' he snorted. 'No, thanks. In any case, I don't see how it helps us. So much of our more poetic language is derived either from the Bible or from Shakespeare, isn't it? Anyone might use it subconsciously.'

She giggled. 'I'd like it to be McDine!'

'I'd never have guessed. But I don't see how we can possibly pin anything on him with such a tenuous connection.'

'Unless we can prove he bunks off school every day to go to a London pillar-box. Or gets a colleague to do it for him.'

'But I can't imagine anyone taking that sort of risk: "Here, just pop this in the post, will you? I don't want my fiancée to know who's sending Biblical erotica to her".'

She pulled a face. 'And I can't exactly get on to every innocent churchgoer in London, can I? Then every Christian who doesn't go to church but studies at home? The whole Bible thing may be taking us off on quite the wrong tangent. But if Stephen Hardy was in London longer than he admitted to, then I need to talk to him again. Especially if we could place him in Ashford recently. I don't want another trip to the Midlands, not at the moment, and I can't see how I could get him down here. And the last thing I want is some Brummie plod stamping in there in his size twelves.'

'You know they don't all wear woad, my love. What about that nice young woman who was so useful in the stolen identity case? DS Afrizi or something?'

'Farat Hafeez? Yes! You're brilliant. I'll get on to her as soon as we get back. Then all I need worry about is protecting Dilly while we find out. Not that I think Stephen has anything to do with it at all. His is genuine love, not some sick fantasy — I'll stake my retirement lump sum on it.'

'So what will you do? About Dilly?'

'Bar supplying her with a permanent presence, I've no idea. And unless the letters get overtly threatening, I can't see how I could justify the expense. So we play a waiting game, I suppose.'

'What if the implicit threat does become explicit?'

'And what if she didn't imagine being followed and having President Bush eyeballing her? Mark, I don't know! I almost wish he would contact her directly — with a box of choccies, or something harmless. Then we can get on to suppliers. A genuine lead.'

'And if he happened to doctor the choccies, that would give us another lead.'

'Let's talk to her about being followed, at least.' She called up Dilly's work number, and left a message. Then she left another on her mobile. 'She must be working out of the building. Drat and double drat.'

'Tell you what, since there's absolutely nothing else either of us can do till we get back to work, let's check out that Elham cottage. It's only a couple of miles out of our way . . .'

* * *

Jill Tanner was on the phone, literally tugging the roots of her hair. But it didn't seem to Fran, standing silently in the open doorway of Jill's office, as if it was to style her hair in that outdated Afro she favoured. At last she flung the phone down, turning sharply. Leaning her arms on the nearest filing cabinet, she buried her face in them.

Before Fran could move across to hug her where she was, however, she pulled herself straight, and made a great show of burrowing in the top drawer for a file, which she flicked through irritably and replaced. But she did keep the next, though slinging it hard on to her desk meant some of its contents sprayed out.

Fran gathered up those her side of the desk and laid them quietly down. 'Fancy a cuppa? I need a sounding board.'

Jill's face suggested for a moment Fran was paid enough to hire a private one. But, sighing so her shoulders slumped, she nodded. 'Of course, guv. Only I'm—'

'Kettle's hot, coffee-maker's primed,' Fran declared. Her office was much more private than Jill's. As she walked through the outer office, in a draught caused by all those flapping ears, she added, projecting just enough, 'I really don't know where I'm going with that case the Chief's landed on me. I thought another pair of eyes . . .'

* * *

'No need to mess around, ma'am,' Jill said, standing to attention before Fran's desk.

Fran was momentarily diverted. When she'd done wrong at school, she'd have stood just like that. What did McDine make his miscreants do?

'For goodness' sake, Jill, take the weight off your feet. I meant exactly what I said. And now you make me think I should have meant something else. What, precisely?' She plonked two mugs of green tea on the desk, and sat. 'Jill, please sit down. And bugger that "ma'am" nonsense.' The phone rang. She leaned across to reroute it. 'You and I know each other better than that. How long do we go back? Thirty years? Well, then.' Stony silence from the visitor's side of the desk. 'Shall I tell you my problem first? Or will you tell me yours?' Tom's auntie's and her own homemade biscuits having gone the way of all things tempting the flesh, on to her hips, Mark had supplied her with much dourer oat biscuits, an eye to their glycaemic index, no doubt. She fished out a packet and put it on the desk. Jill stared as if it were a snake.

'OK. Me first, then. I told you I've got a local celebrity being stalked. The name is need-to-know only, I'm afraid. Like you, I've no leads at all. Except, in my case, the Bible . . .'

She paused, eyebrows raised humorously. Eventually Jill supplied the sort of words she'd hoped for, 'And even in these heathen times, quite a lot of people read that.'

'Quite. So do I offer her terribly expensive protection, knowing the stalker may do nothing, or simply keep a watching brief hoping he doesn't take this for acquiescence and do something dreadful?'

'Sounds like a Bramshill exercise,' Jill managed.

'All too real. Past lover? Present fiancé?'

'Or some guy in a dirty mac who really thinks he has a relationship with her? Watch and wait, I'd say — all reasonable precautions being taken, of course. Maybe watch and pray!' She managed a grin. 'But you didn't really need my advice for that, did you? That was just so no one in the team knew you were going to bollock me.'

'Why should they think you needed a bollocking?'

'Because I'm getting nowhere fast.'

'Either,' Fran inserted, with a grin somewhere between compassionate and conspiratorial. 'So who are you sharing your problems with? Are you an upwards or downwards woman these days? Joe Farmer or one of your team?'

'What problems?'

'The getting nowhere fast problems. Tom Arkwright, now — he's a smashing listener. He kept me going when my parents were so ill last autumn, bless him. Or Joe — he's terribly new and he knows he's only temporary, so a daily natter might make him feel more secure. Especially if he managed to say something useful. Or at least thought he did.'

Jill managed a doleful snort. 'I thought so. He's been grassing me up.'

'For not getting an immediate result? Come off it! Which reminds me, just as a matter of interest, have you any idea what's happening about my assault? I know I said I wanted to be treated exactly like Josephine Public, but surely even she should know what's happening to her assailants. Especially she, actually.'

'You mean no one's from Canterbury's been in touch? That's bloody shocking.' Grabbing a ball-point, she scribbled on the back of her hand.

Fran nodded mildly. 'They're probably rushed off their feet. But I do seem to recall we had some policy about keeping victims informed every step of the way.'

'Which you drew up, if I remember right, guv. I'll snap at a few heels.' She sighed again, exhaling the last drop of energy from her body.

'You're sure you're all right, Jill? You're looking a bit peaky, come to think of it.'

'Oh, the lads will be sure it's my time of the month,' she said with a savage grin.

'One joke about that and I'll have them on toast, Jill. And that's a promise.'

But Jill didn't take up the challenge. 'That or I'm menopausal.'

If she was kind before, now Fran was empathy itself. 'And are you? Because there's a lot can be done these days.' Surreptitiously she patted her own HRT patch, her amulet of good health.

'Not as far as I know. Let's just say my get up and go has got up and gone.'

'What drove it away? And would a game of tennis bring it back?' It all too clearly wouldn't. 'Oh, Jill — come on. You can trust me. As a friend, for goodness' sake! Or if not me, a counsellor. You know you can get an absolutely confidential referral. It's not like the old days when stiff upper lips and post-traumatic stress ruled.' Breezy wasn't working. She dropped her voice. 'I hate seeing you like this, love.'

She'd gone too far. Jill clammed. Her voice ultra-bright, she got up. 'If that's it, then, guv, I'd best get back.'

'Fine.' There was no point in poking a dead fire, as they said somewhere or other. She got up to see her out of the room. 'So long as you remember that the door's always open. Whatever the problem, here or at home.'

* * *

'Chartham mean anything to you?' Mark demanded, as he joined her for their canteen lunch.

'That nice village where Dilly lives?'

'The same. And I've just had these particulars arrive. Fran, my lovely, it looks as if this house might just have our name on it.'

'Like that Elham place did?' she asked ironically.

'Well, they can't all be as bad as that. Look at this.' He dropped some faxed sheets beside her plate of salad.

The cottage he pointed at was the sort of Kentish village domestic architecture that demanded a village green, complete with cricketers, a pub and a church. The second sheet wasn't so clear, but all the same something made her swallow coleslaw the wrong way. 'Do my aged eyes deceive me or is that a suit of armour in that shot of the lounge?'

Mark peered, arm at maximum stretch. 'I'd need a magnifying glass to tell.'

'Or some reading glasses. Come on, presbyopia is a sign of maturity. And you can't say my specs aren't chic. You'd be able to peer meaningfully over them. Here, for goodness' sake borrow mine. They're supposed to be unisex, after all.'

Reluctantly, disdainfully even, he took them. 'You're right. It is a suit of armour. Do you think it comes with the house? Or we could make an offer for that, too! Look — just the right size garden for us. A pond. A terrace. Enough rooms to invite my kids to stay — if you don't mind, that is.'

'Of course I don't.' If only she could believe they would come. 'Tell you what, I could make an excuse to go and see what Crime Prevention have done about Dilly's security and check it out.'

'Er . . .' He looked both cunning and guilty. She was hard put not to reach over and plant a smacking kiss. 'Let's do better than that. Come on: get that down you and let's look at it together. I've got some time-off-in-lieu owing.'

'I thought you'd got wall-to-wall meetings.'

'I could have sent you in as my substitute, but I shall send apologies.'

'Mark!' She was genuinely outraged.

'It just looks so perfect. We won't see it properly if we leave it till this evening.'

She had a very bad feeling about this. But he so rarely thought about even bending a rule, let alone breaking one, she'd better go along with him.

'Dilly's cottage first?' She pulled up short. 'Actually, is it appropriate for us to move in so close to a client, as it were?'

'You'll have sorted Dilly's case by the end of the month. We shall be living in that cottage till we're carried out feet first.'

* * *

Mark might not have been at that meeting, or even at his desk, but he assuaged his conscience by spending the entire journey on the phone, time off in lieu or no TOIL.

Fran was happy enough. She'd always liked driving, and today's light traffic gave her a chance to scan the countryside as she drove. Any day now it would be greening into spring. She might not be an Easter bride but to be an Easter co-mortgagee would pretty well do. What greater way to show your love for each other than by tying yourself into expensive property till the end of time? And this cottage was definitely at the top end of the range they'd allowed themselves, even though retirement lump sums would eventually pay off much of the balance.

Almost as if touching wood, and despite her caveat about putting work first, she chose a different way into the village from the one she'd used to approach Dilly's cottage. This involved a level crossing. It was closed. She cut the engine as she waited for not one but two local trains, which crossed on the crossing. Was this a good omen or a bad? At least the village had a station, even if it was little more than a halt. How many times a day did trains to and from Charing Cross stop there?

Mark still officially chuntering away and now checking something in his diary, she treated the crossing-keeper to what in her younger days would have been a dazzling smile and pressed on. She picked her way through the village and parked right at the cottage gate.

Mark cut the call with unreasonable haste, almost tumbling from the car in his efforts to see the cottage close up.

'Fran, my sweet, this is it! Isn't it lovely?' He put an arm round her shoulders, as if to embrace their new home as well.

She nodded, swallowing hard as she burst his bubble. 'Perfect.' She turned him gently but inexorably. 'Pity about the view.' There, just across a picturesque bubbling stream, was a mill. Not the historic and picturesque corn-grinding sort with sails or a big waterwheel. No such luck. A Forties or Fifties brutalist papermill.

As one and in silence, they got back into the car. Mark didn't make any further calls, and even cut off an incoming one. Fran merely pointed the car towards Dilly's cottage and drove.

She stopped, very suddenly. 'Oh, my God.'

Mark was out of the car as quickly as she was. A huge bunch of flowers sat on the front-door step. A quick glance showed a legitimate Interflora envelope. But it was the flowers themselves that constituted the problem. Lilies, white roses, white freesias, all sorts of other white flowers Fran didn't know the name of made up either a beautiful wedding bouquet or a classy funeral spray.

'Is this just what we were dreading? Has he got hold of her home address at last?'

Mark nodded at the little camera that was supposed to be watching their every move. 'At least that will help ID the delivery driver as genuine. We hope. Or not.'

The camera seemed remarkably uninterested in their presence, though she'd had an idea it was supposed be alerted by movement and to track whatever was making it. She bobbed around. It stayed put. She literally scratched her hair. It ignored her. It ignored her when she pulled Mark's sleeve, like an importunate child, and told him.

'Let's worry about that later,' he said. 'Let's check the flowers first. Do you reckon they're a genuine Interflora delivery?'

Fran eyed the spray. 'You'd have to be a pro to produce an arrangement as good as this, wouldn't you? It's way beyond my stick-'em-in-a-vase-and-hope skills.'

'Any latex gloves in your car?'

'Does swag get carried away in bags?'

Very carefully they eased out the envelope and opened it. Inside was what looked like a *bona fide* Interflora card, with another giving maintenance instructions.

'*With all my love*,' Fran read aloud. 'But no initial, let alone name. I smell — apart from these lovely flowers — a brown furry rodent.'

'So what'll you do?'

'Call Dilly. If these really are from a friend, she'll want them, won't she?'

'I can see you would!'

'If not, she probably won't give them house-room. In which case, I'll give this card to Mike the Miserable in the vain hope he'll find something other than pollen. Then I'll drop off the flowers to wherever Dilly wants them delivered — a hospice or something.' She phoned Dilly's work number, to her alarm getting put straight through to the newsroom without being asked for any ID at all. Someone needed their ears chewing.

Dilly was out on a story, was she? At least her male colleague offered to do no more than take a message.

'You can't give me her mobile number?'

'Absolutely not. It's against company policy. Sorry.'

'But this is very urgent. It's the police.'

'If you give me your number, I'll call and ask her to phone you back. That's the best I can do.'

'It's a very good best. Well done!' Fran identified herself. 'I do have her mobile number in fact, but it's great to see people being careful. Thanks. Now,' she added grimly. 'if you could just put me through to your switchboard again . . .'

* * *

'Flowers?' Dilly sounded completely bemused. 'Oh. You think they're from . . . him, don't you?'

'No idea,' said Fran cheerfully, lying through her teeth. Had the stalker known Dilly's address all along and for the last couple of weeks continued to send the letters to TVInvicta as a bluff? If only she could move Dilly out. Bloody Daniel

McDine and his piggish principles! 'They're lovely. Shall I send you a photo down the line? No? Well, if you weren't expecting them, I'll check them out with Interflora, if that's OK with you. And have a look at anything the security cameras have shown up. Now, do you want to keep them, if you don't know their provenance?'

'Of course! I love flowers!' And she still hoped they were Stephen's, didn't she?

'Shall I leave them on your step or stow them somewhere safer?'

'Round the back, maybe? Behind the water butt?'

Cutting the call, Fran obliged. And then swore, the sort of verbal blast Mark had probably not heard from her in years. 'Look here. Under this flower pot.'

'Bloody hell! Is that what I think it is? Her front-door key?'

It certainly opened the front door. So they stowed the flowers in the sink, locked up and, using one of Fran's latex gloves as an envelope, popped the key through the letterbox.

'Death-wish or denial or what?' Fran demanded as Mark drove back to Maidstone.

'Maybe she didn't even know it was there. Maybe the previous owner? It is a village after all.'

'And she's switched her phone off.' She composed a pithy message. 'Hello, Dilly. This is Detective Chief Superintendent Harman here. I thought you'd like to know what I've done with your flowers, and, more to the point, how I was able to . . .'

* * *

Interflora personified helpfulness. The flowers had been ordered in a central London shop, by a man paying cash. Since Fran was on official business, they handed over the phone number of the shop.

A pleasant voiced woman with the hint of a Yorkshire accent answered Fran's enquiry. She checked her computer, declared that it was she who'd served the customer and said that he'd dictated the message. After some thought she recalled that he wore glasses that reacted to the light, but as he'd stood in direct sun for the course of the transaction she'd not been able to say much else.

Fran's stomach sank. Spectacles. Stephen. Oh, dear.

'Well spoken. Middle years — at least forty-five, but with the spectacles and the hat he wore—'

'Hat?'

'One of those with a wide brim like detectives used to wear in old black and white films.'

'A trench coat too, by any chance?'

But the irony was lost.

Not many people wore hats, however, these days. If they did, they had good enough manners to remove them in public. Was this a disguise? A mocking disguise?

'And when was this?' In her irritation she'd almost forgotten to ask. She jotted the response. 'Two weeks ago?'

'It's quite usual for people to specify a date in the future, Chief Superintendent.'

'And to pay cash — it must have been quite expensive?'

'It was over fifty pounds. Not one of our standard orders: the despatching florist was told to use her own initiative, lilies apart.'

'How much over fifty pounds?'

'Fifty-five. Plus delivery charge.'

'Is there a cash machine near the branch? Sorry, I was thinking aloud.'

The woman at the other end had clearly heard all sorts of strange questions. 'Do you want me to pop out and see? I know there's an HSBC, because that's the one I use myself. But there may be others. Call me back in five minutes.'

Fran's heart was pounding, just as it used to when she was young and involved in a chase. Alas, her fears were that this was the longest of shots was confirmed. There were three banks within walking distance, all with two or three machines. If it was any help, she added, hearing the fall of Fran's voice, their shop till recorded the time of all transactions. This was at 13.27 hours.

'And do you have an address for this man, Mrs Lester?' Fran liked being on name terms.

'Yes. But I'm afraid it doesn't necessarily mean it's the correct one. You see, sometimes if we're busy — and lunchtime is busy for us, same as it as for cash machines — an assistant will just ask for the post code of the delivery address and the customer points at the relevant house number when it comes up on the computer screen. I've done it myself in a hurry.'

'You wouldn't remember if you did it for this gentleman?'

'I would remember because I don't do it at all anymore. Not since I saw what someone could do.' She paused for Fran to agree. Perhaps disappointed, she explained slowly, 'You could easily go and invent a postcode and remember the house number, couldn't you? And then you'd have a false address for yourself.'

'Mrs Lester, you wouldn't care to join the police service, would you? I've got a vacancy for a right hand woman!'

'Police! That'd be even worse than teaching! So thanks but no thanks. Thirty years in the classroom were enough for me. I can't claim my pension yet, you see. Hence the job. But I've got my health and hope back.'

* * *

Health and hope. That sounded like a good basis for a second, later life career. But Mrs Lester was clearly a loss to the classroom. And she was right. The address was false.

She phoned the still unobtainable Dilly. Crossing her fingers, she left a message. Had a long-forgotten admirer worn spectacles? Please God, she added under her breath, don't let it be Stephen.

She checked her watch. The meeting Mark had just got back in time for would have finished ten minutes ago and soon she'd hear his voice over the phone telling her it was time to go home. It had become one of the small but vital pleasures of her day.

So it would be tomorrow before she had to do anything about Jill.

CHAPTER THIRTEEN

Consider the lilies of the field. Solomon in all his glory was not arrayed as one of these.

* * *

Summoned first thing on Friday morning to see how she was getting on with what the Chief clearly saw as his personal case, Fran laid the anonymous offering on his gleaming desk — it was one of his foibles that he polished it himself. Once again the stalker had sent it through the post from London to TVInvicta, but this time it had been properly diverted. Since Mike the Miserable had reported nil returns on everything she'd sent him so far, she'd succumbed to a Dilly-like attack of curiosity and opened it herself at the Chief's behest.

'So he's changed from the Old to the New Testament,' Fran said, leaning over his shoulder to point, as if she had known all the time about Chummie's theological tendencies. 'Just to make sure we know it was he who sent the flowers. Having possibly acquired the cash from one of a dozen cash points in that area of London, at about the busiest time of day.'

'A great help, then.'

'Exactly. Even assuming he didn't have wads of ready cash on him — which, to be honest, doesn't sound like the average clergyman.'

'The one who was your only suspect so far? Up in the Midlands?'

'That's the one. Though I think the Barber Institute and the curry would have been ample excuse to go up there, don't you? The Reverend Stephen Hardy. I truly do not think he was involved, but just in case, I've asked a West Midlands Police colleague to speak to him again.'

His eyes narrowed. Harassing clergymen didn't come easily to him. 'On what grounds?'

'He's been less than accurate in telling us when he was in London. I think he may still have been there when those flowers were ordered.'

'Quite a time lapse?'

'The florist says it's not unusual to place an order in advance. He also has one feature in common with the man who ordered the flowers — spectacles with Reactolite lenses.'

'And if he denies it?'

'DS Hafeez asks for details of his cash cards and we see if we can match them against withdrawals in the area of the shop at an appropriate time.'

'That's the sort of job I got landed with when I was a rookie PC.' He offered a matey smile, to remind her, if it were necessary, that he'd worked his way through the frustrations of rank and file policing, just as she had.

She responded with a rueful grin. 'I know. But that's what police work is, isn't it — long searches for deeply hidden bits of vital information.'

She returned to the visitor's side of the desk.

'More deeply hidden than Ms Pound's key, Mark tells me. My God, under a flowerpot!'

'Yes, sir. She tells me she'd forgotten it was there. Apparently it was the hiding place when she moved in and she forgot that time has moved on from when her ninety-year-old predecessor passed away.'

They shared the upraised eyes and overgrown shrugs of irritated professionals. But she got more than sympathy. 'You are sure you can manage this on your own? All those bank details, for instance. It's one thing making the calls to the banks in question, quite another checking the results. There must be other things you could more usefully be doing.'

She peered over the reading glasses she tended to wear on the end of her nose when they weren't in use. 'A pair of nice young eyes, Chief?' Someone who could deal with that while she got on to the Alpha course leader. Yes, please!

'That lad you praised to the skies last year. The one who was so good in court. Young Arkwright. Tom.' When he could remember details like that, no one wondered why the Chief had got his job. Especially as he asked, peering over his own glasses, 'Wasn't there some family problem? Sick father?'

'Cancer. In remission, thank goodness. I'd love his help. But he's being pretty useful in DCI Tanner's team, sir, investigating this happy-slapping business.'

'A couple of hours a day from a team that size shouldn't deprive her too seriously. Unless the rumours are true?'

There was no point in blustering, even in asking which rumours. Unasked, she sat down and leaned towards him confidentially, dissembling only slightly. 'The job has grown enormously.'

'Like Topsy.'

'Indeed. So much that I wondered aloud to Joe Farmer — the acting Chief Super, sir — if a profiler was called for.'

'And his response was a decided negative. You can see his point, Fran. He wants to pull a big result all by himself.'

'It's an awfully large rabbit and may well be stuck in the hat.'

'So he needs more than a magic wand and an abracadabra!'

'I would.'

'But you've got nothing to prove. Now, the bastard hasn't actually raped yet — right?'

'So far he's confined himself to wiping semen over his victims' faces, apart from one indecent assault. You know, it's almost as if he enjoys making us wait. He must know he's got us on tenterhooks. Us, and all the women of Kent. Get Joe to ask for a profiler, sir.'

'I don't want to impose one on him. You couldn't have a word . . . ? No? Persuade DCI Tanner to press for one? Which reminds me, Fran: this conversation was meant to be about Tanner. A very neat bit of hi-jacking, if I may say so. Straight answer time. Is she up to the job?'

'Of course she is. Especially with the assistance of a profiler.'

'There's a "but" coming up, Fran. Isn't there?' he prompted. 'I can hear it in your voice.'

'I don't think she's well. I've tried talking to her informally in my office—'

He cut across ruthlessly. 'Another but! What about Joe Farmer talking formally in his office?'

'Absolutely not! With respect, sir,' she added belatedly, 'I think she'd have hysterics and walk away on six months' sick pay and leave us with an accusation of bullying hanging over us. Not that I think for a minute she'd want to take action, but you know what these keenie-beanie ambulance-chasing solicitors are like.'

'Not to mention Fed Reps. Very well. So get Cosmo Dix on to it.'

Would she hell. She smiled. 'Come on, Chief, I've been her friend and colleague for thirty years. I'd rather not ask Cosmo, no matter how good he and his team are, to get involved yet. Can I see what an even less formal talk, well out of the office, will do?'

'So long as you get results, Fran.'

'If results can be got!'

'If indeed. Now, anything else I should know about the case? I know it's not your brief anymore, Fran, but I bet you're up to speed.'

'Sir, Joe'd be very upset—' Damn! Wrong word! '—concerned, that is, if he thought I was usurping his function.'

'No one's usurping anyone's function! I'm asking you what you know, Chief Superintendent.'

'Sir.' Drat him for this oscillation between the friendly and the formal. 'DCI Tanner's coordinated groups of neighbourhood support officers. Each team liaises closely with a couple of schools.'

'Does this apply to private schools too? The kids that assaulted you were from that very smart place in Canterbury, weren't they?'

'I'll remind Jill to tell the teams to spread the net as widely as possible. If necessary, I could speak to school heads.'

He chuckled. 'You could put the fear of God into them if anyone could.'

Gee, thanks, boss. She opened her eyes widely. But he was going to say something else, wasn't he?

'That assault on you, Fran. What's happening?'

'Canterbury will keep me updated, sir, as they would any other victim. I told them I wouldn't be pushing for prosecution, but I wanted the living daylights scared out of the little bleeders.'

She was fairly sure he spotted the flaw in her report, the fact that two weeks and more after the incident she was still in the dark, but he said nothing, pushing the anonymous letter in its evidence bag back across the table. He opened his mouth to speak, but seemed to be considering how to put something unpleasant. Something about the knife-wielding child's injury, no doubt. For which she was responsible.

She tried not to ball her fists.

'It's very fortunate that every single minute of the incident was recorded on CCTV and witnessed by a whole lot of interested eyes,' he began slowly.

He might have punched her in the stomach. It was coming. What every cop dreaded. The complaint. The allegation of police brutality. The automatic suspension.

'The Police Complaints Commission? Because I dislocated that kid's shoulder?'

'Someone did mention it to them. Well, we know it's standard procedure. So I had a look at the CCTV footage myself. You're such a senior officer someone even higher up the pecking order has to investigate. And I could hardly ask Mark to, could I? It was quite clear that as you arm-locked the child — and you clearly had to, in view of that knife thrust — another child came up behind you and pushed you hard. A third tripped you. So when they mentioned further investigation and suspension I did the obvious thing.'

She was sweating with relief. 'Which was what, sir?'

'I told the investigating officer to go fuck himself,' the Chief responded, clearly relishing every moment of her shock. 'In absolute confidence, of course.'

* * *

The Chief was one who treated wishes as gently expressed commands, just as much to be obeyed as if he'd stood up and bawled them through a megaphone. She went straight to the Incident Room. But she got no further than the door.

Despite the bright day, the sun slicing its way film noir-style through the blinds, there was a decided air of gloom. A glance at Jill's office door told her why. Joe Farmer was standing at her desk, flicking angrily through the files and slapping them down again. He punctuated this with irate and regular glances at his watch. Regular and ostentatious glances, meant to din into the troops that he was furious with the DCI for being elsewhere. Would they stick loyally together like a class knowing their teacher was in for it, or grass Jill up? Tom was very obviously trying to meet no one's eye, peering deep into a computer screen as if it were his girlfriend's face.

Her presence wouldn't help. She melted out as silently as she'd melted in. Back in her office, she called Tom's mobile.

* * *

He stared at the oatcakes with disdain. 'I'll have to get on to my auntie, like, won't I, guv?'

'You will indeed, Tom. It shall be the first call you make when you're seconded to me later today.' As his face lit up, she shook her head warningly. 'Only a couple of hours a day, and only if you can be spared. And only if you tell me what the hell's going on in that Incident Room,' she added, leaning forward with a smile, as if merely asking for gossip.

Tom knew her better. 'I'm dead worried about the DCI, guv. And DCS Farmer seems to be gunning for her. You'd think he had too many other responsibilities and roles to concentrate on just one person and her case. But it's as if making her seem weak makes him look even stronger.' He sipped his tea, watching under his eyelashes for permission to go further. It came, tacitly, as he must have known it would. 'Mind you, the DCI is asking for it, like. She's late in, home early. Misses briefings, like today. And when she is in, she's not all there, if you see what I mean. I had a word with my mate at Ashford — but this is only station gossip, guv.'

She nodded sombrely. 'And it won't go beyond these four walls.'

'The rumour is — shit, Fran, they say she's doing dope.'

She ignored the accidental use of her first name: they'd been through a lot together, and it was only in private and under stress that he ever lapsed.

'Came in smelling of pot the other day. And it may be worse. She used to wear short sleeves whatever the weather — used to say it saved her having to roll them up when she got busy. Now you'll notice she wears them buttoned at the cuff, all the time. But someone reckons she saw bruises when she was washing her hands . . . You know, bruises from needles, like.' He added, chin up, 'And before you ask, no, I've said nothing to anyone. And if she'd been in bright-eyed and bushy-tailed first thing I wouldn't even be telling you, would I? But someone's got to do something, guv, and I reckon it'd be better you, because you've nothing to prove, than Farmer Giles, who wants a permanent job.'

She made a little circling gesture, to return to an earlier point. 'These bruises, the tracks . . . Have you ever seen them yourself? With your own eyes?'

For the first time he fidgeted. 'I've seen bruises. Yes. On her arms. I wouldn't have called them needle tracks, myself. More as if a pair of hands were gripping too tight.' He put his hands about three inches from her own. 'And I did smell the pot, skunk, to be honest. But on her clothes, guv, not her breath.'

'So you think it's someone else smoking the stuff?' Did it take a genius to suspect Rob? He was about the right age.

'The trouble is, it's not exactly legal, knowingly letting your premises be used for people to smoke themselves senseless, is it?' He swallowed, aware that he'd started well but lapsed.

'Bother the legalese.'

'And now she's missed yet another meeting and I'm afraid the DCS will have no option but to grass her up,' he concluded, a child in the playground again.

They smiled sadly at each other. They could never quite be equals, but friends they certainly were. Perhaps Tom was the son she'd never had. If she got sentimental, she reminded herself that he had a perfectly good mother, better then she could ever have been. As it was, on a day-to-day basis he was precisely the partner she wanted to work with, and the fact that the Chief had decreed it took away any residual guilt she might have had.

However, working on the Dilly case was the last thing she had on her mind at the moment.

'I take it someone's tried to phone Jill?'

'Tried myself, guv: landline and mobile. Both switched off. I'd got as far as checking Traffic — you know, she might have been in a smash, like.'

'Negative?'

'Negative. And so I thought I'd try the William Harvey A and E.'

'And?'

'That was when you sent for me.'

'Try them now. Now, what the hell's the name of the school they send their son to?' She ran her finger down the phone directory while Tom fought his way through the hospital system to A and E. One look at his rounded eyes and mouth were enough to stop her.

* * *

Tom hadn't begged to go to the hospital with her, as she'd expected. Instead, he'd asked for any routine work he could get on with, for her or for Jill. Phoning Farat Hafeez; he could certainly do that. And he should contact the Vicar of St Jude's, simply to ask for a list of Alpha Course members. He could also chase the CCTV footage of whoever delivered Dilly's flowers. Two hours a day? Four might just fill the bill. And it might be more tactful if he stayed in her office to do it all; she didn't want rumours flying round the building, and silence was easier if you didn't see anyone to talk to. He should immediately tell Mark and Cosmo where she had gone, but no one else.

Tom had gleaned no details, other than that Jill had been admitted. It could be anything from pneumonia to a suicide attempt, taking in a twisted knee en route. Somehow Fran didn't see Jill bothering officialdom with anything minor, so, as she picked up an unmarked pound car in case Mark needed his, she braced herself for something bad.

* * *

Fran threw the car into a slot marked Consultants Only, leaving one of her business cards propped against the screen and strode in. The dismal queue parted before her good suit and air of authority, though she always reminded herself that being five foot ten never hurt.

She showed her ID. 'Where can I find Ms Jill Tanner, please?'

Years ago, in her Traffic days, she'd have known every A and E receptionist on the circuit, and each would have got her to the person she needed before she even asked. They had presumably moved up the ladder at the same rate as she. So she was left with this dozy, uncooperative woman.

'I understand,' she said very slowly and clearly, 'that you have admitted DCI Jill Tanner. I would like to see her if it's clinically possible.'

'If you sit down.' The woman gestured. But the flap of the hand towards the vacant chairs transformed itself, almost unconsciously, to point at the most senior nurse at the far side of her desk.

* * *

Jill was lying listlessly on a trolley waiting for someone to ferry her to X-Ray. She was alone — no sign of Brian or either of the kids. In her unforgiving hospital gown, every bruise was visible, including the two hand-shaped ones Tom had mentioned.

'If you're nice to me I shall cry, and it'll hurt,' Jill greeted her.

'Well, you'd better lie to attention then, hadn't you?' Fran bent and kissed her cheek. 'Well?' She took Jill's hand in a warm clasp, retaining it.

'Stairs. I fell down the stairs. They think I may have cracked a rib or two, and maybe my left ankle.'

'A woman of your age falling down stairs in a bright modern house like yours? That takes some doing, Jill, even at the end of a hard week.'

She rubbed her head with her spare hand. 'It all happened so fast. Is it only Friday?'

'It is. And you haven't told me how you did it.'

'I just missed my footing. In a rush, not looking where I was going — you know how it is. That time you fell over the pavement that wasn't there. You remember — Ashford market?'

'Fancy your remembering that!' She'd gone base over apex for absolutely no reason. She'd been lucky to bounce. It must have been around the time Pa had started having heart attacks, when she was under unbelievable stress.

'Teenagers are worse than parents,' she mused, unthinking.

'Teenagers are fine. This case — these cases — they've really got to me, that's all.'

Fran nodded. 'Of course. Like they grabbed you round the forearms hard enough to bruise you.'

Jill flushed vividly. 'That was — well, come on, Fran, doesn't Mark grab you when . . . You know, moments of passion?'

'If he squeezed that hard, I'd go even as he came. Jill — we're both adults and we're old friends. Who has done this to you? Brian?'

Jill turned her face literally to the wall. 'I fell down the stairs, for God's sake.' And she might have muttered under her breath, 'And you can't prove otherwise.'

Equally inaudibly, Fran responded. 'Want a bet?'

* * *

Fran parked herself in the waiting area until Jill had been plastered and bound up. Then she presented herself again. 'You'll need a lift home, won't you? And I don't see Brian.'

'He's on a bloody training session, as I could have told you if you'd given me half a chance. Residential. Good respectable local government witnesses everywhere.' She sighed, with what seemed like resignation but obviously turned to pain. 'Do you suppose you could stow a pair of crutches in your car?'

* * *

Fran had no more than cleared a load of disparate rubbish off Jill's sofa, which conveniently had a built-in lifting footrest, when her phone rang.

'Tom?'

'Bit of a problem, like, guv. The Chief and your ACC like are in a private huddle with some guy from the Transport Police. Absolutely no interruptions. And I don't think you'd want me to discuss this with anyone else.'

She checked her watch. 'I should be with you within the hour if you can hold the fort.'

'I'll do my best, guv.'

Why did he sound so pleased?

She cut the quickest sandwich, found bottled water, the TV zapper and Jill's mobile. 'What time do the kids get back?'

'Fiveish. And Brian about eight tonight. I shall be fine.'

'Of course you will.'

Especially if Fran could make it her business to come back too. There were things she needed to sniff out. Not least the reason for the most pungent plug-in air freshener she'd ever had the misfortune to meet.

CHAPTER FOURTEEN

The rest is silence.

* * *

However rushed and flustered she felt, Fran always tried to look cool. If she'd combed her hair and applied some slap, senior officers believed the flannel she had to fob them off with, and junior officers trusted her to deal with their problems. Like Tom now, for instance. She even popped a confident smile in place as she opened her office door. And stopped short.

'Dilly! What are you doing here?' She stepped inside quickly, closing the door.

The answer, by the looks of it, was that Dilly Pound was enjoying herself, Tom dancing attendance on her. Bottled water, a plastic dish of salad, some uneaten fruit, all on a canteen tray, sat on Fran's desk, with Dilly occupying her chair and Tom his usual one pulled up opposite.

Tom didn't even have the grace to blush. He just gave his usual innocent smile. Without a word about Jill Tanner, he explained, 'Dilly was hungry and I thought no one would notice if I got her the sort of lunch you have if you're in a hurry.'

Used to have. These days her half hour with Mark, however snatched, was sacrosanct unless one of them was locked in the sort of business that had made Mark inaccessible today.

'Well, you'd better work out why I'm extraordinarily peckish and go and find me a supplementary sandwich,' she grinned, appeased by his reasoning. As he left, she turned, amused, to the young woman who seemed to have been absorbed into her unofficial family. 'OK, Dilly, you've obviously explained to Tom why you're here: could you tell me?'

'Of course.' Dilly at least was clearly aware of the potential awkwardness of the situation. 'And I do apologise. I came straight here. I had to. It never dawned on me you'd be out. And your secretary . . . she just showed me in. And Tom was working away at your desk and he told her you'd just popped out — you know, as if you'd gone to the loo or something — and that she could leave me. You know, trust me not to — well, hack into your files, or something. I don't know.' And this was a woman who could talk to camera in long coherent sentences! 'Which was wonderful. Look.' She patted an opened A4 Jiffy-bag. The letter inside was slightly creased, as if something else had been in the bag too. 'It came to me at work.'

In her position, Fran would probably have wanted to be looked after too. Even by Tom, if Mark wasn't around. Today's note, sent by courier to TVInvicta, had shifted from the Bible to Shakespeare — thank goodness she'd done *Hamlet* for A Level — for inspiration. *The rest is silence.* Apart from that it was in the format she'd come to expect: A4, average weight paper, laser printed. She'd bet her pension there was no DNA on it either, or anything else the slightest bit of use to the forensic science team.

'And the note wasn't quite all.' Dilly's voice threatened to break.

'It sounds as if whatever else there was wasn't very pleasant.'

Dilly shook her head. 'Tom put it in an evidence bag. He's had it photographed and sent for DNA testing. Just in case.'

The door opened, Tom sliding in and shutting the door quickly.

'Very Secret Service, Tom. Thanks.' She put the sandwiches on a corner of her desk. 'Now, you've clearly been terribly efficient, but I am, as Senior Investigating Officer, allowed to know what has so upset Dilly.' She added with a grin, 'What is the "it" we're talking about?'

'Just a five-inch bladed kitchen knife,' he said with ironic cheerfulness. 'It came by courier, from Ashford. I checked with their depot. A very ordinary man in shades, false address.'

'*Just* a knife! New? Old?'

'It was the sort my mum brought me when I set up down here. Woolworth's. Stainless blade, black plastic handle. Mine looks just like new, even though I've used it and it's been through the communal dishwasher every day. So it'll take the Forensics team to tell. But what I have done is phone Woollies' regional HQ and ask for details of sales round here in the last couple of weeks. Just in case, like.'

'Well done.'

'The trouble is,' he declared, with a theatrical pause, 'the knife didn't just rattle round inside the bag, ma'am. It came wrapped in something. Didn't it, Dilly?'

The young woman hiccupped on a sob. 'Yes. Fran, it was . . . they were . . .'

'Undies, ma'am.'

'What?'

'A bra and pants set,' Tom said, deadpan now. 'Also bagged for evidence. According to Dilly—'

Fran raised a hand. She wanted this from Dilly herself, whom she encouraged with raised eyebrows and a quick nod.

'It's so embarrassing. Three or four weeks ago I lost a set. Out of my laundry basket.'

'Just like that? You didn't leave it at Daniel's or at another friend's?' She'd be hard put herself to say in whichever house she'd left any item of clothing, of course.

'Daniel and I — you know we . . .' She swallowed. 'At first I thought I must have washed them and they had got stuck in the washing machine, you know, pressed against the sides of the drum. Or hung them on the line and they'd blown off. But I thought, why just them?'

'Why indeed?'

'And then — well, Daniel told me I was imagining things, but you can't just imagine losing a bra. Pants, yes.'

Unwilling, for Tom's sake, to get involved in the philosophy of underwear loss, Fran asked, 'And now your bra and pants are back?'

'Not exactly. An identical set. Marks and Sparks, of course.'

'And Chummie had cut out the labels,' Tom put in.

'So someone got into your house, stole some dirty undies and a few weeks later replaced them with clean ones. What a nice man. The more he does this sort of thing, the sooner he'll bring himself down, won't he, Tom? So you won't have to endure this sort of thing much longer. Now, do you have any work assignments today, Dilly?'

'Not till Monday — I already had this afternoon booked as time off. There was some talk of doing something with Daniel, but it fell through, so I was hoping to do some gardening, but I didn't want . . . didn't think . . .'

'Good. I'm sorry about your pruning or whatever, but you're certainly safer here. As for the weekend, we'll have to give that some thought, won't we?' She fancied she caught a tiny silence: had they already discussed that but decided not to float the idea yet?

Tom coughed. 'Do you want me to get back to the Incident Room with the others, ma'am?'

'Not for a couple of moments, if you don't mind keeping Ms Pound company a little longer.' As if. 'I've got some running around to do. In connection with DCI Tanner's accident. There should be a general announcement to the Incident Room.'

He'd completely forgotten, hadn't he? 'Is she—? God, I—' He smacked his forehead. 'Not much of a multi-tasker, am I?'

'You're male,' Dilly put in indulgently.

'She's safe at home, but with a couple of cracked ribs and a broken ankle. So I've got to go and talk to people. Best if you learn the details when the others do, eh?'

With the Chief and Mark still in their private meeting, she could no more barge in than Tom could, though they would certainly have to be involved in the next move in the Dilly Pound affair. That could wait, as long as Tom was happy to babysit. He might as well make himself useful while he did. She approached the matter obliquely. 'By the way, Dilly, your fiancé told me you'd thought you were being followed at one point. And that you'd had George Dubya himself peering through your window. Why didn't you tell me?'

Dilly looked at Tom, not her, and blushed. 'Daniel said it was all nonsense, and I'm sure he's right.'

'Just in case he isn't, just go through the various incidents with Tom, will you? In as much detail as you possibly can. With dates. Everything.'

She didn't need to tell Tom to be thorough. Thorough was his middle name.

* * *

Her immediate problem, then, was Jill. For once she'd go through official channels. Someone had to tell Joe Farmer he was a significant member of his team light, but for Tom's sake she'd rather he didn't know exactly how she herself got involved.

Cosmo Dix was the answer. It was his job now to redistribute personnel. With luck the Chief's fiat would ensure she kept Tom as her gofer for the couple of hours a day he'd promised. If she were a betting woman, she'd have a fiver on Joe Farmer wanting to take on at least Jill's caseload, popping the rest on to her desk. Five years ago she'd have been the first to put her hand in the air. Now she wasn't so sure.

'Three weeks' sick leave?' Cosmo repeated. 'And the gravy, if I may say so.'

'You may,' Fran said graciously. 'So long as you can tell me what it means.'

'It's what my dear old gran used to say when she meant that and a good deal more. Dudley, Fran — where Lenny Henry comes from. They have a nice line on vivid phraseology up there. Bear with me one tick, would you?' He leaned back to page his secretary. 'The minute the Chief's free, get his secretary to call back. The very nanosecond, in fact. No, I don't want to talk to him — it's the ACC, Mr Turner, I want. Thanks.' He turned back to Fran. 'Might as well get this sorted before the weekend. At least, as sorted as we can. And that means involving DCS Farmer, too, of course. Though I fancy,' he added, eyes agleam under his lashes, 'that the fact you've come on your own means you're making some sort of pre-emptive strike. Who's your nomination, then?'

Fran listed half a dozen names. 'But I want to take a back seat in this. What I do need to do is talk to the Chief before he leaves the building, so—'

'No, you sit back down again.' Back to his secretary. 'And tell Janice that DCS Harman must talk to God before he hies him home. M for must. OK?'

'Cosmo, I'm not supposed to "must" the Chief, you know.'

'Come on, you can rely on Janice to be firm tactfully.'

* * *

Dilly suggested she was in the way, and stopping Fran and Tom doing their job. Unable to gainsay it, Fran asked how she would feel simply staying where she was, while Tom and she did indeed do other things. Tom found her some embarrassingly old magazines from Reception, and they left her to it. Fran's secretary was as huffy as an old-time butler at such an unorthodox arrangement, but these days knew better than to argue.

'Anything new?' Fran asked, as she and Tom stopped outside the Incident Room.

'Bloody McDine's told her to keep schtum about all sorts of sightings. God knows why. But I think Chummie's regularly been doing a Peeping Tom act outside her cottage. You know, wearing one of those masks, like — the sort people wear on demos. And I think he regularly tailed her from her office to her car.'

'Before or after the broadcast?'

'Well before, I reckon. I reckon her going national was just an excuse to step things up further. I may be wrong. But she's so bloody vague about dates and times.'

'And anything else?'

'Not a lot. What she needs if you ask me is a good shrink to find why she's saying so little. In her place I'd be scared witless, but she's so bloody phlegmatic.'

'We'll have to do the shrink act for her, I suspect. Sod it, it looks as if DCS Farmer's on his way out. Get back to the Incident Room — oh, you'll come up with an excuse for going AWOL — and then brief me later. Off you go.'

Farmer, caught in mid-stride as he left his office, didn't take the news of Jill's fall with any enthusiasm.

'I wondered if we should both be present to tell the troops,' she said, though she didn't really fancy a Tweedledee and Tweedledum act.

He pulled a long face and looked at his watch.

'OK,' she said helpfully, 'I'll do it myself and update you later.'

The Sexual Incidents teams greeted her announcement with something like relief that the governor had a genuine reason for absence.

'Will you be taking over the cases, ma'am?' some hopeful asked.

'Nothing's been decided yet. I'll let you know immediately it has. In the meantime, simply press on with what you've been doing. I'll be in DCI Tanner's office if you need me, but I shall be busy, so I don't want purely social visits. OK? Tom? Can I pick your brain, please?' She withdrew to the comparative privacy of the goldfish bowl.

'How far did you get before our visitor turned up?' she demanded, nodding towards the door.

Shutting it, he counted his tasks off on his fingers. 'CCTV at her cottage: for some reason the camera wasn't tracking properly. Something to do with high wind blowing it off its moorings, like.'

'What high wind?'

'Well, it's been a bit breezy, like.'

'Enough to damage a well-fixed camera?'

'Must have been a Friday afternoon job.'

She slapped the desk in exasperation. 'So we've got nothing?'

'Apart from you and the ACC, just a very fuzzy shot of someone's bald spot.'

'Bloody hell. So we get every suspect to kneel for the ID parade, do we? I take it you gave the firm that fitted it an earful on my behalf.'

'You'd have been proud of me, guv,' he said dryly. 'And of the one I gave the Whitefriars security staff for not putting a tape in their recorder. All this bloody technology there to help us and it's no bloody use!'

'It seems too much of a coincidence to me.' As if the idea were new, as if she hadn't floated it to Jill at least twice, she asked, 'Can you get on to the firm installing the cameras and see who made a porridge of Dilly's? Low key. No accusations. Just general information about any installers. After all,' she added, 'I know you're on the happy-slapping team, but all the sex crimes have been out of CCTV range and you do just wonder . . . No, hang on. I'd better see if DCI Tanner got one of the other team on to it. No need to reinvent the wheel. Any progress on the Alpha Course vicar?'

'Seems Friday's her day off. Well, since she'll be doing weddings tomorrow and services on Sundays, I suppose it makes sense. I said I'd phone her tomorrow—'

'Between weddings, I hope!'

'I didn't leave a message. You never know how these things will be construed,' he added, quoting her usual instructions verbatim.

'Good. Now, one more thing — can you get on to the witness protection people? Dilly will need a safe house at least until the CCTV is working properly and all her locks have been changed — you knew she kept a key under a spare flowerpot, did you?'

'Seems she's thought of that: she's got those fixed.'

'Who by? We don't want some load of cowboys doing those, too.'

'I'll go and check, guv.'

She suppressed a laugh — any excuse to go and talk to her again and be the macho but caring cop. And Dilly, who had been so grey and negative with Daniel McDine, would blossom in the sunlight of his obvious admiration.

'But some of those safe houses aren't very nice, guv. I mean, protecting scrotes turning Queen's Evidence is one thing, and they shouldn't expect the Ritz, like. But she's a lady.'

'Tom, Tom, what happened to all that equal opportunities training? There are no such things as ladies anymore! OK, I know what you mean. Tell the protection people you don't want some flea-ridden council house.'

A venture into the Incident Room found everyone engaged in something apparently useful, except for DI Jon Binns, who was staring at a screen crammed with columns of figures. He blinked as she approached, then again, harder, as if his eyes hurt. 'Budget balancing,' he said, running his hands across a prematurely balding pate, to which, for some reason, he hadn't taken the clippers.

'Not someone your rank,' she frowned.

'The last Chief Super was taken ill before he could manage it.' He sounded apologetic, as if it was his fault.

'And DCS Farmer?'

'Has problems with the software. And I can quite see why. It's very cumbersome.' That was loyalty for you. But it deserved a better reward than it was likely to get.

'If you know a better program, jot down the details and I'll take it to whoever. Or Joe Farmer can. You're supposed to be detecting, not number crunching.'

'I was training to do both — to be a forensic accountant. With my background I thought I could be really useful.'

'And then?'

'I fancied something a bit more active. As soon as I got my inspector's exams, I baled out. And here I am.'

She sat opposite him. 'How do you fancy doing a bit of detecting for me? I thought I'd already asked one of the DCIs to look into the CCTV firms, but maybe I didn't.' She explained.

DI Binns looked totally blank, but agreed to liaise with Tom.

'So I need a list of all their employees, from the people in charge of deciding the location of the cameras to the guys actually fitting them. It's rather a lowly task, but could you get on to it? Or delegate, if you wish.'

'I'll get on to them the minute I've finished this lot of figures, shall I?'

'You could do that,' she said not unkindly. 'Figures are important, Jon, but lives much more so. Why not save that page and do as I asked? I'll make it OK.' He looked so young and vulnerable she added, with a grin, 'Promise.'

Shaking her head at her soft heartedness — Jon Binns was thirty-five if he was a day — she toddled off to leave Farmer a concise note.

Surely, surely she'd spoken to Jill about her suspicions! Maybe not. Anyway, things were at last in train on that front.

* * *

Perhaps it was because it was Friday that all the managerial issues were resolved extraordinarily quickly. Jill's caseload, naturally falling into two sections, was put under the supervision of Farmer and Fran, but not under their day-to-day care, with two more DCIs to be brought in. Farmer seemed inclined to argue; Fran had to restrain herself from kicking him hard on the ankle. Let detectives detect, she wanted to say, we've got to administrate. But she said nothing, because her administrative load was almost zero these days, and she had an irresistible urge to detect. And eschew the rest. Especially meetings. Especially policy meetings.

'And most especially of all Home Office policy meetings,' she concluded, as Mark put the car into gear.

'When you know all your carefully worked out plans will be eliminated because of some Downing Street minion scribbling on a table napkin,' he agreed. 'Whatever happened to that idea of marching drunken louts to cash machines to pay instant fines?'

'Someone discovered they couldn't remember their names, let alone their PIN numbers?'

They shared a cynical laugh.

'But how did you fix that Dilly protection business?' he asked. 'A bit *ad hoc*, surely?'

'Entirely *ad hoc*! But clearly the poor woman can't stay in that house on her own, not until someone's fixed the CCTV stuff so a bit of wind won't blow it haywire. And if young Tom Arkwright really does have a spare room in his house share and is happy to spend his weekend minding her when she isn't with that fiancé of hers, that's a damned sight easier than popping her in a safe house which is far below the quality that he seems to think is her due. The Chief, too. He's really smitten, isn't he?'

'The Chief or Tom?' he laughed.

'Both! And I must say, the Chief's wife apart, that is, either bloke would be better than her current options. Especially young Tom.'

'But he's years younger than she is!'

She said, as sharply as if they were in a meeting, 'If the age difference were reversed, you wouldn't raise even half an eyebrow.'

'You're right.' But he didn't seem to accept the rebuke. 'I'd leave that to you. You do it so much better than me, especially now all those bruises have healed.'

'I meant it, Mark. Why, I'm older than you—'

'But only by a month, for goodness' sake. OK, I was out of order. Sorry. Now, do you really insist on us both going to Jill's house? You don't think she might find the two of us a bit intimidating?'

'Not if you hide behind a nice big bunch of flowers. And one of us washes up. Her kitchen was in a bit of a state.'

'So you buy this "fell down a messy staircase excuse"?'

'Let's reserve judgement. So long as we go as Fran and Mark and leave all our braid and buttons behind.'

* * *

Jill let them in herself, hobbling back to her sofa as Fran announced she was about to make a cup of tea and disappeared into the kitchen. The very fact that she didn't argue told Mark she must be in pain.

'You'll be getting an official visit from Pers — from *Human Resources* — to talk about your return to work. I'm more interested in how long it will be before you and Brian can thrash us at tennis again,' he said conversationally.

Now why had Jill glanced at the silver trophies on the mantelpiece and on two shelves of what was designed as a bookcase? He'd seen that involuntary look before, when he was an active cop raiding premises, the sort of eye-movement that told the onlooker that Chummie was hiding something — and, more to the point, where he was hiding it. What was it that Jill didn't want him to look at? After a few minutes' conversation on this year's Wimbledon prospects, Mark drifted over to look more closely at some of the cups. Everything was a little tarnished, but what worried him far more were a couple of clean circles in the dust that covered everything. Big circles meant big trophies. To ask what had happened to them would, he suspected, elicit little more than a string of lies — if Fran were correct in her surmise that Rob was on drugs, it might well be that he'd nicked them to feed his habit. And when had Fran not been right?

'I gather Natasha's taken after you in being sporty? Cricket, if not tennis?'

Jill would clearly have preferred Wimbledon to Lord's as a venue for her possible hour of triumph. 'At least it's not rugby. I couldn't bear that. The risks . . . And it's so unfeminine.'

'I didn't think they did frilly dresses in tennis anymore. Or ordinary shorts, come to that,' he added. 'All that sculptured stuff — looks as if it's been sprayed on!'

She nodded. 'I tried to get a new tennis dress in the Outlet this summer. Bright orange. Imagine that at Wimbledon. Nowhere to stow your tennis balls, either. Quite impractical.'

'Neater than the weird beach clothes the men seem to wear. Like cut off pyjamas.' What on earth was keeping Fran? Small talk with junior officers had never been his forte, especially not at six on a Friday. 'What time do they get in, your kids?'

'When they feel hungry.' Her smile was unconvincing, to put it mildly.

'They're a worry, aren't they? My two — I still want to tell them to work harder, drive more slowly, drink less, give up smoking. But the more I tell them, the less they take any notice. Mind you, they are in their twenties.'

'How do they get on with Fran?'

It was such a direct question he was taken aback, almost offended.

'Well. Very well,' he said with finality.

But she didn't let go. 'They don't see her as a replacement for Tina?'

'Why should they? She isn't.'

'I thought — I'm sorry, I thought — you know, the ring.' Jill touched her left hand. 'At least, it's what everyone assumes. And there was a pile of estate agents' particulars on Fran's desk the other day.'

She was digging herself in deeper and deeper. He made a huge effort. 'Fran and I — Fran isn't looking to be a replacement mother. What woman of any sense would, with two adults? Our relationship — her's and mine — isn't . . . In a sense, it's none of their business.' Nor of Jill's, either. Where the hell was Fran with the bloody tea? Perhaps attack was the best means of defence. 'You and Brian — how long have you been together, Jill?'

'Twenty years, give or take.'

Twenty years sounded a bit too memorable to give and take. It was the sort of length people celebrated publicly. So what on earth did she mean?

At this point Fran came in, almost as if she'd been waiting for some sort of cue. 'So when's the party? Come on, most police marriages don't last half that time. Balloons, a conjuror — you deserve the works!'

'Let's wait till it's twenty-five years,' Jill said. 'Then you can do everything in silver.'

She spoke lightly but he was sure there was some under-current there. He looked to Fran for confirmation. A tiny lift of one eyebrow confirmed his suspicions. But she jumped straight in.

'So how good are Natasha and Rob at cooking? Or is Brian bringing something in? Because if not, I'm no Delia, but I could knock up something for you all. From jars and packets,' she added, her face comic in confession.

'There are plenty of those. I'm sure I can manage . . .'

'I'm sure you can: the question is, should you have to?' Fran bit something back. 'Now, by the looks of you, you ought to be in bed. Can I help you?'

Jill's relief was palpable. But then her face fell. 'That's when it happened. When I fell. I'd just stripped the bed.'

The implication was that she missed her step because she had her arms full of bedlinen and couldn't see where she was going. Was she telling the truth? Was there a monster pile of dirty linen lying somewhere, or had Fran loaded the machine when she'd brought her back from the hospital? A quick glance at Fran showed a studiously blank face.

Fran chipped in quickly. 'No problem. Just tell me where I'll find the clean sheets and Bob's your uncle.'

'Airing cupboard. But—'

Fran did her greyhound act and vanished up the stairs. Craven, he stood and said, 'Always easier with two. Back in two minutes.'

Fran greeted him with a bundle of bed linen and a serious face. 'Load the washing machine. I'll be back down in a second. See if there's anything else to make a full load while you're at it,' she added, at the top of her voice. In other words, go into the kids' rooms too.

He didn't like this one scrap. 'What sort of thing?'

'Socks, T-shirts . . .'

From downstairs came a wail. 'Don't bother. Honestly. Please.'

Quite. All the same, he popped his head round a couple of doors. Of the two rooms, Natasha's was much the untidier — he could have culled a dozen T-shirts, but gathered four at random. But Rob's smelt rank, like a rugby club changing room, full of sweaty garments and testosterone. And something else — not a sporting venue smell this at all! Pot. Strong, heavy pot. Skunk.

CHAPTER FIFTEEN

As Mark got downstairs, arms full, knowing he had to say something to Jill, the front door burst open, and a young woman hurtled into the hall.

'Who are you? And what are you doing with my things? You fucking pervert!' She flung herself at him, grabbing handfuls of fabric and pulling.

Young woman? No, just a young teenager to judge by her face. But she was tall and strong.

'Hang on, Natasha!' Fran shouted. 'That's Mark. He's with me. Your mother's had a fall and we're just—'

'Fran?' Her face lightened, and after one more scathing glance she turned to the stairs. 'Where is she?' The T-shirts fell to the floor as she bounded away.

'I'm fine! In here!' That was Jill's voice.

'Mum? What's up?'

He'd forgotten how noisy family life could be. Automatically he picked everything up and made for the quiet of the kitchen while he could. It was as immaculate as ten minutes of Fran's energy could make it. He loaded the machine, but could see no sign of detergent. It must be in one of the units, but, despite his years of official practice, searching still felt like trespass, so he gave up and dug deep for some control as he went back to the living room. What he ought to do was tell Natasha to stop her hissy-fit and make herself useful.

Instead he hung on as a spectator.

'Rob? How should I know? We're not joined at the hip!'

How old might she be? Fourteen at most.

'I just hoped . . . So you've no idea where he is?' Jill almost pleaded. What a good job her team couldn't see her now. Had he been so spineless with his kids?

Natasha produced a shrug theatrical enough to turn a Frenchman green with envy. But perhaps there was too much guignol: did the girl protest too much?

He stepped in. 'Natasha, would you be good enough to show me where the detergent is? And set the machine — it looks like a flight deck with all those controls.' Always mix steely power with a touch of humour, that was his motto. A smaller shrug preceded her flounce into the kitchen.

'Your mother's had a bad fall,' he said, as on her knees she burrowed under the sink. 'Any idea how it happened?'

Another shrug as she surfaced with the Persil.

'And she's plainly worried about your brother — Rob, is that it? It wouldn't be grassing him up if you told her where he is.'

She couldn't have measured the detergent more carefully if she'd been about to transmute some base metal into gold.

'I think you're worried about him, too. And I think you're worried because you really don't know where he is.'

Her head dropped slightly. She might have been trying not to let him see her biting her lip. Still facing the machine, not him, she made a show of rearranging the laundry and fishing out a vivid pink top. 'You put that in with them everything'll come out pink,' she explained.

He took this as a sign of a thaw.

'That's why I never wear fuchsia,' he said. 'Any help, Natasha. Anything at all.' He placed his card on the surface in front of her, and added Fran's for luck. 'Just between ourselves. Your mum doesn't need any more stress, does she?'

Neither did Natasha. So he drifted back into the living room, slowly enough for her to call out if she wanted to.

* * *

'Your theory is that young Rob is into pot,' he said to Fran, fastening his seat belt.

'Not just a theory — not if your nose is accurate,' Fran retorted, 'which I'm sure it is.'

'And it's having a detrimental effect on his psychological state, to psychosis, even, leading to random violence towards his mother. It's well enough documented.' He gave a rueful grin. 'Of course, it could be simply being sixteen.'

She overrode him. 'Or, if you were right about the gaps in the silverware, maybe she challenged him about nicking her cups and he got violent then?'

He put the car into gear and backed out of Jill's drive. 'We'll have her panicking if we hang about any longer,' he observed. 'And I don't want to do that yet. Would you,' he continued, 'recognise young Rob if we happened to see him walking home?'

'Or hanging out with his mates . . . How about the skateboard park by the sports centre? That'd be a good place to start looking. But not, of course, a casual bumping into.'

'Which I suspect might be the best way of approaching the problem. Especially as you know him. You might simply want to warn him about his mother's accident. Gee him up a bit about supporting her about the house, that sort of thing.'

'And, having got him nicely softened up, go for the jugular with questions about pot?'

'Quite.' He nosed the car gently through the estate. They might have been kids on their first panda patrol. Eventually, having explored every cul-de-sac, he turned the car down to the tiny cluster of shops at the foot of the hill. A number of kids of both sexes were messing round on skateboards, in direct contravention of a viciously defaced sign prohibiting practically everything. Most were simply scooting around. A couple more adventurous souls, no helmets, no protective gear at all, were trying to run the boards down handrails alongside shallow flights of steps. From time to time they'd pause to let a third lad leap from the top of the steps, attempting to land with the board still beneath his feet.

'Supposed to be good for the cardio-vascular system,' she remarked. 'And certainly better than computer games.'

'You don't want to go and remonstrate with them for breaking the by-laws?'

'Emphatically not. Not unless you really, really, really think I ought to go and ask them if they've seen Rob?'

'I think one of us ought. No, it'd better be me. You've had your share of teenage violence.'

He was out of the car before she could argue, affecting a casual slouch he'd never have permitted himself in everyday life. Hands in pockets, shoulders hunched against a chill wind the kids seemed oblivious to, he retrieved a board as it shot from under some hapless lad, offering a suddenly avuncular hand as he crumpled at his knees.

The others swarmed around the fallen hero. Fran herself was ready to call an ambulance. But soon he was on his feet, ostentatiously pulling his hoodie around his face, and apparently giving Mark lip. He responded by raising a placatory hand, and she could see his lips moving.

Suddenly she couldn't move for terror. Her tongue stuck to the roof of her mouth. What if they knifed Mark? What if they aimed for that enticingly vulnerable area of shirt front? She was halfway out of the car when he turned towards her. No dark patch of blood. No fingers clutching an entry wound. She gibbered with relief as he returned to his seat and fastened his seat belt.

'They said they'd last seen him at school. Two hours or more ago. There was something else, though, a tiny look there, a nuance here . . . Get on the radio, would you, and ask for anyone in the area to have a look.' He set off with a spurt of gravel that made the kids turn in apparent admiration.

'All we're after is a little sod who smokes pot and may have had a row with his mother,' she pointed out.

'I just have this feeling, sweetheart — indulge me. It's a long time since I had feelings like this.'

'Feel away,' she said, 'so long as you don't have to indulge in heroics. Not part of your job description. You're supposed to do boring things behind desks.'

In the event, they were called on to do nothing. There was no sign of anyone at the school, cleaning staff apart. They joined the uniformed constables rooting behind the bike shelters and bus stops. At last, cold and hungry, Mark gathered everyone together and called it a day.

'Hang on,' she said, suddenly catching his anxiety, as they returned to the car, 'let's get a call through to A and E at the William Harvey. Just in case.'

Nothing.

She rubbed her face. 'So why are we so worried about a rotten kid who's probably doing the round of local fences to off-load his mother's silverware?'

'Of course he is! And do you know what? I don't even know who the local fences are anymore!'

'Me neither. But I'll bet I know a man who does.'

* * *

Knowing Tom would be otherwise engaged all weekend, for a while Fran toyed with going to Sunday morning service at St Jude's to speak to the vicar about the Alpha Course members. But tact and discretion were called for, and charging up to the poor clergywoman in front of the whole congregation and possibly even the perpetrator himself was neither tactful nor discreet. She would just have to hope Tom remembered to phone the vicar between Saturday weddings.

So how could she fill a whole weekend without work? Even now, she felt she ought to be in transit to Devon, just as she'd spent practically every weekend for the past few years, cooking or gardening for her aged parents. Now Pa was dead, and Ma, under the beady eyes of her elder daughter, Hazel, had retired to a Scottish care home where she passed her days telling the staff what they were doing wrong, an activity so important she viewed Fran's visits as an irritating interruption. So apart from occasional and irregular flights to see her, Fran's time was pretty much her own.

Without Mark the void would have been terrifying. As it was, he had to put his foot down firmly as Fran embarked on frantic spring-cleaning sessions, either at her own home or at his. These days he tended to plan outings, even to local Kent beauty spots neither had seen for years because of work or family commitments. And now, of course, there was the thrill of the chase, in house-hunting terms at least.

And today there was Jill to visit. To her shame, Fran felt the same stomach-clench of apprehension as she'd always felt on the drive to Devon. Mark chickened out, opting instead to be dropped off at Ashford nick to talk to the duty CID inspector about stolen silverware. In any case, it would have been hard to look informal and supportive with the two of them sitting in Jill's living room.

When she arrived, Brian was running the vac round the rest of the house. Of the kids there was no sign. She'd have put money on Tash being already up and doing something sporty, and Rob still lying somnolent in bed.

Jill looked far worse than she had the previous day, with more bruises coming out and a sort of limp exhaustion that Fran had never seen before. Her smile was decidedly wan.

Fran hardened her heart. 'If it were you visiting me and me lying there,' she began awkwardly, 'you'd be itching to ask me about the accident, wouldn't you? Did she fall or was she pushed, that sort of question. And what answer would you expect?'

'I fell down the stairs, Fran,' Jill said with a challenging lift of her head.

'Of course you did. And in what circumstances?'

'We went through this yesterday. All the clever questioning in the world won't get me to say anything different.'

Fran didn't doubt her. Brian had dusted the trophy shelf, and there was no sign of the circular patches. She fancied he'd rearranged the silver too to fill the gaps.

'Did Rob get home all right? I know Tash was worried about him.'

There was a minute pause. 'He's growing up. She doesn't like the extra freedom he gets. I know you had the worry of your sick parents, Fran, but you've never had kids. You wouldn't understand these things.'

Any other time or person, Fran would have gone into orbit with fury. Unfortunately, anger made her more tenacious. 'I certainly wouldn't understand letting someone get away with domestic violence. Or with nicking my tennis trophies to feed his drugs habit.'

Jill flushed. 'Get out!'

'Don't be daft,' Fran said. 'It's either me or Joe Farmer you need to talk to. The troops have noticed the smell of pot on your clothes. There's open gossip about it. I'd bet my pension it isn't you who's using. I don't want to accuse anyone, just protect you!'

Now Jill paled. 'People think I've got a habit?'

'No. They say you're not well and can smell pot on your clothes. They put two and two together and made half a dozen. When I did it I came up with a different total. That it was Rob, about whom you were obviously concerned when we talked just the other day, who was smoking it. And it's worry about him that's making you take your eye off the ball at work. And no, before you say anything, this isn't management harassment of a sick colleague. This is entirely off the record, just Fran talking to Jill. And I'm happy to talk equally off the record to Rob. You know, aged auntie sort of stuff. But I wouldn't do more than pass the time of day with him without your permission, Jill. You know that.' There was no response, so she persisted, 'Is he happy at school, do you know?'

'Why do you ask?'

'People often take drugs because they're unhappy. Or, in the case of kids, because of peer group pressure. And that must make a lad from a decent home very anxious. What does a bully like more than an anxious schoolmate?' She got to her feet. 'I'll leave you now. Talk to Brian about what I've said. And to Rob, if you can. And if all else fails, call the fifth cavalry, and Auntie Fran'll be here like a shot.' She bent to kiss Jill's cheek, but the younger woman pulled away.

'Just get out.'

Brian came downstairs as she stepped into the hall. How much had he overheard?

Trying to keep her voice normal, Fran said, 'She's very shocked, still, isn't she? Keep her away from work as long as you can, eh, Brian? Chain her to the sofa if you have to. Now, the Occupational Health people will soon be descending on her — they have to, when anyone's likely to be off work for some time. And they'll make sure she's on light duties until she's one hundred per cent fit.' She was being craven, wasn't she? So she added, 'And if you think there's something wrong with Rob, or you suspect something's bothering him, I'm here to help. Bullying, for instance. Or drugs.'

Before he could do more than lean forward confidentially and open his mouth, the living room door opened and Jill shuffled to join them, preferring the support of the wall to her crutches. 'I told you, get out. Stop poking your nose in. Just go.'

Brian looked from one woman to the other, gaping. 'We were only saying the other day—'

'Shut up. How many times do I have to tell you to leave?'

Fran stood her ground. 'For God's sake, Jill, some senior officers would blame you for letting him smoke pot on your premises. It's a criminal offence, after all. But I'm your mate. Can't you trust me to do a damage limitation exercise?'

'You've no proof—'

'But Brian's got suspicions.' He'd turned away guiltily. 'Isn't that enough? Please, just talk to each other, and to Rob. And when you're ready, just pick up the phone.'

CHAPTER SIXTEEN

Just as Mark was reaching for their Sunday night malt whisky, she had a text message. How like the young to choose a nice swift medium that the middle-aged needed their reading glasses to decipher. 'It's Tash. Natasha, I suppose. What looks like a website address. Nothing else.'

Abandoning the crystal glasses — Mark liked to make the nightcap an event — they switched on Mark's computer, tapping in the website address almost idly. To get snow. Electronic snow, at least. He peered closer. Then leaned back. In irritation, she whipped off her reading glasses and handed them to him. Unable now of course to see herself, she pointed to the screen.

'Password access only,' Mark said.

'Irritating to know all those little scrotes can access whatever's here just like that,' she said, snapping her fingers, 'while we're locked out. And if we play round with passwords, it'll probably exclude us permanently. At least Tom and his mates should be able to sort it.' She looked at her watch. 'It's a bit late tonight.'

'Surely it'll keep till tomorrow morning.'

'I suppose. And if our home grown geeky lads can't suss it, there's always the forensic computer scientists — if the budget will stretch that far?' She eyed him hopefully.

Before he could respond, her phone sounded again. Another text, again from Natasha. This one said, 'No Rob whole weekend.'

'She must be worried to abbreviate so little,' she said, trying to return the call and failing. She left a message asking for more details, and a request to phone back ASAP. 'Do I phone Jill now or leave it till tomorrow?'

'Neither, not after your reception yesterday. If she wants to report him missing, she'll do it to the proper people.'

'But he's . . . and on Friday you were worried enough to drive round all the unlovely parts of Ashford looking for him.'

'Not all, surely. OK, OK. And I admit I was worried enough to talk to Ashford nick about the missing silverware. But there's a fine line between being there in a time of trouble and interfering. You'll kick yourself if you cross it.'

* * *

Sometimes she wished she were young enough to see anything to do with a computer as a manageable challenge, not as a matter of ill-suppressed terror. Tom and Harbijan Singh, who was about thirty, Tom's age, and one of the few Sikh officers Fran had come across in the Kent force, looked like children offered another Christmas when, sitting in Jill's office at eight on Monday morning, she gave them the details.

'Probably nothing too tricky,' Tom said with the cheerful air of someone whose weekend has been a marked success. 'Only schoolkids, after all.'

Harbijan gave a polite smile, which showed quite clearly that he disagreed. When prompted with raised eyebrows and a grin, he said, 'Oh, my kid brother can beat me hollow, ma'am, at anything to do with computers.'

'If you think it's too problematic, then, get it straight to the forensic computer scientists — I'd rather you didn't waste your time or bugger up the task. On the other hand, you could always draft your brother in, Harbijan.'

'I doubt if the budget would run to him, ma'am. He's already designed and sold his own computer games — his royalties are way over my pay cheque.'

They were returning to the Incident Room when she called Tom back. 'Your weekend's protection duties,' she prompted.

'Went very well, thanks, guv. Until her poxy fiancé turned up and got very snotty with me. And with her. I wanted to smack his head. So did Dilly. Eventually she went off to his place with him.'

'When would that be?'

'Sunday breakfast. He dragged her off to church. And made it quite clear she'd spend the rest of the day at his place.'

'Well, they are engaged.'

'Not engaged enough for him to invite her to stay the night. Just enough to snarl when one of my housemates said our spare room was always available. And there's a funny thing, like. You know the Post Office is redirecting all her mail here? There's been nothing since Friday. When those knickers turned up at TVInvicta. Nothing Saturday or today.'

'Really?'

'Perhaps the bloody pervert's run out of quotations. Or he can't gift wrap a machete. Do you want me to phone them to make sure no one's slipped up and let anything through to TVInvicta?'

She grimaced. 'That doesn't require brains; the computer stuff does. In any case, I'm going across to Canterbury to talk to the vicar of St Jude's, so I can pop in and check up for myself.'

He nodded. Almost as an afterthought he asked, 'What about you, guv? How was your weekend? See DCI Tanner, did you? I hope you sent her our best. I'm organising a bit of a whip-round, by the way. I suppose I couldn't touch you for a quid?'

Fishing out a couple of tenners, she said, 'If it looks a poor haul, let me know.'

He removed an A4 envelope from a pile in a filing stack and tucked the notes inside. 'How's the house hunting?'

She smiled in recollection. 'We found a lovely black and white timbered house near Hythe. Right in the middle of our range. Perfect in every way. Except right next door, and I mean right next door, is a used car lot. Cars all over the verge everywhere. And loud music from a ghetto-blaster meant to help a bored lad valet the things. Perfect.'

'You'll find the right place one day soon. You mark my words. OK, guv, we'll have this sorted by lunchtime, with a bit of luck.'

As she left, Acting Detective Chief Superintendent Joe Farmer was deep in conversation with Jon Binns, the DI she'd briefed to check CCTV installers. Farmer was shaking his head so emphatically in disagreement she decided it would make Binns' life a lot easier if she put off talking to him till she'd got back from St Jude's.

Why the silence from Chummie? Yes, it was only a couple of days, but he'd not missed a single one before. And this business with an Ashford-based courier? On impulse, she turned back and asked the nearest DC how the sexual assault tally was going. It was still rising, apparently, with an especially frightening attack in a village just outside Canterbury on Thursday.

'The victim didn't get a chance to ID him or anything like that. And there's no CCTV, of course. And no mobile reception, so she couldn't dial 999. She ran home and her brothers were so furious they went looking for him and totally messed the scene. So nothing new — except it's definitely the same man. He left a hair on her coat.'

'Nothing since?'

'Not with the same MO. But there has been something else. The Acting DCS is going to make an announcement.'

So why hadn't the bugger chosen to tell her? Was there time to wring his neck now? But apparently he was in with the Chief, so she'd better restrain herself. It wasn't her case, after all. Was it?

* * *

Canterbury had some of the oldest and most beautiful churches in the country, possibly the world, Fran amended generously, and she was quite looking forward to seeing this example. It would make a welcome contrast to poor St Philip's, back in the Midlands. But as she got deeper into the sadder side of the city, out to the east, she became less optimistic. With a sinking heart, she saw a Fifties concrete bunker mercifully half covered by a wind-torn Alpha Course banner. Yes, that was St Jude's. What perversity made Dilly and Daniel come here when they could have worshipped in any number of inspiring buildings?

Perhaps the answer lay in the priest in charge. Kicking herself for not phoning ahead, or even getting the number from Tom, Fran tried to decipher the number from the notice board, so thickly sprayed with graffiti that hardly any of the original colour was visible. As she keyed it into her mobile, however, a woman materialised at her elbow.

'I hope you don't mind my saying so, but that's a terribly posh looking piece of equipment to be waving round just here.' She emphasised the point with a jut from a very solid jaw. In fact, everything about her seemed solid, reassuring in an auntish sort of way. Fran realised with a pang that that was much as others might see her. Auntish. When she felt seventeen inside.

Fran pocketed the mobile. 'Leading into temptation, am I?'

'Not me personally.' She pronounced it *pairsonally*.

'What's brought a Glaswegian this far south?'

'Work. Not just mine. His.' She nodded her Pre-Raphaelite shock of rusting red hair at the church.

'So you're the Reverend J something-or-other Falkirk?' Fran sounded doubtful: there was no odour of sanctity about her, not even a dog-collar as far as she could tell.

'Janie. And you are?'

Fran flipped open her ID. 'Fran Harman.'

Janie Falkirk narrowed her eyes. 'A Detective Chief Superintendent? Out on the beat, are you? Are they short of PC Plods? Ah yes, of course they are: that's why we never see one round here.'

'I'll get on to that,' Fran assured her. 'Actually, I was looking for you.'

'Not for speeding in my Beamer on the M2 again!'

'Don't you just wish? Alas, I need information about someone in your flock.'

* * *

In contrast to the church, the vicarage was a huge sprawling Edwardian edifice. 'A bomb got the church, but not this. I could wish, in the cold, that it had been the other way round. Actually, all the time. The church was Norman, very lovely, by all accounts. This pile could never have been anything except a refrigerator. I inhabit the kitchen, as the only place I can afford to heat, if that's OK by you?' She slipped off her a hand-knitted scarf, revealing under her duffel coat a polo-necked jumper that either supported her chin or became another one. 'Tea or coffee?'

'I'm fine, thanks.'

There was not a mod con to be seen, though perhaps the scullery was large enough to accommodate a washing machine and a fridge, even a freezer. But there was something pleasing about the wooden slatted drying rack hanging from the ceiling and the big rectangular table, once scrubbed by armies of minions and now by this practical-looking woman not much shorter than herself. Everything about that round, slightly pugnacious chin and the strapping frame inspired confidence. Perhaps that was why Dilly and Daniel worshipped in such an unfashionable place, when she'd have seen Daniel as very much a cathedral man.

'Now, how can I help you?' From somewhere — how could such a sturdy woman move so silently? — Janie produced a tin of shortbread. 'I've got to be out in half an hour, so we can't settle for a nice chat, not this time, anyway.'

No unnecessary explanation. Fran liked that in a person. 'We speak in absolute confidence?'

'Is there any other way?' Janie sounded amused rather than pious.

'One of your congregation is being stalked. There's no reason to believe the stalker is known to her, but I'm checking all eventualities.'

'You? Aren't chief supers a bit like bishops? Desk bound?'

'The victim is high profile, so the officers dealing with it are strictly need to know.'

'High profile? Are we really talking about St Jude's, Ms Harman? We have a congregation barely reaching a score most of the time, and many are known to the police in quite a different way.'

'The young woman in question came to the Alpha Course about a year ago. Dilly Pound.'

'Ah, before she became the face of crime on TVInvicta. So she did. And that man who's since become her fiancé, I understand.' She crunched her face and snapped her fingers in an effort to recall his name.

'Daniel. Daniel McDine. You don't sound very enthusiastic about him.'

'It's not I who am engaged to marry him. Neither worships here anymore, I'm afraid. I think they prefer the anonymity of the Cathedral, and who can blame them, now she's public property.'

'Funny — he implied he still came here. But — since your time is limited—'

'I'm due at the prison, Ms Harman. Not a very flexible institution.'

Fran nodded. 'Do you keep records of people who come on your courses? Names, addresses?'

'We tend to know regular attenders, but people drop in off the street, and some distinctly prefer anonymity. Who are we to argue if they just give a Christian name? Some might not even have addresses — we've had people sleeping rough come along, more for the warmth and the tea and bikkies than for God's word, I suspect.'

'Why don't you chuck them out?'

Janie shook her mop of hair. 'Chief Superintendent, that's a disappointingly conventional question. You wouldn't expect the Sally Army to throw out street people: why should we? Remember what Christ said about the poor.'

'Not that bit about them being always with us,' Fran laughed.

'Touché.' She glanced at her watch. 'You look up all the other references yourself, as penance.'

It might have been a joke, but Fran suspected the intention was not. 'I just might. They may turn out to be the reasons I joined the police,' she said seriously. 'Now, would you recall — I'm aware that this is a stupid question, but bear with me — would you recall any oddballs on that particular course? Any man obviously attracted to Dilly?'

'Her fiancé apart, you mean?'

'An oddball? That's a bit unkind.'

'We are talking in confidence, are we not?' Janie chortled. 'OK, let's just call him a control freak.'

'Agreed. But the logistics of the stalking make it hard to put him in the frame, much as I'd like to.'

Janie frowned. 'I don't remember any poor souls that might turn to stalking. Have you tried Dilly's writing group? I seem to recall from my own attempts to write the Great British Novel that such things attract what you might call psychic cripples.'

'I didn't know she went to a writers' group.'

Janie shook her head. 'Maybe I'm mistaken. Maybe it was someone else. Senior moments, Chief Superintendent. But, tell you what, I'll have a wee root round in the records and if I come up with anything I'll contact you on the instant.'

* * *

TVInvicta in the form of Huw Venn greeted her like a long-lost cousin, but had no mail to pass on. 'We've hired a bodyguard to accompany her when she has to go out for a story,' he beamed, settling behind his desk, hands across his stomach. 'He accompanies her right back to the office. And if you want, he can drive her back to her home. She's a very popular part of our team, both with viewers and her colleagues.'

Surprised by such a headmasterly encomium, delivered as if it were a job reference, she smiled quizzically. 'It's good to see such cooperation, Huw. I don't suppose you'd like an exclusive story when everything's done and dusted? If one were on offer?'

'I think we might, you know. If one were on offer, of course.' He stood. 'Coffee? I've a new machine I'm dying to have an excuse to try out. Or is it a capital offence to blow up a Chief Superintendent, even by mistake?'

'Probably. But we could risk it. Tell me, is Dilly around?'

'Out on a job with her new guard. I bet her miserable fiancé won't like that, not if he didn't like her spending the night with a lovely young policeman,' he added, in full nudge-nudge-wink-wink mode. Now, how did he know about that? 'Do you know what she sees in Daniel, Fran?' He passed her what smelt like a very good espresso.

She shook her head, almost repressively. 'Who knows what anyone sees in their partner? Oh, this is excellent. Thanks.'

But he didn't take the hint. 'Partner! Don't let him hear you use that term! He's a proper fiancé! Oh, I wish we could find her a really nice young man.'

'Nailing her stalker's all I've got on my mind at the moment. Now, is she likely to be back soon? If not, could you ask her to call me when she has a moment . . .'

* * *

A Post-it greeted her on her return:

Guv
We've sorted the website
T and H

Three minutes later she was in the Incident Room, greeted by Tom, seated in front of a screen currently showing nothing but a screen-saver, and Harbijan, standing hands-in-pockets beside him.

Harbijan shifted his feet. 'Guv — some of it's not very nice.'

'Come on, lad, I was in Vice for three years — I bet there's nothing much here I've not seen before.'

* * *

'Well, here you are.'

Tom fiddled with the mouse. Adjusting her glasses, Fran peered over his shoulder at the screen. 'Bloody hell! That is pretty hardcore stuff! Now, why should a teenage girl refer me to this site?'

'The visual equivalent of get stuffed?' Harbijan ventured.

She straightened. 'Well, someone certainly is. And in a rich variety of ways.'

Her laughter was cut short. To think that thirteen-year-old Tash must have seen this . . .

'Or did she want you to see something on it?' Tom pointed. 'Those heads — they don't match the bodies. They're too young, surely. That guy there — with the dog. Look at this! Body courtesy of a lot of time in the gym, face of a weedy little chap.'

Her stomach turned. That face was dreadfully familiar, though she'd not seen it recently. It couldn't be Rob Tanner's, could it? Could it? Best to say nothing yet. Not until she'd shown the video to Jill.

'And this kid? An ordinary teenager doing that with that particularly well-endowed young man?'

'She can't be more than twelve, thirteen at most!' Harbijan sounded as outraged as she felt.

'What does it feel like to have your face kidnapped?' Tom demanded. 'And to be put in that sort of sexual position? And to have all your mates sniggering about it?'

She leaned back. 'Bullying, that's what this is. A vicious variant of that happy-slapping scam you're working on. Any chance you could save all this as evidence and still close down the site?'

Harbijan said, with a patience she thought commendable, 'That's what we've done with all the other sites, ma'am. Trouble is, knock out one, you get three more.'

'Do you want to see the rest, guv, or have you had enough?'

'Just save it all for me on something portable. There's someone else I want to see this, for reasons I can't explain, I'm afraid. Not yet,' she added. She didn't want them to feel excluded unnecessarily. 'Strictly need to know stuff.'

'D—' Tom blushed scarlet, as well he might.

'No. Another strictly need to know,' she said firmly. 'And if you can find out the school the perpetrators of that vile stuff go to, I want to know immediately — before you even think of contacting the head, or whatever Jill's policy was.'

'Also need to know, ma'am?'

'Oh, Harbijan, do call me guv. Otherwise I feel like the Queen. And yes, please. Definitely need to know only.'

Tom was hovering near the ladies' loo when she emerged. 'Dilly, guv. She now tells me she thinks someone stole her credit card, like. One she kept locked in her desk drawer at home "just in case". And someone changed her toothpaste tube for another make.'

'Not Daniel thinking hers wasn't upmarket enough? Sorry, just joking. Anything else missing or disturbed?'

'She thinks someone had been through her undies drawers too. Clean ones, this time. "Daniel likes her to leave everything tidy",' he added in an irritated mimicry of Dilly at her most supine.

'Even knickers? In places he shouldn't be looking?'

'Especially things in places he shouldn't be looking. And now the credit card's back, for God's sake.'

'Do we have an exact sequence of events?'

He shook his head. 'That's what I asked her for. But she only thought to tell me an hour ago, and I was too busy to press her. Trouble is, you don't know whether to be kind to her or shake her for being so bloody stupid!'

CHAPTER SEVENTEEN

'I'm not telling you how the rumour reached me, Chief Superintendent. What I want to know is if you know about it and if it has a foundation in fact.'

Fran stood at attention. If the Chief Constable wanted to be formal, she wouldn't argue. They both knew that she could have been lying in the sun somewhere, had it not been for his pleas for her to stay, and they knew equally well that his strings were being pulled by the Home Secretary, who expected him at the very word 'drugs' to huff and puff with the full force of rank behind him. Sooner or later he'd simmer down. She hoped so, for the sake of his post-lunch digestion. That apart, the quicker the better: she had real policing to get on with.

Meanwhile, all her years in the force meant she faced him across the acres of polished wood with more anxiety than she cared to admit. He was so good at being fierce she replied with great formality, 'Sir, I would stake my reputation on DCI Tanner being as drug-free as you or me.'

He took a couple of paces, then spun on his heel. If only he'd get on with this mandatory yelling so that she could get back to proper work.

'How else would you explain a perfectly fit woman falling down the stairs and injuring herself?'

'With respect, sir, it's not impossible. As you know, teenage children and tidiness are hardly synonymous,' she ventured, though she suspected that the Chief Constable had begotten and bred a paragon of virtue, 'and she believes that she tripped over something when her arms were full of bedclothes. Her injuries are certainly consistent with such a fall.'

'It's not the fall I doubt, Chief Superintendent, it's the cause. I understand she's come in smelling of cannabis on a number of occasions. And that perhaps she's used other substances too.'

Which evil, conniving little toerag had come snivelling out of the woodwork with this? 'As it happens, Sir, ACC Turner and I went to visit DCI Tanner at her home on Friday evening and again on Saturday morning. There were bruises on her arms, but not needle marks. Heavens, she doesn't drink, so I can't imagine her even succumbing to a quick spliff.'

'So how would you explain the bruises?'

'They were as if someone had gripped her too fiercely. She claims her husband is a passionate man. I suspect there may be another explanation, which I am trying to discover.'

He sat down abruptly, waving a hand at the chair opposite. 'You're on to it already?' His hectoring tone was replaced by his private voice. Any moment now they could stop playing games.

'Mark and I, sir. I didn't want anyone else involved. As soon as I picked up — and tried to quash — the first rumour. Off the record, it's one of her kids, guv. And I reckon she fell because she was pushed. And I think we shall find that if her son is taking drugs there are some extenuating circumstances.' She leant forward confidentially. 'You couldn't just slap down whatever lowlife grassed her up and leave it in my hands — and Mark's — for a bit?' It would give her time to check the MisPer file again — there'd been nothing earlier. So perhaps Rob was safely at home, in which case Mark had been right not to let her interfere, or perhaps for some weird reason Jill didn't want to involve any of her colleagues.

The Chief was smiling. 'So long as you sort it, Fran. Good and proper. Now, what's the news of the delectable Dilly?'

She briefed him as swiftly as she could. He seemed affable enough, so she asked, 'There's a rumour about other sexual assaults, sir. Can you tell me what's new?'

'I thought you were off that investigation?'

'I am. Technically it's nothing to do with me. But as a woman I'm interested. I went for a solo prowl round Ashford the other night.'

'Solo?' he repeated sharply.

'I had to be there for something else. I found it's a very scary place when you know our friend could strike again at any moment.'

Before he could say anything, his secretary tapped and came in. The Chief Constable of Sussex was in the building, and had been waiting five minutes already.

'We'll talk more about this,' the Chief said, grabbing his jacket. 'Meanwhile, Farmer's doing a full briefing any moment now. Why not gatecrash?'

* * *

Joe Farmer was in mid-spiel when Fran made her way into the Incident Room. '. . . no more minor attacks just out of range of CCTV cameras,' he was saying, 'since the end of last week. What we have had is three far more serious attacks, in full view of cameras. The trouble is that one has been committed by George W Bush, one by Tony Blair and one by Margaret Thatcher — those hideous face masks, in other words.'

Fran caught Tom's eye. Could this be the breakthrough they all needed? He responded with a particularly curly thumbs-up.

Others were less enthusiastic.

'Bloody hell, you'd have thought shafting entire nations would be enough!'

'Nah, he wouldn't have the brains to dodge the cameras.'

'Silence!'

But the titters continued. Someone, *sotto voce*, was wondering what other world leader might enjoy a spot of sex.

As much to re-impose discipline as anything, Fran put in, 'It's as if he's taunting us.' Then she wished the words unsaid, because it wasn't her meeting and she shouldn't be anything more than an observer. Having said that, however, she might as well continue. 'He must know we're bound to have realised he knows the whereabouts of every single CCTV camera—' she broke off to eye-contact Binns, who blushed to his ears and shook his head in a small but decided negative '—in the county, so he's changing his MO. But surely lots of people will have seen such — er — eminent people wandering round the streets of—?'

'Maidstone and Ashford, guv,' someone put in.

A young woman shook her head. 'Party nights, Fridays and Saturdays. Kids getting bladdered and puking in the streets. Lots of people wear party gear. They wouldn't remember the odd fake politician.'

'So where did he put on his masks?' Fran pursued. 'No, don't tell me — out of the range of any CCTV cameras.'

Binns got up and silently left the room.

'It's got to be the same guy, hasn't it?' the young woman insisted.

'We've no evidence of that, Sue,' Farmer said, earning points from Fran for learning names so quickly. 'None at all.'

Sue didn't permit herself so much as an eye roll. Fran did — but only in her head.

She could think of no tactful way of putting it. 'I know it's a mammoth task, but surely if we checked the CCTV of all the shops in the area that sell those masks we might get something.'

Farmer cast a venomous look in her direction but could hardly argue. But he was going to. 'Which of your team can you spare to do the footwork?' he demanded waspishly.

Stupid bugger. She offered him her sweetest smile and herself the promise of revenge. 'I'll let you know.' Should she grass up Binns, not to mention Farmer himself, for failing to follow up her CCTV theory or remain professionally silent? She compromised. 'Meanwhile, I think DI Binns may be talking to the firm installing the CCTVs, not just because of Chummie knowing where each one is but for another reason. In a separate case, I have reason to believe—' hell, how long since she'd used that old cliché? '—that a new camera may deliberately have been badly fixed.'

* * *

Fran had scarcely sat down at her desk when the phone rang.

Farat Hafeez from West Midlands Police. How strange that although Fran would have sworn her English was accent-free, over the phone it came over pure Brummie. 'I'm afraid I've nothing to report, gaffer.' Fran smiled at the Midlands version of guv. 'Reverend Hardy's gone on his holidays. According to the church secretary, they've been booked for months.'

'And I never bloody well asked about his intended movements. Shit and shit and shit! Sorry, Farat.'

'Be my guest. Do you want me to put out a call for him? He's touring in Cornwall.'

'In this weather? Poor sod.'

'I suppose it's cheaper off season. Anyway, what I did do was get on to the diocesan office, which provided the name of his bank. They were efficient, too. They wouldn't give me all the details I wanted, but they did say his debit card hadn't been used in London at the relevant time. That doesn't mean he couldn't have paid cash for the flowers, of course.'

'Did he make any large withdrawal that week?'

'A hundred pounds from a bank here in Brum. Digbeth coach station. In the concourse, in fact.'

'Travelling to?'

'I tried the ticket office: nothing booked with them, but of course, he could have booked in advance using a credit card I haven't found out about yet. And he may even have been returning from somewhere else, gaffer.'

'Of course. One last thing, Farat — find out if Mrs Hardy has gone to Cornwall with him.'

* * *

'Creative writing group?' Dilly repeated after a long delay, as if she were asking permission from someone in the room before she replied. For goodness' sake, she wasn't about to admit to being a part-time lap-dancer. 'Do you mean the one here or the one in Birmingham?'

Fran suppressed a desire to fling down the phone. How could so bright a woman be so switched off? 'Either.'

'Well, here it's just a small group of women. We meet in the house of a wonderful lady called Marion, who really keeps our noses to the grindstone. Only she wouldn't let me say that, would she? It's a cliché.'

'I won't tell if you won't tell. And in Birmingham?'

'That wasn't really a group. It was more a class. Run by one of the colleges. But I can't really remember any of the people in it. I wasn't very — it was a difficult time. I had my mind on other things. So I never finished the course. But that's a long time ago — it must be nearly ten years. You forget, don't you?'

Fran could have reminded her that some memories never died. Those of the love of your life, for instance. No doubt her relationship with Stephen had been one of the things on her mind. 'Could you give me the teacher's name?'

'Lecturer,' Dilly corrected her, pedantic as McDine, 'since it was a college, not a school.'

'Very well, the lecturer. And the college.'

'Walker. Mary Walker. But she's married and moved. I actually ran into her at Euston Station once — we had a cup of coffee together.'

'And you don't recall her new name? OK, it doesn't matter,' Fran declared briskly. 'It's part of the college's legal duties to keep records. So if you can tell me the name . . .'

'I thought I had. William Murdock. It was supposed to be an access course for university entrance, but most of us just went for interest's sake so they closed it down. Or it may have been because Mary left. I don't know.'

'It doesn't matter. Tell me, Dilly, are you all right?'

'I'm fine.'

'Work all right?'

'Yes!' She sounded positive for the first time. 'They've brought in an extra security guard. Apparently if I have to cover a story, he'll look after me.'

'Excellent!' Fran said, as if it were news to her. 'And where are you staying tonight, Dilly?'

'Has the security camera been fixed at home yet? I've had all the locks changed, after all.'

'Are you absolutely sure you want to stay there on your own?' Fran squeaked despite herself.

'I shall be all right.'

'I'll do my best to organise a regular police patrol, but rural forces are always stretched to their limits.' She grasped the nettle. 'Look, why don't I ask Tom if that bedroom's free at his house?'

'No, thank you. I have Daniel's feelings to consider, after all.'

'Does he consider yours, Dilly? Has he invited you to stay with him tonight?'

'There's some school function. He won't be back till late.'

If only Dilly had managed to say, 'And if he were the last man on earth I wouldn't stay with him.' But she hadn't.

Fran continued, 'What about Tom staying in your spare room?'

'Daniel . . .'

As if on cue, Tom knocked and entered. Fran pointed to the handset, mouthing 'Dilly!'

Predictably he held out his hand, then made a praying gesture and finally shrugged when she shook her head. But she held his gaze when she told Dilly, 'There's only so much we can do without your cooperation, Dilly. If you want us to help you, you have to help us. Very well, I'll get on to that college, get a list of students and call you back. Or get one of my team to. OK?' She cut the call without waiting for a response. 'Sit down, Tom, and tell me how you've so offended Daniel McDine that he won't let his fiancée anywhere near you.'

He blushed so furiously that anyone else might have deduced that he had debauched the young woman in her own bed. 'We played Scrabble and Trivial Pursuit — Dilly and me and my housemates. I asked her to lock her room from the inside. I slept at the far end of the house. But she came down to breakfast in her dressing-gown, as we all did, and McDine thought we'd had an orgy. Talk about a Victorian father.'

'No hanky and zero panky then?'

'Zero, zilch, whatever — I can't think of any other zeds,' he concluded, grinning at himself. 'Mind you, guv, given half an eyelash of encouragement I'd have been there. Despite the fact she kept on talking about Steve, the guy she left behind in Brum. You know what,' he added, 'I reckon he was as big a control freak as this McDine guy. They met because he told her off about leaving books open and damaging their spines. Him just a student and her the librarian. Can you imagine it?'

She thought back to Stephen's sad, lined face. Was there something implacable about the set of the jaw, the tightness of the lips? She'd assumed it was the pain of his self-denial that had caused all those frown lines.

'What's this about a college and a list of students, then, guv?'

'It seems she's forgotten that she was a creative writing student at one time up in Birmingham. You wouldn't like to phone William Murdock College for me and get a class list, would you? There's just a chance there might have been a male in the group besotted with Dilly.'

'I should think they'd all have been besotted with her — I mean, ten years ago she'd have been — well!' he rolled his eyes. 'Sorry, guv. What about the teacher?'

'Female. Mary Walker. Now with a different name and a new address.'

'Also being stalked?' he asked eagerly.

'Calm down. She got married, Tom. As people do. Even lecturers.' But not her and Mark, of course. 'OK. Off you go.'

He looked at her under his lashes. 'And would you want me to phone Dilly to ask if any of the blokes made a move on her?'

'Who better?' she replied blithely. But wondered even as she spoke if she'd done the right thing.

He was halfway out of the door when he stopped. 'Almost forgot what brought me here, guv. We've shut down that obscene website. We couldn't manage to trace it back to source, but we've got the forensic computer scientists on to it. I asked for Amy Lu: she's the best. And I asked for it ASAP.'

'Well done. Any news of Jon Binns and the CCTVs yet?'

'Only that Farmer Giles went ballistic about him slipping out of that meeting and told him he should have been doing his own team's work, not someone else's. Tough, especially as it only took him two minutes to ask for a list of technicians by five tonight. So we can reckon on nine tomorrow, in my experience.'

* * *

She was ready for Mark's phone call to say he was ready to leave, but there was something very odd about his voice when he made it.

'Would you be kind enough to pop round to my office a moment? Thanks.'

It reminded her irresistibly of the way he'd prefaced any bollockings he'd had to deliver in their past. Trying to unclench her jaw and her stomach muscles, despite herself she started to review her activities to see if she'd broken any major rules. But her conscience was as clean as she'd known it would be, and she wondered if he simply had some lovely surprise to spring.

So she was beaming when she put her head round his door.

He wasn't.

He stood as she entered, but stayed his side of his desk. Then he leant on it, knuckles down and shoulders braced. 'The Chief tells me you went on night patrol round Ashford. Would you care to tell me when?'

She replied easily, 'The night there was an assault in the town. You were busy with some papers, weren't you?'

'So who did you patrol with?'

'What do you mean? I was on my own, of course. Just casing the joint, as it were.' And now getting uneasier by the minute.

'Just putting yourself at risk. And putting yourself at risk at a time when you were far from fit, and probably even more vulnerable. What the hell did you think you were doing?'

'What I always do.' Unease had mutated to anger.

'Did. When you were a middle-rank officer. And you'd have had a partner. I take it you didn't bother with body-armour or CS spray or even a radio? For God's sake, someone in your position being so cavalier! You should be setting an example, someone of your rank.'

'An example to whom? And how?' She'd moved to furious, in one breath.

'We get the media to tell all women to be on their guard, to go nowhere ill-lit, preferably to take cabs and always to stick in groups. And you swan round disregarding our own advice! Wouldn't it have looked good if you'd been a victim — not just of the rapist but even of a set of juvenile bag-snatchers? More happy-slappers? You'd have been a laughing stock. We'd all have been a laughing stock.'

Hell! All those years of conditioning — must accept a senior officer's rebuke, mustn't answer back. But her own lover speaking to her like this, her lover, her partner, the man she wanted to spend the rest of her life with. How dare he? How bloody dare he?

The conditioning swamped her.

'Will that be all, sir?'

'For now. Thank you.'

She'd have slammed the door off its hinges if it hadn't been for three or four officers in the corridor outside discussing their forthcoming evening's boozing. Boozing. When she'd be silently retrieving all her stuff from his house and knowing it was totally impossible to rebuild her life without him. She wanted to howl with the pain of it.

But women of her rank didn't retire to a loo and sob. What did they do? And what did she do? She'd better get back to her office, because whatever her face was supposed to be doing, it wasn't obeying orders. And she'd better take the shortest route, away from any casually interested eyes.

The last person she wanted contact with was the Chief, who emerged as if by magic from his office as she went past. He was obviously seeing his Sussex opposite number off the premises.

But he hung back a second. 'Harman, I hope Turner did a good job? You deserved every word. You know you did.' He quickened his step and fell in with the other man.

Did knowing that Mark was acting on orders make it better or worse? Still staggering with the shock of it all, she made it back to her office. Her secretary was just shrugging on her coat.

'Urgent message on your desk, Fran!' she said. 'I gather you're looking at another house tonight. Let's hope this is the right one.'

Fran hoped the muscles formed a smile, hoped the voice sounded as if Fran were merely thinking about something else. Yes, there was an urgent message on her desk. In a sealed envelope addressed to her in Mark's writing, *Fran*, not *DCS Harman*.

I had to do it because it was a direct order and what I said was right. What I couldn't say was that had you been hurt — or worse, for God's sake — my world would have collapsed about my ears. Can we stick to our rule about no work talk after working hours? See you in the car park in twenty minutes?

At least she made it to the loo before she was sick.

As she blotted her face, she stared at herself in the mirror. Should she act on her first impulse and end everything between them? Or — and this really hurt — should she admit that she had indeed been in the wrong and accept his remarkably gracious explanation? Was it just the implications for their lives at work if they broke up, all the covert glances, the open sniggering that were influencing her decision? Or was it something else?

She'd know when she saw him. But it would be best to speak before they reached the car park. Surely it would. After all, as he'd said, they had their ban on shoptalk to consider.

Did that mean she'd made a *de facto* decision?

Hadn't she once said that they must continue to treat each other exactly as they'd treat other colleagues in a similar situation?

And she'd been in the wrong. No doubt about that. She'd have said much the same to Tom.

She headed back to his office to apologise. She got as far as, 'I'm sorry.'

He didn't speak, but switched off the lights and locked the door.

* * *

Baying and snarling, the two Dobermans hurled themselves against what appeared to be a terribly frail wire barrier between the kitchen and their scullery.

The cottage must have been five miles from its nearest neighbour, and six from anything like a main road.

'The rush hour would be two tractors, not one,' she murmured into Mark's ear.

The vendor — a pallid woman whose too-tight jumper showed the outlines of an inadequate bra — was working up huge enthusiasm for a clargester, a means of disposing of human waste neither had ever heard of. At the end of three minutes, both knew that they didn't wish to push the acquaintance further.

The dogs certainly didn't.

From time to time, the woman asked them to be quiet, in the hopeless tones some mothers use when addressing vile toddlers. The dogs took as little notice.

Would Mr and Mrs Harman like some sherry? It was time to declare themselves teetotallers on the way to an AA meeting and scoot. Even as they turned the car in the lane outside, the dogs hurled themselves at the gates. Another off the list, then.

'I think we've taken a wrong turn,' he said at last, the grass growing in the middle of the lane brushing the car's suspension.

'Best find a gate to turn in,' she said absently, wrestling with an OS map and an inadequate torch — the oracle seemed to have thrown up its hands in horror.

'What about this one?' Cutting the ignition and releasing his seatbelt, he murmured, 'Look at those stars.'

'Careful how you get out — cowpats!'

'Who said anything about getting out? Fran Harman, come here!'

CHAPTER EIGHTEEN

'Do you reckon Tom will have worked his charm and persuaded Dilly back into his care?' Mark asked, as he drove them into work the following day. Neither had referred again to the bruising encounter of the previous day or to the sexual passion it had engendered. They'd been neither more nor less loving or tetchy with early morning irritation than usual. But he thought she was still wary; God knew he was. He'd meant to read her a reasonable lecture, but the thought of the danger to which she'd so blithely exposed herself without even talking about it afterwards had made him explode. Just as he'd have exploded at any other colleague doing something so stupid.

Possibly.

'Technically, it depends whether he had any news to report about the Birmingham writing course,' she said.

'If I'd been him I'd have phoned her, even with nil returns!'

'Are all men really attracted to pretty faces rather than personality?' she asked, almost wistfully.

He was glad the traffic had congealed into a solid jam: it meant he could look at her properly. This tone was getting familiar — nothing to do with yesterday evening. It dated from their Birmingham trip. What had happened in Birmingham to shake her self-confidence like this? Surely it wasn't the simple fact that there had been no clothes in one shop that had been to her taste? Was she really so frightened of growing old? She was hardly middle-aged, and certainly didn't look even that. Why, in any other profession than the police, there'd be no question of her retiring till she was sixty. The government were already talking about raising the national retirement age to sixty-seven, for goodness' sake. Only talking, he hoped. It was all very well for people behind desks, but how could labourers or even front-line police officers for whom fitness was vital continue to such an age? And what a national outcry there'd be when the first 67-year-old officer died of a heart attack chasing a young yob. But would it be age discrimination to move older people on to permanent light duties?

Meanwhile, he must find something to lift Fran's spirits, to prove to her that she was still attractive and desirable — though he'd have thought their sex life should have been demonstration enough of that. Or was she afraid that his long abstinence after Tina's death was the reason he wanted her, not her body? And her mind, of course. Fran, all of Fran.

'I'd have thought most men would have wanted to wring Dilly's neck. Men with any sense. Me, for instance,' he amended, with a grin and a squeeze of her hand. 'Helpless women don't do anything for me. I'd bet that's why Tom's so fond of you. And — Dilly's good looks apart — I'd guess he sees looking after her as an additional way to get your approval.'

'My God, I'm not his mother! Nor his head teacher.'

'In a sense, you're both. And a good friend, too. And I suspect he wants not so much to wring Dilly's neck as to shake her into independent action. She's proved she can do it, after all. It must have taken guts to embark on a new career, especially one where she actually talks to millions of people unscripted, after that cloistered existence of hers.'

'She's better at talking to the masses than one to one, you know.'

'How strange. Perhaps she doesn't see them as people. Perhaps it's the camera lens she talks to. My God, what would a Freudian psychologist make of that?'

'She certainly goes in for unyielding and implacable men. So Tom may be on to a loser. Though of course, since he's a policeman, albeit a plain clothes one, he could be an authority figure too. In which case the pattern will repeat itself and he won't have an equal partner but a doormat.'

'He might want that but I wouldn't.' Was that enough positive affirmation? Or should he go further? *I want a woman like you, fierce in your independence but vulnerable, a woman I can talk to and take to bed with equal delight.* It was true, but too effusive for a traffic jam at eight in the morning. 'I'd rather have you,' he said, with a handclasp he hoped would make up for the lack of fine words.

She returned it, with a lingering smile. Perhaps it had been enough. But one day he'd try harder and find the time and the place to spell everything out.

'I'm going to have to phone Jill,' she said, doubtfully, almost as if asking for his approval.

He shot an anxious look at her. Where was his feisty woman?

'Rob's just a kid,' she continued. 'And she needs to see the evidence, too. We've got to be grown up about everything. Damn it, we've been friends for nearly thirty years.'

'And you're a senior officer she unleashed the old verbals on. So don't expect too much of a welcome. But you'll always get one from me,' he added, with another squeeze of the hand. Suddenly he found himself lifting hers to his lips and kissing it. His reward was a blush as pink as any Victorian miss's.

She got no response at all from Jill, just an answerphone. She left what she hoped was a neutral message and rang off.

'You're good on those things,' Mark observed. 'I always give too much information or sound as polite as a machine gun.'

* * *

'Wow! Look at you. Don't tell me, you've found the right house?' Tom greeted her, an hour later.

Why on earth should he think that? She shook her head. 'Alas, several Hounds of the Baskervilles had got there first. Redecorate? You'd have to fumigate the place. No, another dud. But we shall find the right one sooner or later. Now, what have you been up to? Did you find Dilly's stalker?'

'Have I buggery. The bloody college has just moved premises, and can't find the paper records for so long ago. Paper records? I gave them paper records. And I gave them not find, too. Let me have the material by noon today, I said, or I'll do the management team for concealing evidence. What I did get, however, is the married name of that Mary Walker woman. Mary Wolford she is now.'

'Address?'

'No idea. But — big but — apparently she's a writer. You know, those that can't, teach. Well, seems she can, well enough to be published so I shall get on to her publisher soon as they wake up, like.' His tone implied total disbelief that not everyone in the world of work was at their desk by eight-thirty.

'Do that. No arguments about confidentiality. I want contact details by ten. And let's hope her memory's less selective than Dilly's. How did she react to the college news, by the way?'

'It's always hard to tell with her, isn't it? I couldn't persuade her to stay over at our place again, and didn't dare say I'd take her sofa if she wanted. But I did take her out for a meal. Before I left I checked under the beds, in the wardrobes and anywhere else an intruder might have concealed himself and then I made sure she locked up after me. The intruder systems seem to be working. At least I hope so.'

'You don't sound sure.'

'Funny how faulty devices seem to attach themselves to the world's victims. If you had a system — you probably do? — every whistle would blow, every bell ring, absolutely to order, like. With someone like Dilly, you know her car's going to break down the day after its warranty expires and that she'll have completely forgotten to renew her AA cover.'

She laughed, but asked seriously, 'How do you work that out?'

'Look at that fiancé of hers. Any initiative, like, he'd be the one to take it. And if you don't act on your own initiative, you get swamped.'

'You'd still like it to be McDine that's faking the stalking.'

'Love it to be. But we've just had in a lab report on the paper you nicked from his waste bin.'

'Nick? Me? I never! And it says?'

'Different weight, different brand. Sorry.'

'Bugger. OK. And — Tom — don't forget to put that meal on expenses!'

'Can't, guv. She put it on hers. Honestly. You could have knocked me down with the proverbial.'

'Me too.'

To Fran's surprise he was back within minutes, just as she was dialling Jill's number. She hung up without waiting for a reply.

'You've located Mrs Wolford!'

His face fell, but only for an instant. 'I'll get on to that in half a tick. But before you bawl me out, we've managed to locate the webmaster of that obscene website! A kid called Field. Noel Field. It took Harbijan all of yesterday, and probably most of last night, and don't ask me how he sorted it . . .'

'I hope to God that brother of his knows the words "strictly confidential".'

'You don't think . . . ? Shit. Anyway, Harbi says Field's a kid living near Ashford. Does that figure?'

'It certainly does. Any more details?'

'I got on to the council, and they gave me the name of his school. It's the Thomas Bowdler, quite an old established co-ed grammar. Grammar schools, guv! Like something out of Billy Bunter! Why do Kent have them?'

'Same reason they don't have proper roads, I should imagine. Right. I think this is where I sally forth.'

His face fell so hard she almost laughed.

'I'm sorry, Tom: I told you from the start that this was need to know only.' It was like denying a favourite dog walkies.

He looked her full in the eye. 'It's young Rob Tanner, isn't it, in some of those shots? Pictures of him on DCI Tanner's desk, guv. Harbi noticed first, but I swore him to secrecy, and I know he likes the DCI too, so he won't say anything.'

'Of course he won't, any more than you would. But I want this to be as low key as possible, and even when you're dressed for the allotment, Tom, as you are today, you still look like a police officer.'

He laughed. 'You think you don't! There was something in this A Level book I had to read once: "Every inch a king". And I always think of you, like that.'

Fran supposed she should be flattered by the comparison with a senile old monarch, but shook her head nonetheless. 'To paraphrase another A Level text: to have one police officer on the premises may be regarded as a misfortune; to have two begins to look as if a crime has been committed. And that's the last impression I want to give. I need you to organise surveillance of his home and make sure his computer stays where it is. And, come to think of it, he can't even touch it when he comes home.'

'Plain clothes?' he asked hopefully.

'Of course plain clothes. But you can take your mobile and make the calls to that novelist's publisher while you lurk. OK?'

'OK, *ma'am*!' he said, saluting and exiting at the double. He popped his head back. 'You do realise he doesn't need to touch his own computer to change the website, don't you, guv?'

'Doesn't he? Bloody hell. I suppose you'd be able to tell if someone had tampered with the site?'

'Oh, yes, both the time and date of any changes. Possibly even the computer originating the changes.'

She shook her head. 'Time I went to college again. OK. Maintain an unobtrusive presence, then. But if I say move, you bloody move.'

He gave a mock-salute. 'Bloody move it is, guv.'

* * *

She had two swift visits to make before she left, the first to the Incident Room.

'Jon, how did you get on with the people fitting the CCTV cameras?'

'They promised to phone back last night with a list of employees. I thought I'd give them till nine this morning before I roasted them.' His mouth turned up like a banana.

'But it's after ten, Jon.'

'Sorry, ma'am.' And he was reaching for the phone before she turned her back.

The second errand was to update the Chief Constable. His office door was open as she went past, so she popped her head into the room. When he nodded, she stepped inside, closing the door firmly. But she suspected neither would refer to the previous day.

'I'm fairly certain I have a lead in the business of DCI Tanner and drugs,' she announced. 'But a stink may follow.'

'Stink?'

'At a good grammar school.'

'Not the one where the animals that assaulted you come from? Any news of that, by the way?'

'None yet, sir. I'll make sure you have a full report—'

'Fran, you were the victim.' He made a note. 'It's your colleagues who should be presenting a full report to you! Anyway, if there's going to be a stink about the other business, let there be.'

'It's the school where your son's doing his A Levels,' she said quietly.

* * *

Grammar school Thomas Bowdler might have been but Greyfriars it was not. There were probably some older elements lurking beneath the Sixties facade, but nothing to dilute the blue painted concrete and blank windows frontage identical to that of endless cheaply built education establishments. Was there some firm that had prided itself on producing blinds that drooped so despairingly?

She surveyed it as she got out of the car. Had she seen a single attractive public building during this case? Houses apart, of course — and goodness knew none of them was without imperfections. Why didn't she take Mark off to Bruges when this case was over? Bruges or for that matter Bath — some decent civic and domestic architecture was definitely called for.

It was a long time since she'd had to visit a school in anger, as it were, and she was nonplussed by the security buzzer system. It seemed she wouldn't be admitted till she'd given her name and title. 'Doctor' sounded altogether more convincing in this scrubland of Academe. But it got her nowhere.

'We're not aware that any of our pupils has medical needs,' came the flat voice.

'You mean, needs to see a doctor?' she snapped back. 'This is Detective Chief Superintendent Fran Harman of the Kent Constabulary, and I need to speak to the headmaster now.'

'I thought you said you're a doctor.'

'I happen to be both a doctor and a police officer. Kindly open the door.'

'Put your ID through that flap.'

'My ID card never leaves my person.' She could feel her blood pressure shinning up the little silvery column, waving as it went. After such atrocities as Dunblane and Wolverhampton, tight security was admirable, but this was taking it to absurd and discourteous heights.

Having at last penetrated the sacred portal, she now faced what appeared to be a bullet-proof Perspex screen, through which she had to speak to what was presumably the uncooperative woman who'd admitted her with such reluctance. The smell of new wood and paint was overwhelming.

'ID, please,' the receptionist said unsmilingly through a circular grille.

Fran held it up. 'Detective Chief Superintendent Frances Harman,' she repeated. 'To see the headmaster.'

'The *Chief* Master is busy,' she responded, stressing the correct term with an emphasis Fran found patronising rather than helpful.

'I think he'll see me. Or one of his deputies will.'

The dragon pressed a button, but doubt dripped from her voice. 'You have an appointment, Superintendent?'

'*Chief* Superintendent. I come on urgent police business that overrides the necessity of an appointment.' The Chief Constable himself would have been proud of her burst of polysyllabic pomposity. She looked ostentatiously at her watch and settled for a wait.

After some four minutes, an inner door was flung open by a man of her age, with a full head of blondish hair and a body regularly spending time in the gym. His eyes were a darker blue than Mark's, and his teeth brilliantly white in a face that might just have acquired its tan outdoors. In any other location she'd have tipped him as a marketing executive. Did schools have such commercial posts? She responded to his effusive smile with a professional one of her own.

'Dr Challenor. Giles. Welcome to what I'm afraid resembles Fort Knox, Chief Superintendent,' he said, adding swiftly, 'I'm afraid we've had to resort to this horrible security ever since a civil war erupted between our lads and the comp down the road. Little swine.' He did not specify which lads he was describing. 'And now that, on the advice of some of your junior colleagues, we've banned phones, we've had some very irate parents down here.' He pointed to a series of wooden bins, labelled by form. 'There's a dump-bin for staff phones too, only we keep that locked in the staff room. What brings you out on such a miserable day?'

He'd walked her briskly to a set of doors that he opened with his swipe-card. Ushering her through, he caught up to walk alongside her. 'A visit from someone your rank is very rare. We usually get smaller fry altogether.'

'The matter is entirely confidential,' she said, 'so you'll forgive me if we don't discuss it till we reach the privacy of your office.'

Suddenly they were into cod Tudor, with linenfold panelling on the dark oak dado, and a particularly impressive grained door, all completely at odds with the exterior of the building.

Chief Master
Knock and Wait

'Study,' he couldn't resist correcting her. But he added, 'We can shed the genial welcome but we can't shed years of tradition.' He produced a key, and unlocked his door.

'I hope in the midst of all this history you'll have technology to watch this.' She produced the CD Harbijan had burnt for her.

'Coffee first?'

She said flatly, 'CD first.'

She observed his face as he watched the screen. She would have laid bets his shock and outrage were genuine.

'My officers have prevented any further access to this particular site, but I've shown it to you because they believe it was created by one of your pupils. And features, as you saw, several others.'

'Dear God, I've never seen anything like it, apart from adverts for hotel porn channels. Tell me, Chief Superintendent, how did you discover this — this outrage?'

'You know I can't reveal my sources. Especially when bullying of this order is involved.'

'It puts happy-slapping into the shade. Which reminds me — I've at last placed your face. You're the officer those young people assaulted, aren't you? Are you completely recovered?'

'I'm fine, thanks. Unlike the victims of that little adventure.' She pointed to the screen. 'We've traced it back to one young man: Noel Field. I could just take him out of school and charge him. But I suspect that such an enterprising youth may have other interests, too. Drugs, for instance. I'd like any rumours, any evidence, anything — I want to nail this young man for as much as I can.'

'He's our Head Boy, Chief Superintendent. With a place at Cambridge.'

'That sounded like more than a factual statement. It sounded like a plea, Dr Challenor.'

'For more than our position in the results tables, I assure you. He's a young man with a brilliant career ahead of him. His father's a consultant at William Harvey; his mother's the first solicitor to be called when there's a problem over an asylum claim.'

'So young Master Field is not to be treated as a criminal,' she observed dryly.

'He's not — not a criminal. Surely not.'

'Well, Dr Challenor, how would you describe him?'

* * *

'Strictly *sub rosa*,' Dr Challenor told his colleagues, hastily summoned to his room.

Fran wasn't sure that all had had an education including Latin, so she said definitively, 'Top secret. Absolutely confidential. Nothing must come out of this room that could lead to a possible criminal getting off the hook. Is that understood, gentlemen?' Whatever had happened to co-education? And were there no teachers from ethnic minorities? Deputy Chief Master, Head of Upper Sixth, Head of Pastoral Care — all were white, male and middle class. The only thing in which they differed was their age. 'What I want is any rumours about anything untoward in the school: bullying, sexual harassment, drug dealing.'

'Theft? Cheating in coursework?' An oyster-eyed man nearing retirement age suggested.

'Everything. Especially computer-related. And — you can understand the need for your complete discretion — especially related to computers and to your sixth-form pupils.'

A very chipper young man, scarcely thirty, said with an irritating drawl, 'Students. We call them students.'

'Do you indeed?' she asked with a calm interest that would have Tom running for cover. 'So they're in receipt of loans that leave them in debt till their thirties or forties? Gentlemen, we are not here to discuss nomenclature, but to investigate what may be a very serious crime indeed. Do me the courtesy of accepting that my professionalism is equal to yours. And that my status is somewhat senior,' she added under her breath, but with her most steely smile.

CHAPTER NINETEEN

Mark was due in meetings all afternoon, so she was lucky to be able to grab half an hour with him for lunch, which they ate, as usual, in the canteen. With so much noise, she guessed that no one would realise that the two senior lovebirds weren't tweeting sweet nothings to each other.

'So,' she began, putting down her fork, 'we seem to have a veritable hot bed of minor crime, but only one really serious accusation so far. The website.'

'All of which the headmaster—'

'*Chief Master*!'

'—Would prefer to deal with internally?'

'Naturally. In a most gentlemanly way.'

'I'm sure that went down a treat with you.'

'Quite. Especially as it'd involve just a manly heart-to-heart and a bit of wrist-slapping. But it's far too serious for that.'

'Absolutely! So what does Jill think?'

'I haven't got hold of her yet, nor young Rob: I've just left messages for them to contact me urgently. Now, I want to consult you. Should we bring in the young persons' protection team? There are a lot of youngsters on that website whose faces have effectively been stolen. And I must talk to our Chief, too: it seems his son's one of them. At least the teachers, who prefer to be called masters, were able to put names to the faces, boys' and girls'.'

'Masters? Not mistresses?'

'In your dreams. There might have been women teachers, of course, but no senior female members of staff, not that I saw.'

He fielded the last shred of lettuce. 'Bring in a whole team of counsellors. It might just help the kids and will certainly sound good when the media get hold of it. Noel Field apart, how many kids are running the site?'

'It may be a one-man band: he's not just a paragon of old-fashioned virtue, he's already outstripped his computer teachers. But I've always found that bullies hunt in packs.'

'Or even coerce other people into doing their work for them.'

'Quite. So I've told Challenor to prepare a complete dossier of crimes young Field might want to put his hand up to and get it to me by the end of school. At which point Tom and Harbijan will pick him up.'

Mark smiled. 'Harbijan Singh? What a good choice. You know he came down here because he'd been bullied in his home force, don't you?'

* * *

The moment she returned to her office from lunch the phone rang.

A woman's voice she didn't know, one with a hint of the Midlands about it, asked, 'Is that Detective Chief Superintendent Frances Harman?'

Fran enjoyed a direct question. She gave a direct answer. 'It is.'

'Good afternoon. It's Mary Wolford here. I understand from a young colleague of yours that you wanted to speak to me about my college classes.'

The courtesies over, Fran asked, 'Did DC Arkwright explain how you could help us?'

'I'm afraid I never spoke to him: he spoke to my publicist, who passed on your details. I'm getting more curious by the minute.'

'And who could blame you? What I want, Ms Wolford, is information about students in a creative writing class you ran some years ago.'

'Back at William Murdock College? Heavens, you're asking a lot, Chief Superintendent!' The surprise brought out her accent more strongly.

'It's very important or I wouldn't ask.'

'Any student in particular?'

'Any male students in the same class as Dilly Pound. You might remember her as Delia Pound.'

'I might if I could remember her at all!'

Fran mustn't let her frustration show in her voice. 'A very quiet young woman, probably pretty underconfident?'

Wolford sighed. 'That's the last sort of student you remember. You remember the outstanding ones — because they're troublesome or because they're brilliant. Why, what's this Pound woman done?'

'She's just had some success as a crime presenter for our regional TV news, TVInvicta.'

'She must have something about her, then. Look, obviously we don't get TVInvicta up here in Yorkshire, so I really could do with your prompting me with a photo. I pride myself on never forgetting a face, even if I can't always attach a name to it.'

'If you've got mod cons I could send you her photo through the ether.'

'I meant a good old-fashioned Box Brownie type photo.'

'I'll get one in the post. But it's not a case of identifying Dilly so much as any man in the group who might have conceived a passion for her,' Fran added.

There was a depressing pause. 'I suppose I could get on to my old college for a copy of the registers of classes I taught. Do you know the precise year?'

She gave it.

'I was teaching two or three creative writing classes a week, out of a total of twenty or so hours' class contact. And the college was never the most efficient when it came to administration.'

Fran didn't try to suppress her bark of laughter. 'We know that already. DC Arkwright had to get pretty fierce. But at least they promised the information today.'

'Which in college-speak means "when we get round to it but don't hold your breath". Tell you what, Chief Superintendent, let's cut the Gordian Knot. You give your Dilly Pound my phone number and we'll have a nice gossip about old times. I'm sure we'll come up with some names between us. And faxing through anything William Murdock gets round to sending you might speed up the process. This is my fax number.'

Fran jotted. 'In that case I'll fax you a photo too. Grey and grainy it may be, but it might still help.'

* * *

Fran didn't have time to leave more than a terse message for Dilly, asking her to make the call to Wolford at the first opportunity. Another call was waiting.

'This is Janie Falkirk, Chief Superintendent.'

There was no doubting the claim. The telephone amplified the accent as much as it had Mary Wolford's; whereas Mary's voice had been controlled and what Fran's mother would call ladylike, Janie's might have been heard above the roars of Braveheart's forces.

'The folk attending the Alpha Course Dilly and Daniel attended,' she announced. 'I've got a list.'

'Excellent. Is there any chance you could fax it through?'

'Are we not talking Data Protection Act here, Chief Superintendent?' Janie demanded. 'After all, these good folk gave me their details in the belief that they would be confidential.'

Fran couldn't dispute what she was saying. But Janie was an intelligent woman and surely had a better nature, to which she would appeal. 'Please tell me you're not asking me to obtain all the official paperwork. Please.'

'Ah, well . . . But faxing the whole is not an option, all the same. A good three-quarters are women, and I would assume from the nature of the crime the perpetrator is likely to be male.'

'Likely to be,' Fran conceded.

'Three of the names on my list couldn't be committing the crime in question anyway. I know one is in Broadmoor, because I phoned his primary carer, one is in Canterbury Jail, because I visited him the day we met, and one is with a peace team helping rebuild Pakistan after the earthquake — he emailed me a couple of photos this morning. Pretty good alibis, eh?'

'Unshakeable.'

'Apart from the earthquake laddie!' It sounded as if the vicar had thrown her head back to laugh.

Fran joined in.

'Which leaves us with two names. Paul Lewis is definitely an epistle short of a testament, and I doubt if he'd have the literacy skills required. But you can have his details if you wish?' She dictated an address in Canterbury. 'And there's Dean Fellows.'

'Dean as in a first name, not as in a church dignitary?' Fran asked, hoping her grin would travel down the phone.

'Indeed.' It sounded as if Janie were returning it. 'Now, if I were a psychologist I might well describe him, in the strictest technical terms, as a weirdo.' She paused while Fran laughed. 'He lives in a caravan — he does seasonal agricultural work, picking, packing produce. That sort of thing. I think you'll find him in a village near here called Linsore Bottom. No jokes, please.'

'Would I dare?'

'To be honest, you're wasting your time with him too, unless he's got a computer stowed away somewhere in his van. And he was truly more interested in finding God than chasing women. In fact, I wouldn't have had him down as the marrying sort.'

And it didn't sound as if he were mobile enough to send mail — or flowers — from London.

'I wish I could recruit you on to my team,' Fran said, meaning it.

'I wish I could recruit you on to one of our courses.' It sounded as if Janie meant it too.

'I'll let you know how I get on with them, shall I? And you can give me the dates then. Now, my phone's telling me I've got another call waiting, so thanks, and good bye for now.'

'Goodbye. And God bless you.'

He might bless Farat Hafeez, too, calling with the news that Stephen Hardy was apparently touring Cornwall alone in an elderly Fiesta. According to Mrs Hardy, still apparently swallowing the police story that they needed vital and totally confidential information about an ex-parishioner, he had always had an interest in the silver mines of the area.

'She gave me the name of a couple of guest-houses he might stay at,' Farat added.

'And?'

'He checked out of one at the end of last week. He hasn't appeared at the other, but since he'd not made a booking no one thought it suspicious.'

'Phone contact?'

'Only one call to say he'd arrived. The mobile company confirmed it was from the right area. Near Launceston. Apparently he doesn't text, and only has a prepaid mobile, so he rations his calls and the time he spends on them.'

'Have you got his mobile number?'

Farat dictated it, adding, 'And would you be surprised that it's switched off every time I've tried to call him?'

'Nothing about this man would surprise me.' Except the proof that he was guilty. All the same, she asked, 'Has he made any withdrawals from cashpoints?'

'One for a hundred and fifty the day he left his guest-house. I suppose if he lived frugally that might keep him going till now. Maybe he's a cheque and banker's card man.'

'Whatever he is,' Fran said decisively, 'I'll get a national alert out for him. Can you remind me of his car reg? Right, let's be having him . . .'

* * *

Clutching at a cup of green tea as if it were neat gin, she made another attempt to reach Jill. Again the phone rang unanswered. All sorts of unpleasant scenarios began to play themselves before her eyes, most involving Jill lying on the floor with further injuries. She checked the computer again: still nothing on the MisPer records. On impulse, she phoned the school. Had Rob been in that morning?

The woman at the far end of the phone might have come from a different planet from the one guarding hell's gate, personifying cooperation, as soon as she heard Fran's rank.

'You'll understand that this sort of information is usually confidential to the parents, Chief Superintendent.'

'Of course: I appreciate your cooperation. And your discretion. Is young Rob Tanner in school?'

'No. And his attendance in the last few weeks has been remarkably poor, according to my records.'

'No phone calls to explain his absences?'

'None. In fact, I have a letter in front of me awaiting his Head of Year's signature to warn his parents of the likelihood of suspension.'

Suspending someone who was missing classes had always seemed an odd way of dealing with the problem, but Fran didn't comment, merely thanking the woman for her help. Now what?

Natasha? She'd trusted her enough to let her know about Rob going missing but not enough apparently to call her back. Her phone was switched off. Fran would have to leave another message.

* * *

Another incoming call. The handset still warm from the previous call, she picked it up to hear Tom's news. Uniform had confiscated Noel Field's computer and were searching his parents' house. He and Harbijan had arrested Field himself; he was already being processed by the custody sergeant. In five minutes she should be observing the interview.

But there were other things to do first. William Murdock College had sworn they'd faxed the details Tom required, so her first port of call must be to the basket next to the machine. Yes! Excellent. Except they'd sent every single register for that year, all hand-written and none benefiting from the fact that the machine was warning that it was at the end of its paper roll by smearing pink across the sheets. For some reason, some classes didn't even have their titles anywhere on the page. A quick scan, all she had time for, revealed nothing. Definitely a job for someone who had enough time to consider stuffing mushrooms for his or her supper.

Now, what about Jon Binns' success with the contractors fitting CCTV?

He was back in front of his computer crunching numbers.

She could either scream or ask quietly, 'Any luck?'

'I'm expecting a fax any moment, ma'am. They've had two standard bollockings and one of my specials.'

'Excellent. Now, when the names come through I want to know if any matches the name on these lists — perhaps you should photocopy everything and pop it on Tom's desk?'

'Everything?'

She reflected. 'Any sheets you can identify as being creative writing classes. Though of course, he may have been in a different class altogether and smitten from a distance.'

'Their eyes met across the crowded canteen, that sort of thing?'

'You put it beautifully — perhaps you should join a writers' group yourself. Now, how's the profiler getting on with your main case?'

'Profiler? What profiler?'

For God's sake, hadn't they set one up yet? 'I just heard a rumour . . .'

'Budget. Every briefing we have, someone asks for one. Seems there's no cash left in the pot. You couldn't do a *quid pro quo*, could you, guv? Find a few quid for your poor relations?'

* * *

For all she knew she was invisible and inaudible to everyone in the interview room, Fran tiptoed in and settled herself as quietly as if she'd arrived late at in a theatre auditorium. One of the cast, Noel Field, had already taken his place, and was preening in front of what he believed was a mirror while awaiting his interrogators and the highly expensive solicitor his family had conjured up. Apparently his mother thought it would be unethical, given her legal background, to sit in on the interview, but Fran suspected the poor woman would have given her right arm to be able to lurk undetected as Fran was doing. Police courtesy, however, didn't compel Fran to offer to share the facility, much as she wanted to respond to the anguish written all over the woman's face.

Tom and Harbijan were to conduct the interview on the grounds that their skills with the young were likely to be far better than her own. They could also talk with authority about his website's contents, not to mention the computer, currently in the hands of the forensic computer science team. Giving no hint that he knew they had an audience, Tom made all the introductions by the book, carefully explaining about the tape-recording. Not even the top brief would be able to fault anything.

Unfortunately it was equally hard to fault Noel Field. It would have been easier if he had slumped yobbishly back in his chair, his baseball cap on backwards, demanding his rights and a fag. As it was, he personified an old-fashioned courtesy that involved sitting up straight, listening without interruption, and responding with carefully chosen words. No wonder Dr Challenor and the other Thomas Bowdler staff didn't want him cast as a criminal. He'd have polished the school's reputation at Cambridge. It would also have been easier if he'd seen himself as a criminal, but he listened with genuine — or very well-feigned — shock when he was told his antics were against the law.

'But it was all just a bit of fun,' he protested, contriving to be both innocently wide-eyed and to have a puzzled frown.

'Fun is usually at someone's expense,' Tom pointed out mildly.

'So did you get the consent of the film-maker to use his material?' Harbijan asked.

There was the merest hesitation that wouldn't have pleased his liberal-lawyer mother, as if young Master Field wished to convey a smidgen of surprise that the young Asian should have spoken. 'No. But you know, it's not exactly as if I'm stealing great literature.' He gave a winsome smile.

'What about the people whose faces you superimposed on the bodies? Did you ask their permission? I notice your own isn't on there,' Tom added ominously.

'I told you, it was a joke. You don't go up to someone and say, "D'you mind if I play a joke on you", do you?' Winsome morphed into truculent.

'I suppose not. Nor do you go up to a person and ask if you can happy-slap them.'

'Happy-slapping? That's kids' stuff.' The authentic voice of one of our country's elite, Fran thought, dismissing the lower orders.

'Of course. Remind me what subjects you're taking for A Level, Mr Field,' Harbijan said.

Field's smile came tinged with patronage. 'I don't believe you asked me, so I fail to see how I can remind you. But I'm happy to impart the information—'

His lawyer raised a minatory finger. Obviously mocking the poor plods was not the tactic they'd agreed.

'Chemistry, Physics, Biology, General Studies and Computer Science. On the basis of my A/S results, I'm expected to obtain A's in all of them.'

Harbijan's eyes widened. 'Five good A Levels! It's a pity you're not likely to be taking up your university place next year.'

Did he ignore the threat deliberately or did he genuinely miss the point? 'Of course I won't. I shall be taking a gap year. A friend of my parents has a laboratory in the USA; I shall do some work experience there, and then move south to work on a rain forest project.'

'You'll be sorely missed, then. You'll be looking at a custodial sentence, you see,' Harbijan said, shaking his head sadly.

It was news to Fran, but she made no attempt to rein in the young men.

Yes. At last he was shaken. 'For God's sake! It was only a bit of fun. No harm done.'

'Breach of copyright law, of course. That would be a civil offence. But putting people's faces on a website is an offence under stalking legislation. And the courts take that very seriously indeed.' Harbijan looked to the solicitor for confirmation. He got it.

Field would have got to his feet had not the solicitor restrained him. 'For God's sake, jail for a bit of blogging!'

'There are one or two other things we wanted to talk about,' Tom said, very mildly. 'But maybe you and your lawyer would like to take a comfort break and a cup of tea. You may have things you want to talk to him about, after all.'

* * *

'Your hospitality is exceeded only by your concern for the young man's bladder,' Fran commented, as the young detectives joined her in her observation room. 'What might he need to talk to Mr Sandys about?'

Tom took the initiative. 'Drugs. Some very promising looking E's under the bed. Almost industrial quantities. And a large amount, more than for personal use anyway, of very strong cannabis.'

'The stuff they call skunk?'

'Yep. And a lot of cash in smallish denominations. All immaculately kept in one of those purpose built offices, only his has a bedroom at one end and an en suite bathroom. Hi-fi, computer system to die for, plasma screen TV. His own little empire. I shouldn't wonder if he has room service.'

Harbijan shook his head sadly. 'Poor little rich boy, eh?'

Fran nodded. A bit of decent mucking in getting the tea had always seemed to her a good principle for keeping families together, though of course it was one she'd never had to put to the test. But she said nothing. How on earth did working mothers keep tabs on their kids? If Jill was working round the clock on a case, how did she check the contents of her son's room? 'We need to know his suppliers. He's obviously not up to speed on the principles of sentencing, so pull him along with the idea of coming clean and getting a lighter tariff. I wouldn't mind knowing his customers, too.'

'Got one of your hunches coming on, like, guv?'

'I may just have. I get these feelings, Harbijan, I always take note of,' she explained as he stared at her. 'They very rarely let me down.'

'Intuition? Second sight?' He was quite excited.

'Probably just years of experience,' she said, though she wasn't entirely convinced and didn't think he was either. She foresaw a long conversation with him when they weren't busy. 'OK, you're doing very well. Now, it's seven o'clock—'

'Doesn't time fly when you're enjoying yourself!' Tom agreed.

'Go on as long as you want, so long as you're not seen to be overly heavy. Or send him down to the cells. Or hand him over to his mother on the strictest understanding he's not allowed into his own room in any circumstances.'

Harbijan shook his head. 'With due respect, ma'am, let him near any computer, any mobile, even, and he could bugger an awful lot of leads. Incommunicado, I'd say. A night in the cells might do him a world of good. He's legally an adult, after all.'

'By three days,' Tom put in.

'It might indeed clear his head. On the other hand, we don't want to appear to be vindictive. Talk to his solicitor, as if asking his advice. Be terribly reasonable and soon it'll be his idea. Rule number one in high-profile cases, watch your backs. So another hour maximum tonight. Mustn't exhaust little diddums, must we?' As they left the room, she added, 'And maintain absolute and total discretion. For all our sakes.'

* * *

Late as she was, Fran still had to wait for Mark, deep in some meeting from which he emerged looking strained and exhausted. She fought back a wave of nausea. What if all this pressure was doing his heart no good? Spending time with her meant he'd spent less in the gym, good old jokes about ten mile runs notwithstanding. It was her birthday soon; she could ask for a rowing machine or a multi-gym, ostensibly for her but really for him. She couldn't risk him having a heart attack or a stroke. Quite literally, she couldn't imagine living if anything happened to him.

Yesterday's panic returned, with a strength that quite terrified her. She'd heard widows of murder victims tell her they didn't know what clothes they were wearing, whether their shoes were even a pair. She'd sympathised, deeply, but never before empathised. If Mark were to die, how would she prepare food, knowing she had to eat alone? How could she ever sleep in a bed he had left empty? How would she even breathe, if he were not there to breathe for?

He was too tired to worry with even an inkling of her fears, so she smiled and held out her hand for the car keys. 'My place tonight. I know just what's in the freezer and I'll reheat it while you have a bath.' Forget about going round to Jill's to show her the CD and talk about young Rob — her place was with Mark tonight.

He surrendered the keys without a quibble. 'What would I do without you?' His voice changed. 'My God, what would I do?'

And in the middle of the car park they clung to each other like children afraid of the dark.

CHAPTER TWENTY

Jill froze the frame. Fran had brought the CD round before going into work, and they were watching it in what seemed to be a communal office, GCSE coursework jostling with reports on housing associations and Fran's own memos. 'Yes, that's Rob.' Jill's voice was little more than a whisper.

'I'm sorry you had to see this. But I thought it might explain . . . something,' Fran said. She added quickly, when she saw that Jill could no longer speak, 'It's one thing to watch things like this in Vice, isn't it, when it's part of the job. You know, it's nine o'clock in the morning so it's bestiality time. It's quite another when it involves images of someone you know, even if they are electronic fakes.' She put her arms round Jill, holding her tightly while she cried. 'I suppose it's a bit early in the day for a nip? No, you don't anyway, do you?'

'Not having seen my father go that way. A cup of coffee might go down well though.'

Fran fished a packet of tissues from her bag. Leaving it within reach, she headed for the kitchen. All her good work had been undone, but as she stood arms akimbo regarding the chaos she realised it might just have been the results of one supper and one breakfast. At least someone could have loaded the dishwasher. Or they could have if anyone had bothered to run it after the last load.

'Rob's job,' Jill observed, startling her. She was leaning heavily against the door-jamb. 'I've an idea we've run out of dishwasher tablets, though.'

'Maybe if we use the hottest wash without detergent it'll be OK,' Fran said. 'And if you give me a shopping list I can collect some things on the way back here to talk to Rob after school.'

Jill dropped her eyes as if ashamed. 'You don't have to come back. Not today. He's with his grandmother. In Sheffield. He bunked off on Friday. We've been worried sick. He told her if she phoned us he'd run away somewhere else.'

'Somewhere as warm and comfortable with homemade food?'

Jill managed a smile. 'Well, when she called his bluff he stayed. I'm so worried about him. Some days he won't go into school at all.' All flat sentences, all heaving with emotion.

'Would you, if your mates were doing that to you?'

'Fran, what do I do?' Her voice cracked with despair.

Fran suppressed two tart remarks, one about answering her phone, the other more serious. How many days ago had Jill informed her that non-mothers weren't qualified to advise? And she was here as a friend, not as Nemesis. 'Get back on your sofa for a start, while I wash up. I always find ten minutes with hot soapy water does wonders for my thought processes. And your sitting down while I do it might help yours, too, because I still think there's stuff about Rob you haven't trusted me with.'

But even when the crockery and the kitchen sparkled again, Jill's face was still set in stubborn lines, and Fran had to get back to Maidstone.

Where there were still no more letters to Dilly. And no further reports of sexual assaults. Apparently Farmer was out at a meeting, so she still couldn't scream at him over the absence of a profiler. But she wanted to be angry with someone, so she summoned Tom and Jon.

'And how's young Master Field this morning?' she asked, hoping he'd insulted someone so she could have an excuse to go herself and put him in his place.

'Chastened by the primitive conditions in Maidstone nick,' Tom said. 'And, I fancy, by a long conversation with his solicitor. And his mother.'

'Poor woman.' Her anger ebbed away. How would the poor woman cope?

'Often happens, according to my mother,' Jon observed. 'Professional parents — you know, teachers, doctors, even police officers — seem to have a dreadful time parenting. High expectations, too strict or too liberal. Mum's a college lecturer,' he added.

'But she brought you up OK.'

He grinned engagingly. 'Nope. I was supposed to be a merchant banker.'

'Well, there you are. And Master Field? How will he end up?'

'The CPS think he'll get a custodial sentence. Not for the website, but for the drugs. They'll certainly ask for one. A long one. Which will come as a bit of a shock to Master Field's system.'

'If he doesn't end up running the whole prison,' Tom suggested darkly.

'Come on, it's bad enough if you're used to a comfortless home. Imagine swapping his suite for a cell.'

'Maybe a hefty fine and a lot of community service?' Fran said hopefully.

'Guv, he had enough in his bank account to pay off the national debt of a medium African country. OK, a small one. He's bloody loaded. And how does he get it?'

'By making and selling drugs?' Fran hazarded

'Yes, guv. And by getting kids hooked by giving them freebies outside school. Just like a hardened old pro. If it were up to me, I'd fasten the bastard to the school gates, like, and get everyone to throw their rotten fruit at him. You know, the pillory. Worse than the stocks because you can't put your hands up to cover your face.'

'Has he identified all his victims? Both his customers and those on the film?'

The young men looked at each other, embarrassed and reluctant to speak.

'Let me confirm one. Rob Tanner. I've spoken to his mother so it's OK to admit it.'

Their sighs were audible. 'Sorry, guv.'

'It's not my problem, though I'd rather it wasn't common knowledge. It's hers — poor Jill's. And his.'

'And ours,' Jon corrected her. 'Ashford CID phoned: they've found some of DCI Tanner's silverware. We think young Rob nicked it to pay for his habit.'

'I'm sure you're right. We'll talk to him as soon as he comes home. He'd scarpered. To Sheffield.'

'Probably because he owed Field a couple of hundred quid and had no way of paying for it.'

Fran whistled. 'That's a hell of a lot of drugs. Were they all for personal use or was he supposed to be selling them on? I take it Field wouldn't have let him off with a kindly warning.'

'A strong warning, like, and find three more customers,' Tom said. 'That was the deal. Oh, and come up with the dosh within a week. Or else. Or else never came into it, apparently. He's a nasty piece of knitting, as my auntie says.'

'Talking of your auntie, Tom — have you had another consignment of biscuits recently?'

'As a matter of fact, she sent me the recipe to pass on to Dilly. Maybe Dilly'll bake us some, as a thank you, like.'

'That might be a bit premature. The stalker may be taking a break,' Jon warned. 'Or sick.'

'Or is saving himself for the biggie,' Tom agreed.

Or is at the bottom of a Cornish cliff, Fran added silently.

* * *

As the young men left her office she willed the phone to ring. When it failed to, needing a spot of human kindness, she called Janie Falkirk to thank her for her help.

'Has young Dilly come up with any other hidden bits of her past?' Janie enquired.

'It's like extracting hen's teeth, isn't it?'

'Blame that young man of hers. The fiancé. He wants a respectable wife, not Someone with a Past.'

'Surely anyone over the age of thirty's got to have some past?' Like her and Mark, for instance.

'Och, aye. I dabbled with prostitution once, Fran, to pay for my booze.' She might have been talking about taking a newspaper from W H Smith's without forking out the right change. 'But the Good Lord decided that wasn't for me, or no doubt I'd have been laid out on some morgue slab with a nice dose of cirrhosis long before this. I'm sorry, that's a bit of a conversation stopper, isn't it? Maybe that's why young Daniel McDine prefers another church.'

Fran couldn't deny the information had taken her aback. But she adopted their usual joking tone. 'A sinner-free zone?'

'He'd be hard put to find that, even at the heart of the Cathedral. Talk to the lass again, Fran. That's my advice for what it's worth.'

'I shall take it.'

As pleased with Janie as she hoped Janie was with her, she cut the connection. No, still no incoming call. So she would talk to Dilly again. She jabbed the numbers, and beat a tattoo as she waited. Now, should she be calm and controlled or as forceful as she wanted to be? At least she managed to be polite to the girl on the TVInvicta switchboard.

'I–I thought it was a bit early,' Dilly stuttered, 'to phone Mary out of the blue.'

'You could have phoned her last night!' Forceful won the day.

'But Daniel—' Dilly bleated.

'Come on, Dilly, it's your life we're trying to protect. It's not making a fuss, it's not making an exhibition of yourself

— it's taking sensible precautions. Hell's bells, if we didn't believe your life was at stake, do you think we'd be spending all this time and effort on you?' She gave full rein to her exasperation with a few more choice sentences.

When she finished, there was an inaudible murmur.

'Well, then. Now, I shall be at my desk for the next half hour. I shall expect you to phone me back and report on your conversation with Mary Wolford. Do you need the number again?' Perhaps she'd missed her calling; perhaps she should have been a headmistress.

A tap on her door announced the arrival of one of Jill's CID team she'd not actually spoken to, but who had asked intelligent questions at Farmer's briefing. She was a young woman in her twenties, with red hair to rival Janie's, except that hers looked freshly ironed.

'Good morning.' If only she had Joe Farmer's facility with names. 'What can I do for you? Come on in and sit down.'

'DC Hall, ma'am,' the young woman said, remaining on her feet.

So they'd told her Fran's problem. 'Well done for reminding me. It's Sarah?'

It seemed the young woman's initiative stopped there. But after a moment, she smiled. 'Sue, actually.'

'Sue, I'm so sorry. Do, please, sit down. What can I do for you? Or is it more what you can do for me?' She raised a hopeful eyebrow.

The young woman responded with a polite half-smile. 'You remember the other day you asked about CCTV footage of shops in the area where people could buy those facemasks? Bush and Blair and so on? Well, I thought I'd check out as many as I could over the weekend. Maidstone, Folkestone, Canterbury and Tunbridge.' She ticked them off on her fingers. 'I've got a pile of videos on my desk. But I've only had time to skim through them, and all I can see is loads of innocent-looking people going in and out of lots of shops.'

'No one with "SUSPECT" branded on his forehead? Drat! But that's admirable work, Sue. Absolutely excellent.

All that time — and mileage. Don't forget to claim. I mean it.'

'We're no further forward, though.'

'Don't put yourself down. If we do get a suspect and we can link him to a fancy-dress supplier, we're quids in. Well done. Oh, and claim for some TOIL or some overtime — I'll authorise either.'

'Thanks . . . Ma'am — do you think DCI Tanner would mind if a couple of us went round to see her this morning? That whip round brought in ever such a lot of cash, and I thought some flowers would make a nice start. But there's a lot left over. Any ideas what I could get?'

'For a start, dishwasher tablets,' Fran said dryly. 'Tell you what, she never, ever has any time to herself. Is there enough for a voucher for a day's pampering at one of those posh spas?'

Sue pondered. 'If we got a smaller bunch of flowers. I could order one over the Internet.'

'She'd need someone to ferry her wherever it is and back, so she'd have no excuse not to go.'

'No problem there. Ma'am, that's a brilliant idea.'

Fran shook her head. 'I always try to give presents I'd like myself.' She fished in her purse. 'Here. Now you won't have to worry how many carnations you can afford.'

She sat back with a silly grin of satisfaction delighted that there were still young men and women with initiative in the service. And sat up as the phone rang. It was the Devon and Cornwall Constabulary. A gentle male voice told her they'd found Stephen Hardy's car. Her heart stopped.

'But no Stephen Hardy?' Had the enquiries driven him to suicide? Or was his illicit love for Dilly responsible? The bile rose from her stomach; she had to swallow hard not to vomit.

'Not yet. But the Moor's a big place, ma'am. And it's snowing up there at the moment.'

'You're throwing all your resources at it?' Cheeky, that — but she seemed to have got away with it.

'We are indeed. Choppers, sniffer dogs — it's standard procedure when some grockle goes walkabout. They think because it's so far south it's like taking a walk in the park,' he added, the bitterness at odds with his burr.

'Any development, whatever time of night or day, you'll phone me — OK?'

* * *

How long had she sat there watching her hands shaking, and wondering if she could ask Janie to have a word with her employer. Why not? She left a terse message.

Meanwhile, she needed to get someone to talk to the men Janie had mentioned, even if it were the longest of shots. The trouble was, who? The replacement DCIs were now in place, taking over from her and Farmer, but she didn't want to bully them into handing over bodies, not when they were so new in post. Harbijan? He'd done his share, and his expertise was clearly with matters requiring more intellectual skills than farm labourers.

No argument, then.

As she passed his office door on her way out, Farmer yelled to her. She went in, cocking her head enquiringly and shutting the door behind her.

'I'd appreciate it if you stopped interrupting my team members when they're doing urgent work, Chief Superintendent.'

'And I'd appreciate some cooperation, Joe. Come on, even without the profiler I'd have thought was an obvious resource, there's a good chance Jon's running to earth our flasher, who just may be in the frame for a case I'm working on for the Chief. As for DC Sue Hall, in her we have an officer whose worth is beyond rubies, more than capable of working on her own initiative and on her day off, too.' She explained.

'Well, what *I've* done,' Farmer said, rather like a schoolboy demanding a pat on the head, 'is ask Interpol for help. It seems to me Chummie's MO is so distinctive he might have done something similar elsewhere. There's been nothing like it in this country, not according to the computer, but it's so efficient, so beautifully timed — we could ask him to do our accounts for us, it's so meticulous.'

That was the nearest to an apology she was going to get, and more than she'd expected. After all, they were the same rank, both of them supposed to be responsible not for day-to-day minutiae, but for the grander scheme of things. But she found she couldn't forgive him. She said nothing.

'And maybe he's returned to wherever and is doing it again there,' Farmer continued. 'Hence the sudden cessation of incidents.'

Fran sat down uninvited. 'What a good idea.' Her enthusiasm was genuine. 'The funny thing is, our anonymous letters have stopped coming, too.'

He shrugged expansively. 'So I thought of standing down some of the teams. Hence young Binns earning his corn with a bit of accountancy. But I didn't want to interfere with the section, not with DCI Evans new on the scene. She wants results, preferably yesterday. She's sent your Tom Arkwright out on some errand, by the way,' he added waspishly.

'Sounds like my sort of woman.' He wouldn't catch her criticising a colleague that way even if all that William Murdock paperwork must still be lying unchecked.

'D'you reckon? A DCI at thirty? Fast-tracked, of course. Very politically correct. We had to earn our promotions, Fran. Damn it, I'm still trying to earn mine!'

'Yes, it's all very well for old lags like me. It's easy to forget, Joe.' Which was the nearest he'd get to an apology too.

* * *

Judging Dilly to have had plenty of time to make her call, Fran returned to her office and phoned her. Her line was still busy, which Fran chose to interpret as promising. Should she hang about for a few more minutes, or take advantage of the gap in the weather to whiz over to Canterbury, to talk to Lewis or Fellows — both if she was in luck?

A squall of rain against the window made her press the redial button.

'Hello, Fran.' This time Dilly didn't sound apologetic. 'I've just spoken to Mary. I'd forgotten how nice she is. We're going to do lunch in London my next day off!'

As if their reminiscences could wait that long!

'But she remembered some of the people in my group. Well, we both did. Funny how the memory works, isn't it?'

'It is indeed,' Fran agreed, trying to smother the sarcasm. 'So who've you come up with?' Anything to make the task of picking out the right class register easier.

Dilly reeled off four or five names. All female.

As mildly as she could, Fran said, 'Sounds like a feminist group. Any men allowed?'

'Of course. Now, we had a bloke who used to work in CGHQ, but had had a breakdown. We think he was Roddie Muir. And Tom List. He went on to become a professional tennis player. But that's it, apart from a quiet man who didn't attend all that much. We think his name was Jim or Tim, but neither of us could remember his surname.'

'Do you recall anything about him at all?' She wanted to ask if he wore glasses, but didn't want to induce false memory syndrome.

'Not really. There were a couple of others, but we're truly stuck for names.'

'That's a big help,' she lied encouragingly. 'Now, do you recall any fellow students on other courses who might have been attracted to you? Lads in the canteen, that sort of thing?'

'We didn't meet in the main building — horrible place. I gather they're pulling it down. I wonder what horrible secrets they'll find. Ugh.' Dilly produced the sort of exaggerated shudder she'd once given herself as a kid after *Doctor Who*.

'I can't wait to find out,' Fran observed repressively. 'So no other students.'

'None.'

'Well, if any do come to mind, just phone Tom.'

'That's what I told Mary. He's such a nice boy, isn't he?'

Poor Tom. Reduced to that, by a woman heading for forty. Fran opened her mouth to observe he'd make a lovely toy boy, but stopped herself just in time. That really was beyond the bound of what was professionally acceptable. The news about Stephen Hardy? Should Dilly know he was missing? 'Sufficient unto the day is the evil thereof' — now which part of the brain had that sprung from?

* * *

Linsore Bottom: what would Mark think about that for their new address? Apart from the obvious connotation, in her mind's eye it was as picturesque as villages came, complete with thatch, mill, church, green and a few sheep. The reality, waiting halfway along a lane inches deep in mud, was different. Sheep there were, and horses, but the only dwellings were rows of tatty caravans parked near a farmhouse that was now the office of what looked like farming on an industrial scale. Logo-bearing lorries and vans came and went briskly as she looked for someone — anyone — to ask for help. At last a weary-looking security guard and a sullen-looking dog rounded a corner. The dog switched to hostile in the flash of a warrant. The guard switched to sullen.

'I'm looking for Dean Fellows.'

He gestured with his thumb and muttered something. She'd have loved it to be directions to the Hundred Acre field, or something equally bucolic. Instead, it was apparently to a packing shed.

Trekking through the mud, squelchy enough for a TV period drama set, she pushed open the nearest barn door. She sucked in deep breaths of celery-scented air. Magic. Less delightful were the unprotected hundred and fifty-watt bulbs hanging at almost scalp height. They gave almost enough light for a team of ill-kempt youngish men to chop messy outer leaves and roots from celery and shove them into plastic baskets. Once a basket was full, it was carried to the far end of the barn for washing. The operation took place against a background of canned music, possibly Eastern European in origin, without much conversation.

She raised her voice. 'Dean Fellows?' And to parade ground level. 'Dean Fellows?'

A tiny brown-skinned man, scarcely to her shoulder and fine-framed as a child, put down the baskets he was hefting. He nodded to one corner, putting his hands together, as if in a namaste. She replied, in kind, bowing her head even lower and searching for the correct Hindi phrase.

'Prayer,' the man said. 'Prayer. There. Prayer.' His accent wasn't Indian.

Nonetheless, she gave him another namaste, and followed the jerk of his thumb, the ball criss-crossed with scars old and recent in the filthy skin.

An even skinnier man was on his knees in the far corner, in the straight-backed, head-upright style she associated with Tudor tombs. Eyes closed, he was muttering under his breath, the same thing, she thought, over and over again, so quickly the words ran together, as at Mr Polly's wedding — amazing how flickers of her school curriculum would keep popping back these days.

She coughed, as reverently as she could. Unoffended, he got to his feet in an amazingly easy movement and treated her to a wonderful beam. She responded, hoping her halitosis wasn't as powerful as his.

'Dean? Might we talk somewhere? Your caravan, for instance?' She showed her ID and gave her name and rank, but he evinced nothing except mild interest.

Another beam, and they were on their way. The smell of paraffin hitting her as he opened the door told her that her mission was in vain. Unless Dean had got himself one of those wind-up computers that world leaders insisted would save Africa, he wouldn't be sending any computer printed letters.

The other smell was roughly the same as Rob's bedroom, minus the cannabis.

'How can I help?' His voice was surprisingly middle class.

'I just wanted to ask you a few questions. Do you ever watch television, Mr Fellows?'

He gestured. There was no set, and how would it work anyway? 'We do have a sort of common room,' he said. 'More a canteen, I suppose. There's a television in there, but it's mostly tuned to overseas stations, and who am I to argue? My colleagues are so far from home it comforts them to hear their own languages spoken.'

'And you — don't you want to see the News or other programmes?'

'I watch *Songs of Praise*. No one minds that. But my news is in here, madam.' He touched his heart. 'And it's good news.'

'The news the Reverend Janie Falkirk shared with you?'

She'd pressed the right button there. 'You know Janie! What a wonderful woman.' His face glowed with pleasure.

'She's a delight, isn't she?' Fran agreed with absolute sincerity.

'I thank God every day for her.' He pointed to a tiny bookshelf. She could see a Bible and a prayer book, and a number of other small volumes. 'And for those.' He reached forward, making her step back sharply. But all he picked up was a leatherette covered New Testament. 'For you,' he said. 'Please.'

* * *

'Damn and blast it!' No mobile signal! Fran abandoned her mobile and pulled back on to the road. Dark ages or what. Very well, if she couldn't phone HQ, HQ couldn't contact her. Since she was so close to Canterbury, she'd drop in on Paul Lewis, probably to do no more than confirm Janie's opinion, which had been pretty sound, after all, in the case of Dean.

Picking her way through narrow streets of old houses given Georgian or even Victorian face lifts, she found the place she was looking for. No earthly chance of parking legally within half a mile, she reckoned. Would a drive-by appraisal do? It was very tempting.

But she managed to squeeze the car into a space in the next street, so do the job properly she would. Other people had had even more of a struggle than she, and several vehicles had wheels on the pavement, or were sticking out at awkward angles. Shamed, she had another go, succeeding only after three or four more backwards and forward shuffles. She patted Dean's little gift with what was meant to be irony. But her hand froze. Tapping his way along the street was an elderly man apparently totally reliant on his white stick. All those protruding car boots and bonnets for him to walk into. Fran was out of the car and offering help before she knew it.

'Ta, love.' He took her arm unselfconsciously. 'The one thing I can do, to drop my neighbour's stuff in the post, and all these cars make even that difficult.'

She guided him along, asking, as much to fill the silence as anything, 'Why do you act as post boy?'

'It makes her think I think I'm being useful, see. She's got it into her head she needs to cook for me, and it has to be said she has a cooler hand for pastry than I do. So I get out of her kitchen by taking odds and ends to the pillar-box, see.' Clearly there was more to this relationship than she had time to uncover. 'Here we are. Now, if you'd just warn me if there are any bits and bobs on the pavement the other side of the road, I shall be fine.'

'Let's go together. Tell me, do you know where I might find Paul Lewis?'

'Are you another social worker? You might as well give up, lady. Unless you grasp the nettle and pop him in the madhouse.'

* * *

'And are you going to?' Mark asked, topping up her lunchtime water.

'I'll have another go at social services. I don't think Lewis is doing anyone — even himself — any actual harm: it's just that he sees life in terms, as far as I can make out, of musical keys. I'm G major. He's in a D minor phase, I gather.'

'Which might make sense if I were a musician.'

At least she knew enough to explain briefly. 'But he's thin enough to be anorexic. And all the utilities have been cut off,' she added, with a retrospective shudder.

'Which someone ought to deal with. But not you, Fran, not you.' He spoke tenderly, not in boss mode.

'I can make the phone call to Social Services and get Gary Tranter to make it all happen, though. He owes me for help above and beyond the call of duty and now he can pay, with interest.'

He reached for her hand and squeezed it appreciatively. 'That's my Fran — why bother to nag an underling when you can twist the arm of the guy at the top?'

CHAPTER TWENTY-ONE

Rain having set in again, a quiet afternoon doing the good old-fashioned police work of her youth seemed almost appealing. So Fran gathered all the William Murdock photocopies that the lads hadn't yet tackled and dumped them on her desk. Some tutors had computer printed their paperwork; others had written them by hand, with varying degrees of legibility. With only one name, the task would have been dispiriting, but even the few Dilly had recalled made it comparatively easy to locate the anonymous creative writing group.

At last, half an hour's eye-popping toil later, she found a match. It was a good job, she thought dourly, for Mary Wolford's publisher, that they didn't get manuscripts in long-hand. Spidery, small, nasty long-hand. And — as far as the names here were concerned — scant respect for alphabetical order. But there it was: Pound, Delia. Alongside were the names Delia had come up with: Roddie Muir and Tom List; Tim Edwards; Jim Holder.

Buzzing with adrenaline, she reached for the list of Watchbrief CCTV employees.

Not a Muir, List, Edwards or Holder amongst them. But a Holden! Could that be the same person, his name changed by a simple slip of the pen?

She dialled so hurriedly she had to stop and start again. It took an age for TVInvicta's switchboard to connect them, and she jumped in without preamble. 'Dilly, do you recall a fellow student from your William Murdock class called Jim Holden?'

There was a pause so long she suspected she'd interrupted a conversation Dilly, hand clamped over handset, was determined to finish.

'Dilly? Are you there? You said there was a Jim or a Tim. Could it have been Jim Holden?'

At last Dilly condescended to reply. 'Might have been. Yes, it might. If it was, he wrote rhyming verse. Oh, yes. Yucky stuff.'

'In what way yucky?'

'You know, sentimental. To his absent princess. Sub-greetings card.'

'Oh, dear. And where did he sit? In relation to you?'

'Opposite, usually. He needed glasses, but he kept taking them off and polishing them and leaving them on the table.'

'What sort of glasses?'

'Fran, after all this time!'

'It's important, Dilly. What sort of glasses?'

'Just glasses. Only he'd been in some sort of accident and he couldn't face the sun, so he'd swap them for dark ones on a very bright day.'

Ah! 'Did you ever talk to each other?'

'Quite often. We used to have coffee sometimes. And when it got dark, he insisted on taking me to my bus stop. But he was very quiet. Never said anything. And if you hadn't mentioned him, I'd never . . . You don't think it's him, Fran? Jim Holden? No, never. He wasn't — I didn't . . . It was never like that. What's he been saying?'

Fran sighed. 'It's not so much what he's been saying, is it, Dilly, as what he might have been writing.'

* * *

On Mark's advice the Chief had summoned Joe Farmer to join him and Fran, who was looking as vibrant and sexy as he'd ever known her. Middle-aged? Old? In the gloomy late afternoon light her energy and excitement lit the room.

'As you may be aware,' the Chief began, pausing portentously, as was becoming his habit these days, 'Chief Superintendent Harman has been working on a strictly Need to Know case.'

Farmer shook his head, irritated as he might well be. But he was wise enough not to carp about missing officers diverted from their day-to-day work.

'Good. Because the matter was — still is! — absolutely confidential. Someone from the Media World—' he spoke with a reverence others might have reserved for senior statesmen or clerics '—has been stalked. Fran has made a connection between a possible stalker and someone who may — and may is still the operative word — be responsible for the sex attacks throughout the county.' He explained.

Fran contrived to look both modest and raring to go.

'It's a very tenuous lead,' Farmer said at last, ungraciously.

The fool! Couldn't he see that bad-mouthing an officer entrusted with a special assignment wasn't a wise move, especially in the presence of another senior officer known to be her lover?

'Do we have any others?' the Chief asked mildly.

'No, sir. We don't, sir. So I shall get my team on to this immediately,' he added, more positive and enthusiastic with every syllable. It had clearly dawned on him that it was, after all, the Chief Constable he was addressing.

Fran's mouth was twitching with amusement. Mark had a feeling she dared not catch his eye, any more than he risked catching hers.

Could the others feel the electricity sizzling between them? He hoped not. All he dared do was nod with professional sagacity. What he wanted was to whip her back to his office and make love to her. Since that wasn't an option, he'd bloody well take her shopping on the way home and buy her the modern equivalent of a new hat. Or would do if they weren't both working late on this case. What had fired him up as it had fired her? Surely more than the thrill of the chase.

'I'd rather we kept back the news about our "celebrity",' Fran put in, as the two DCs left the room. 'Just treat it as an anonymous lead for now. But copy me in on every scrap of information about Jim Holden. Everything.'

'The way you've kept me informed?' Farmer asked sourly.

It was a pity for him he wasn't out of earshot. The Chief said nothing, but sighed heavily, catching Mark's eye and looking heavenwards. And he would be the one to chair the interview panel when the post was ratified.

Mark wondered how Farmer would react to a word in his ear? In the spirit in which it was meant or simply as a grouse from a colleague's lover?

* * *

Farmer continued his downbeat mode in the privacy of his own office. 'There's nothing about a Jim or James Holden on any of the computer databases.'

Fran breathed out very gently. 'Chummie's DNA isn't on record, either,' she reminded him. 'Indulge me, Joe. Let's just go with this until he's out of the frame. Let's bring him in and talk to him, very low key.'

'We don't want him suing us for wrongful arrest.'

Was this why the investigation had dragged? Because the poor man was so afraid he was going to get blots on his copybook that he didn't dare take risks?

She smiled. 'Bring in those two new DCIs and tell them I'm having a brainstorm and to indulge me. Tom Arkwright's up to speed on the stalking case. And as you know Jon Binns has been burdened with my thoughts on this one. So I think they should be involved, too. Let's bring in DC Whatshername — Sue something. Bright lass. Lots of auburn hair.'

'Do you mean DC Hall, by any chance?'

She ignored the sarcasm. 'That's the one. I told you how committed she was. No need to involve the whole unit unless things get interesting. My responsibility, Joe. If everything goes pear-shaped, you can blame it on the whim of an aged old biddy, and when I retire you can tell everyone it was about time too. No need for you to lose face.' If she expected him to protest, he didn't. Old, was she? She'd show him.

'The new DCI has insisted on a profiler, by the way.'

She gasped.

'Oh, he's come up with the usual wishy-washy psychology. Problem childhood, unusual relations with women, you know the sort of thing.'

'Nothing more specific?'

'To tie him in with your suspect? Well, he's probably got two eyes and a nose, hasn't he?'

She stopped herself punching either her colleague or the air. But she wanted to do both. Celebrate she must. If she had time, she'd take time out after work to buy some truly sexy undies. No better way to celebrate than with an evening doing what she and Mark did best.

But the work must come first.

Jon Binns had had Holden's personnel details faxed over. 'A lot of blanks in the CV,' he reported to the cabal in Fran's office. Everyone else must know something was up, just from the sudden scurrying around, but they would have to wait.

'Let's hear what you have got,' Fran suggested.

'Jim Holden. Born West Bromwich, 1950,' he said.

'I suppose someone's got to be,' Tom interjected, like an excited puppy.

She frowned him down.

'Educated at Bristnall Hall Secondary Modern, Chance Tech, Gosta Green College of Advanced Technology. A variety of qualifications. Lots of jobs in industry, most in car factories. Period at what became MGRover. Car crash in the Eighties. Off work for some years.'

'Years!' Fran interjected. 'Must have been a bad smash.'

'Worth checking if there was any other reason for his not working, ma'am?' Sue Hall put in. 'Such as prison?'

'Of course. But the crash might have been bad enough. Any more, Jon?'

'Starts picking up qualifications again, mostly non-vocational, hobby-type subjects. French, Spanish. Creative writing.'

Tom whistled. 'Bloody hell.'

They exchanged a huge grin.

'Tell them, Tom. Just remember, everyone, that this is highly confidential.'

'Dilly Pound—'

'Hang on,' Sue Hall interrupted. 'That's the reporter who was so persistent at your news conference, right? And the one who interviewed you for TVInvicta when you were assaulted?'

'Good-looking woman,' Jon nodded.

'OK for a bit of arm candy,' Tom said, 'but not all that much between the ears, like. Anyway, some bugger's been stalking her — sending anonymous letters pretty well every day and maybe doing other things — and she asked the guvnor here for help. You can't say she's been exactly forthcoming and helpful, but she managed to dredge up the names of some men from her past. And it seems she fancied writing a bit of poetry, like, and turned up at a creative writing class too.'

Jon smiled, the lovely long smile of a man solving a crossword puzzle clue. 'Where she met our friend Jim Holden. Ah, ha!'

But Tom was shaking his head. 'Doesn't work, guv. All the letters to Dilly were posted in London, remember. And if he was living in—?'

'Canterbury,' Jon said, running his finger down the record sheet.

'—And working full-time, like, he couldn't have posted them. Not if he was popping up all over Kent to assault young girls.'

Fran felt herself deflate. But for the sake of the others she mustn't be seen to let go. 'Let's just forget that, just for a minute.'

'With respect, ma'am,' Sue said, 'you can't just ask someone to post what were presumably quite unpleasant letters for you. They'd ask questions. Especially if it was every day.'

She shook her head as if they were importunate insects. 'Maybe he could.' But she couldn't see how, not just yet. It was there, wasn't it, tucked into some part of her brain?

But Tom rushed in. 'Maybe he's got an accomplice who shares the thrills. Maybe they're in cahoots over the assault business too.'

'Hence Chummie's ability to pop up all over the bloody county?' Jon murmured.

'Yes!' Sue joined in. 'What do we know of Holden's personal circumstances? Is he married?'

Jon shook his head. 'No record at any point. Mind you, people don't always, do they?'

People like her and Mark. She didn't want to be soiled by analogy. But she said, she hoped without missing a beat, 'Check, please. Live-in lover; mother; maiden aunt; whatever.'

'It would figure if whoever it was has recently been taken ill, wouldn't it?' Sue Hall said. 'So he lost his post person and had to stay in to care for him or her?'

Where had she dug that up from? It was a hell of a leap of logic.

But reluctantly, Sue was shaking her head. 'But that wouldn't work. Whoever it was would see the same name on the same letter day after day and start asking questions.'

'Unless,' Fran said quietly, the idea surfacing at last as the memory of her encounter in Canterbury came to her mind, 'whoever posts the letters can't see the address on the envelope. What if his post person is blind?' She could feel the atmosphere chill. The guvnor had clearly lost it, hadn't she? 'OK. Let's call a halt now. No point in speculating, not when there are hard facts out there. Jon, to Watchbrief, or whatever they call themselves. Sue and Tom, off to his home address.

Tact,' she added, nodding to Joe Farmer, 'is the order of the day. If you think a search is called for, get the warrant first. We'll play this absolutely by the book.'

To her amazement Farmer looked at his watch. 'It's after five already, but it'd be nice to do as much as we can tonight. I'll get overtime authorised,' he said. 'Now, remember to keep it low key.'

'Don't worry, I'll remember,' Fran said dourly.

Everyone, Farmer to Hall, stared.

'I've earned this last collar,' she said.

* * *

She should be ashamed of herself, muscling in on the youngsters' fun like this. Truly, deeply ashamed. And part of her was. Mostly she felt the old exhilaration — she wouldn't have missed it for anything.

The traffic was heavy, and the rain sheeting down, so she was glad to let Tom take responsibility for driving. He and Sue exchanged a prolonged banter. Dilly Pound, eat your heart out. So she sat quietly in the back, texting Mark to explain what she was up to and receiving a message in return: !!! LOL.

Then a call.

'Jill?'

'Rob's home,' Jill said flatly. 'Brian's just picked him up from the station. Do you want me to bring him straight over?'

'Actually, I'm out on a job. In any case, are you asking me as a police officer or as a friend?'

'What's the difference?'

'As an officer I'd like him grilled now. As a friend — and therefore a nice cuddly human being — I'd suggest you all go out for a nice curry and talk family talk.'

Jill snorted with laughter. 'There's only one problem with that. Can you tell me where in Ashford I can get a nice curry?'

* * *

Jim Holden lived in a Victorian terraced house within spitting distance of Canterbury West Station, his work van parked twenty yards or so down the street. Someone had made an attempt to brighten grey pebble-dash with window boxes, but at this stage of the winter the pansies looked frowsty and bedraggled. The door was painted the most vivid yellow she'd ever seen outside a children's fairytale book.

She nodded at the entry. 'Tom, just make sure he doesn't try the back door route, would you?'

'Ah. The ginnel probably runs two ways, doesn't it?'

'The what?'

He pointed.

'You foreigners!' Sue laughed. 'You mean the back alley!'

Fran joined in the laughter, but looked at her watch. 'Come on, we're not here to discuss the vagaries of dialect.'

Sue Hall knocked the front door, doing the honours when a middle-aged man appeared. He peered from one to the other, and finally, without saying anything, stepped back, letting them in. His appearance was as anonymous as it could be: greyish skin, greyish hair, greyish clothes. And spectacles with lenses that darkened as the light hit them.

The front door opened into a tiny vestibule, with another door, complete with a rather fine stained glass insert, only six feet or so from the first. So they processed in single file past a closed door into a good-sized living room, presumably with a kitchen and possibly a bathroom beyond. The fireplace might have been original; the ceiling rose certainly was. There were bookshelves either side of the chimney breast, one side occupied not by books but by individual audiotapes and complete audio-books. The Bible — Authorised Version; Shakespeare; Dickens; modern crime fiction — someone had catholic tastes. To Fran's mind the walls called out for mirrors or paintings, but they were bare. There was an expensive sound system, but no TV. Fran's heart considered sinking. By the look of her, Sue's already had.

Fran smiled, 'No television, Mr Holden?'

'This is my sister's room,' he said, as if that explained everything. 'Bigger than mine. Tidier.'

'Is she in?'

'Eve? Still on the train home, I should think. Her first day back at work. She's had the flu — very nasty.'

'Perhaps we should be talking in yours, then. Because we wanted to ask you about what you watched on TV. Or more precisely, who.'

There was no sign of guilt, let alone panic.

'Shall we look, Mr Holden?'

'If you want.' He gestured back to the tiny entrance hall and the room off it. As he said, it was small, but equally tidy, with a crucifix on the chimney breast and another Bible on the mantelpiece. If she'd hoped for pictures of Dilly to cover the wall, she was disappointed. But there was a laptop closed on the table below the laden bookshelf nearer the window, with a printer on the floor beneath. A plasma TV screen dominated the further alcove. It must be clearly visible from the street. Another day and she might have given him a lecture on crime prevention.

'Tell me what you watch on TV,' she said gently.

'Not very much. I'm not at home much. I work a lot of overtime.'

She felt less sympathetic. 'So you don't watch the news? On TVInvicta?'

'Why should I?'

Was he genuinely naıve or busy pulling wool? 'To renew your acquaintance with a fellow student. Dilly Pound.'

He smiled reminiscently. 'Delia's a much nicer name. Dilly! Where did they think that one up? These media types.'

'So you've been writing to her, have you?' Sue asked.

He nodded. 'I keep hoping for a reply.'

'I think you'll find, Jim, it helps if you put your address on the paper,' Sue observed, her irony earning a minute shake of the head from her boss. 'Which reminds me, what brought you down here? A long way from home, aren't you?'

'I got made redundant. MGRover. I'd got a job in security, when they said I was fit to work. Rover went belly up. My sister was always on at me to move down here. And I thought, why not? And then I saw Delia!' His face lit up.

Candy from baby time. She let Sue carry on. 'On the local or the national news?'

'Both, of course. I was so proud of her when she was being broadcast all over the country, I had to write to her.'

'You wrote letters, not poems?' Sue demanded.

'She didn't like my poems. She used to laugh at them, the way they rhymed. I don't use rhymes anymore.'

'Where do you get your ideas for writing now?'

He turned and patted the Bible. 'And Shakespeare. And,' he added, reaching for a volume from the shelves, 'DH Lawrence. They say he's out of fashion these days, but I still read him. I suppose it's a Midlands thing.'

Sue didn't get involved in lit crit. 'Before you saw Dilly on national TV you did nothing? Even though you knew where she was working?' she persisted.

'I don't want to talk about this any more.'

'That's a shame, because we'd like you to come along to Police Headquarters to talk about it. Shall I leave Eve a note?'

He turned on her with something like exasperation. 'If you did, how would she read it? She's blind, officer. Blind.'

Sue gasped audibly.

Fran raised a minatory eyebrow and took over, still speaking gently, reasonably. 'So how would you let her know if you were going out? Phone? Or would you rather talk a bit more here? We could have a cup of tea, if you want one? Sue, can you oblige?'

He shook his head. 'No, no. Everything has to be just so. If you start messing about in the kitchen and leaving things in the wrong places it'll really mess up her system.'

'OK, no tea, then,' Fran agreed. 'Now, Jim, we know you've sent Dilly some letters and some flowers. They were gorgeous, by the way. You must have spent a lot of money on them.'

'If a job's worth doing, it's worth doing well, that's what my grandma used to say.'

'And you went to London for them?'

'Eve wanted me to go with her for some hospital appointment. Women's troubles,' he added.

'But you didn't want them to arrive that day?'

'I wasn't sure if she'd like them. I thought I could always cancel. But when I saw the way she smiled at me I knew it'd be OK.'

Oh, dear. Would he be fit to answer formal questions? Would he be fit to plead when the trial came up?

'And you wore masks when you were looking through her windows,' Sue said, obviously trying not to glace in triumph at Fran. 'Why did you do that?'

'Look at me, officer. I'm no oil-painting. I didn't want to put her off, did I?'

Sue looked at her in anguish. Was he really as off beam as this?

'Where did you buy them?'

'Shop local, that's me. Down the road — the place near the Cathedral. But I only wore them at night. A lot of people wear them to party in, don't they?'

'So when you followed her during the day, you didn't bother? Tell me, Jim, why did the CCTV cameras never pick you up?'

'Chance, I suppose,' he said doubtfully.

As if.

'It's so lovely to see her again — renew our relationship, you might say,' he said, confident again.

Fran might, if there'd ever been a relationship.

'The trouble is, Jim, she didn't want to renew your acquaintance. She didn't like all your visits and letters. Pestering someone like that is called stalking, and it's against the law. And,' Fran added, suspecting the innocent bewilderment in his face was entirely feigned, 'I think you know it is. Otherwise why did you post all the letters in London?'

'Oh, that wasn't me. That was Eve.'

She really ought to get the FME to check him over to see if he was fit enough to be questioned. 'Did she know what she was posting?'

'Of course not! She wouldn't have liked the idea of my having a young lady in case it upset our living arrangements. It may well, of course.'

Sue smothered a giggle.

'Competition entries or bills — that was what she thought they were.'

'Jim, stalking's quite a serious offence, you know. Have you got a solicitor whom you could talk to? Because there are one or two other things we want to talk to you about, too. When Eve comes home. And we'll be applying for a search warrant.'

'You will remember to put everything back exactly where you found it? I don't want Eve to fall over anything.'

'Have you always looked after Eve?' Sue asked.

'I don't look after her! Only when she's ill. She was so bad last week I had to take time off work so she could stay in bed. Normally she's an independent woman, holds down a very good job, far better than mine, I can tell you.'

'But you've never married.'

He produced a wistful smile. 'When I met the only lady I ever wanted to marry I wasn't in a position to propose. I'd been in a very serious car crash, ladies, and hadn't been able to work for years. A nervous breakdown, on top of the physical injuries, you understand. And memory problems. Eyesight, too. So it came to nothing. Until now. And now I've found her again,' he declared, his face as rapt as Dean Fellows'.

'Didn't you have any other girlfriends at all in Birmingham?'

His face flushed puce. 'I . . . er . . . you're both ladies. I wouldn't want to talk about it.'

'You mean you saw prostitutes? But not here in Canterbury?'

'My sister . . . what if she found out?' He turned to face the TV, knuckles white as he gripped the back of a chair.

Sue looked at her watch. 'Time's going on, Jim. How would you normally tell Eve you were going out?'

For answer he turned tail and bolted, heading for the back door. They gave chase, with a silly after-you moment, in which Sue, the young, fitter woman, thought she ought to invite Fran to take the lead. At least it gave Tom, by now soaking wet, something to do.

CHAPTER TWENTY-TWO

Though it was nearly ten, Fran still looked flushed and happy, leaning back in her chair while Mark sat on the corner of her desk, toasting her with water.

'Two birds with one stone, eh?' Mark grinned. 'Stalker and flasher in one neat collar.'

She shook her head. 'We can't be absolutely certain that Jim Holden's the flasher. Not yet. Jon and his team haven't finished searching his house. Tom and Sue are still talking to him.' Tom, who'd been soaked to the skin, wore, at her insistence, borrowed clothes that didn't quite fit. The medics had agreed that Holden was dotty, but sane enough to be cautioned. The duty solicitor was in attendance.

'What's the circumstantial evidence?'

'His work schedules for one thing. We know he fixed or maintained the cameras in many of the locations where the assaults took place. We know he had a variety of masks. But we can't actually prove he assaulted anyone, not yet. None of the victims say they could identify their assailant.'

'For God's sake, surely one out of all those women—'

'You'd have thought. We shall begin interviewing them all again tomorrow and certainly go for conventional ID as well if we possibly can. I don't like a case resting simply on DNA — it always feels a bit of a cheat.'

'Like being LBW, not bowled . . .'

She looked blank.

'When we're both retired, my love, I shall convert you to cricket. And then you'll at last appreciate the finer intricacies of the English language. Now, what are you going to do with him overnight?'

'In about half an hour, I shall get them to shove him in a cell down in Maidstone nick. I shouldn't think he'll ask for bail. Meanwhile, let's hope for a full confession. But I want to go at it obliquely.'

'You?'

She nodded, amused. 'Me. Devious old me. I'm just going to drop into the interview room for a minute.'

'Can I watch?'

'You won't learn anything. It's the oldest trick in the book. In fact,' she said, getting to her feet, 'you may want to play it yourself. Go on, it's a fair offer!'

'So's this,' he said, slipping from the desk and grabbing her as she brushed past. She liked being kissed hard, so he obliged. 'For two pins,' he continued, as they surfaced, 'I'd lay you here and now on the carpet.'

Her eyes gleamed.

The phone rang. Her transformation from excited lover to cool professional choked a laugh from him as he turned to face the window to calm down. It was one thing for everyone to know about their relationship, another to demonstrate it quite so clearly.

'Not at all. It's good of you to phone me.' There was a note of impatience in her voice. Clearly someone lowly the other end was going through all the formalities due to her rank. 'So how is he?' she prompted at last, making circling movements with her right hand as if to elicit the news more quickly and rolling her eyes as the thin voice from the other end continued to spout verbiage. But her face was instantly serious as she asked, 'But he'll live?'

More talk. Couldn't whoever it was give a nice monosyllabic yes or no?

'Of course . . . Of course . . . I understand . . .'

Who was she talking about? It sounded as if she really cared, or was that simply another of her skills?

'No, I quite appreciate . . . Oh, I should be back at my desk by nine . . . I'm still at it, that's why!' And, this time laughing wryly, she cut the call. 'Cheeky sod. Only giving me lip for not starting at seven. It's that vicar. Dilly's vicar. Stephen Hardy. They've found him.' Suddenly she looked tired.

He put his arm across her shoulders. 'But not in perfect health, I gather?'

She shook her head. 'Broken back and exposure. Not a good combination. Fell down a disused mine working on Bodmin. Touch and go. Poor Dilly.'

And poor Fran. She was genuinely touched. Why? She'd only met the man once. She stared at the phone.

'Will you tell her?'

She moved away from him, shaking her head sadly. 'Only if he dies. I think that's what he'd want. As for her — who knows what she wants? Come on, let's go and talk to Jim Holden.' She picked up her jacket, case and bag, and, as they left the office, turned to lock it. 'That's it for the night, whatever happens.'

'Knackered?'

'Not while there's this much adrenaline coursing the old veins. Getting to sleep, that's always the worst problem, isn't it?'

Grinning, he fished a small elegantly wrapped package from his own case and shook it enticingly before her nose. 'Courtesy that nice new shop in Fremlin Walk,' he said. 'And no, you certainly can't open it till we get home.' He tucked it away again, but shook the case in front of her from time to time as they made their way down to the interview room where Tom and Sue were still talking to Jim Holden. A glimpse through the window in the observation room next door suggested that fatigue had set in all round. Even his solicitor seemed three-quarters asleep.

Mark stayed where he was, to watch the proceedings, as she breezed in. He'd fully expected her to leave everything she was carrying with him — wasn't it a mite unprofessional to show quite so clearly you were going home? But no, there she was case and all.

'Right, gentlemen, how are we getting on?'

Tom eased himself to his feet and drew her to the door, turning so that Holden couldn't see his mouth. It also meant Mark couldn't hear. But the young man's body language suggested that Holden was still playing the innocent, and would continue to do so until science proved him a liar.

Fran turned back into the room, concern all over her face. Spurious concern, if he knew her. 'Look, Jim, I'm sorry this is all taking so long. Do you want to phone your sister to tell her where you are? She must be worried sick.'

His face glimmered with bravado. 'That's not necessary. I'm never at home in the evening. Rarely till midnight, sometimes later. She won't stay up.'

'Good. Because I want you to explain to these nice young officers exactly how you spend your evenings.'

'But—'

'You see, I think you've been spending your evenings doing something far worse than going with prostitutes. I think you've been assaulting a lot of young women. And some older ones too.'

'You've got no evidence—'

His solicitor shushed him.

'A simple gob swab will provide us with all the evidence we need. But we'd all much rather you made a clean breast of it all. We might even tell the judge how cooperative you were. Come on, Jim — then we can all go home. Oh, no, Jim: not you. We've got accommodation set aside in Maidstone nick. Just as tidy as your room. But somewhat less cluttered.'

Mark was in the corridor miming applause when she came out. Instead of punching the air, she was shaking her head. 'They always give themselves away somehow, don't they? OK, I'd better let Dilly know she can sleep soundly tonight.'

'It's a good job someone will be able to,' he said, patting his case again.

* * *

Fran made it to her desk by eight fifty-five, not bad at all considering the time she and Mark had finally settled to sleep. In fact, if she knew her body, she'd be bright all day, and a zombie tomorrow. She rubbed her hands. She'd best make the most of today, then.

The phone rang bang on nine. As she picked it up, she had a vision of some piskie of a Cornish policeman watching the second hand of the station clock jerk slowly onward until he dared pounce on his handset. Was she as scary as that?

'Fran, it's Jill. Rob's refusing to get out of bed. Literally. Absolutely doesn't want to talk to you. Insists he's going to leave school.'

'Not a good curry, then?'

'The pits.'

Fran suppressed a sigh. The obligations of friendship. But someone like Rob could go good ways as easily as he could go bad ones, and maybe a nudge from her might help. If it didn't? She'd better make sure it did.

'A spot of tough love from Auntie Fran? Because I can really only do tough, Jill.'

'Liar. OK, I've seen you reduce grown men to tears, but I've also seen you hug them better if they needed it. I can't do it; Brian can't do it. Actually, it was Tash who suggested you. She rates you. And Mark.'

'I must remember to tell him,' Fran responded dryly enough to make Jill laugh. 'Look, I've got a few things to sort out here, then I'll come and get him. If you think he'll still be there.'

'I'd stake my teeth on it. And — Fran? — he did nick that silver.'

'I know. I'm sorry. And those bruises? On your forearms?'

'Yes. But Fran,' she almost shouted down the phone, 'I did fall down the stairs. That was nothing to do with him. Honest. I promise.'

'OK, Jill. Now, don't worry any more than you have to. I'll be round as soon as I've got things under way here.'

Before the phone could ring again, in came Tom and Sue, quite as pleased with themselves as they were entitled to be, and maybe a little bit more. She saw Mark and herself mirrored in them.

'Just the paperwork to do now, like, guv. Jon and his team found enough to put him away for a good long stretch.'

'Pity about that sister of his, Eve,' Fran said, half ashamed for raining on their parade.

'Don't you believe it, ma'am,' Sue responded. 'According to Jon she kept on and on about how miserable he was. She blames the accident. She said he had a bang on the head bad enough to bring about a personality change. A cheerful, outgoing lad, she said he was — it's all on paper and on tape. Says she hopes at last he'll get some proper treatment.'

'In today's prisons? She's got to be joking! Pile 'em high, shunt off to the next nick quick. Oh, and send their stuff to a different nick. I heard all about it from Ian. A friend, many years ago. An OU lecturer. He died. He tried to help loads of cons through courses, and the prison system seemed hell-bent on preventing any sort of continuity. Some hope of rehabilitation!' She got a grip. 'Now, I'm going to bring in young Rob Tanner. He's got a habit he supports by nicking from his mum, and possibly other people.'

'From DCI Tanner! Bloody hell! Those bruises—'

A look shut her up. Sue'd soon learn there were some times you had to put your brain in gear before you opened your mouth.

'That young scrote Field admitted to getting kids hooked — mightn't he have done the same to Rob?' Sue almost pleaded. 'She's a decent guvnor, DCI Tanner. She's a better cop than she looks.' She stopped abruptly, and blushed deeply. 'Sorry, ma'am.'

Fran managed something between a sigh and a laugh. 'I've known that since before you were born, Sue. And for God's sake, if we're going to work together, learn to call me guv, like the others.'

* * *

'Jill, with your permission, I'm going to treat him more as a victim of crime than as a petty crook. We may get more out of him that way?'

'OK. I'll just call him.' The doubt in Jill's voice suggested she wouldn't do so particularly loudly.

'You get the coffee on. I'll sort it.'

'His bedroom — I've tried airing it . . .'

'For God's sake, Jill, I've seen scruffy pads before now!'

But at the door she almost turned back, revolted by the smell of unwashed male feet, old pot, cigarettes and testosterone. What had happened to the old Fran, the Fran who'd been known to adjust an accident victim's head to give mouth to mouth, only to have it come off in her hands? Who'd picked through clouds of blowflies to identify a putrefying mess as a dead old man?

The bundle under the duvet might look endearing or exasperating depending on your viewpoint. Fran just saw the giant maggot, with a tiny lock of hair escaping, as infinitely vulnerable, despite its unattractive habitat. She threw open a window. If you listened carefully you could hear the urgent calls of birds responding to the spring. They always made her feel that life was to be lived. Poor Rob simply huddled deeper. She braced herself. Off with the duvet in one swift, unkind movement. Rob huddled in aged T-shirt and boxer shorts. His legs looked absurdly thin, despite the tufting of coarse hair, and the feet, in tennis socks, enormous.

'Fuck off, will you. Just fuck off!'

‘It’s not your mother. It’s dear old Auntie Fran. The shower’s running, and since there’s a water shortage you’d better not waste any more. When you’ve showered and washed your hair, you can shave.’

‘What the fuck?’

‘You’re coming along to police headquarters to answer a few questions. And I don’t want you looking like a dog’s breakfast and upsetting my officers. Get it?’

‘Fuck you.’

‘Rob, that shower’s going to run out of hot water any moment now. And I tell you this, you’re having a shower and a shave even if the water’s ice-cold. Up to you. Now, move.’ This time she removed the bottom sheet.

* * *

‘I still can’t understand,’ he said, drooping as far from her as the seatbelt would permit, ‘why you wouldn’t let me bring Mum.’

She hardened her heart against a yob suddenly turning needy infant. She’d seen it so many times before, but once she’d loved Rob. Perhaps she still did, though she certainly didn’t like him very much at the moment. ‘I didn’t think you’d want her, a grown lad like you. Besides which, I’ve something to show you that you might prefer her not to see.’

‘Whatever.’ There was more anger and resentment, she fancied, than curiosity.

‘You’ll see it when we get to Maidstone. And when you’ve had some breakfast. Then one of my lads’ll run you back to school.’

‘Fuck school.’

‘And all your GCSEs no doubt. OK. Not my problem. Now, just be quiet while I drive.’

‘Some cop! Can’t drive and talk at the same time!’

‘Not if I don’t want to.’ She snapped on Classic FM. Let him chew on that.

If spring was really springing, she might just treat them both to a dose of countryside. She couldn't imagine that he'd enjoy looking at the greening of the fields and trees, but she would and she was the driver.

She was slowed down by a small van, one with an estate agent's name on the back, obviously looking for a turning. On impulse, she followed him when he found the right lane. When he stopped, she stopped. He was erecting a For Sale sign, on the verge, an arrow directing those interested along what was little more than a track.

'What the fuck?'

'Who rattled your cage?' she responded.

'But a lane, man! A fucking lane!'

'Detective work,' she snapped. No, she wouldn't follow the arrow, not with a passenger — to do Rob justice, not with any passenger except Mark. She jotted down the name of the agent and the location, did a nifty job of a many pointed turn in a narrow space, and set off once again to Maidstone.

* * *

'The silent treatment and a lot of food,' Fran told Tom. 'We'll see what that'll do. Then we'll get the Child Protection people to show him his movie. They're trained and we're not, that's why.'

'Plus you think he's a snotty little runt, and you don't want to upset DCI Tanner by telling him so.'

She rewarded Tom with a look. 'Just get on with it. But let me know when he's going to be shown the film — I want to watch his reaction.'

She left Rob in the capable hands of him and Sue, possibly pleased to delay the mountain of paperwork heading inexorably their way. They'd strict instructions to feed him the most nutritious brunch they could find — she was sure his refusal to contemplate food was more to annoy her than because he wasn't hungry.

There was no one from Child Protection available till lunchtime, so Rob was left to cool his heels and talk to them about whatever came into their heads. Eventually, they accompanied him to the Child Protection suite, where victims of abuse were normally interviewed. Its emphasis on the youngest in the age group, biologically correct dolls, Lego, teddies and other comforting distractions clearly made Rob feel superior. Until they produced the disk of the revamped porn film.

Standing behind the soundproof screen with the officer video-recording Rob's reactions, Fran saw him crumple from arrogant guy with street cred into a terrified kid.

'I promised I wouldn't tell. Now they'll kill me. I tell you, they'll fucking kill me!'

CHAPTER TWENTY-THREE

It was hard to leave Rob in other people's hands, even though she knew specialised colleagues would do the job of extracting information and, just as important, putting him back together as a functioning human being better than she ever could. Or Jill, for that matter. And Jill would be frantic by now, so she gave her a reassuring call.

'He'll be all right, Jill, honestly. If he's been blackmailed into buying and using pot, not to mention other things, he's probably got some cold turkey to do. But we'll get the Drugs Referral officer in too.'

'I wish I thought I was doing the right thing.'

'Parents never do the right thing. Even the best ones. Every kid knows that.' They shared a laugh. 'And sometimes kids don't respond even if their parents are perfect.' She could have told Jill about the cold shoulder systematically applied by Mark's kids, but she wouldn't break his confidence. 'But people survive. Parents and kids. Anyway, I'll make sure he's back in one piece in time for supper.'

'Could you and Mark bring him and stay for a bite to eat?'

'Not this time, thanks.' She added, 'I've an idea it won't be a very comfortable meal, and the presence of comparative strangers—'

'You're hardly a stranger!'

'Mark is. In any case, Jill, I've got to take the team out for a quick jar, haven't I?'

Which was hardly the most sensitive remark, given whose team they were, and how their proper leader wouldn't be getting much credit for the way she'd managed it. The police could forgive her being injured, preferably in the course of duty, but not for the rumours of her inefficiency that had circulated beforehand, whatever the cause.

'Send them my best. And thank them for the present. Joe Farmer may have brought it round, but I can't imagine the idea was his. It's brilliant, Fran. Thanks.'

'Joe! Well, he does have a human side. Well, well, well. Good for him.' Who on earth had asked him to do the honours? 'Ah, I've got a call waiting. I must go. I'll be back in touch as soon as I can.'

Should she feel guilty that the incoming call was from the estate agent whose van she had tailed earlier? She tried very hard to. But this, she felt in her bones, was important. On the other hand, Mark had had so many feelings in his bones they could be a symptom of arthritis.

'It's just come on the market,' the smooth young man announced. 'If you're interested, I could pop the particulars in the post tonight.'

'Georgian vicarage. Four bedrooms. Two acres of garden. Why don't you fax them to me now?'

* * *

Still no news from Cornwall. Perhaps they thought she'd meant nine in the evening? Where was their number? This pile or that? Her desk was as messy as it always used to be. Well, that was the end of a case for you, always masses of paper. And a good deal more to come. The kids would have the lion's share, but she'd have to make her own contribution. She ought to start now.

Would she hell! She legged it down to the fax machine, trying to look casual.

She'd long since learned that the trick in any organisation was to keep your head down and study documents even as you paced the power-soaked corridors. So long as she kept her face serious and eyes lowered, no one would guess that she was reading about her future home.

Tidying her desk would have to wait. As she settled to gloat over the details of the house, the phone rang. She had visitors waiting in Reception. Courtesy was supposed to cost nothing, wasn't it? So should she send her secretary down to bring them up or pop down herself? Poking the layer of flesh on her hips, she knew the answer.

Dilly and Daniel. How touching. Hand in hand, for once, and bearing a stiff bunch of flowers. Much as she'd have liked to grab it and run, she ushered them into the lift and along the corridors with maximum patience, and offered tea and coffee.

In return they proffered an expensive white envelope containing, oh yes, a wedding invitation. The Cathedral crypt, no less, would host the happy event.

She hoped she said all that was proper. Clearly congratulations were in order, even though she thought Dilly was making the worst mistake of her not very happy life. They sat rigidly opposite her, faces forward, like some figures in an American primitive painting she'd once seen, sipping in synchrony. Neither initiated any topic of conversation, and the one thing she knew Dilly would want her to talk about — Stephen — was clearly off the menu. How would they react to her deflecting some of their thanks to Janie Falkirk?

'She had some excellent points,' Daniel opined. 'But really we prefer a more . . . appropriate . . . setting for our worship. And we're lucky that one of the Cathedral clergy is a school governor. So she shall not only have her meringue day, she shall have it in the finest of buildings.' He patted his fiancée's hand possessively.

Fran's mother would have demanded, 'Who's she? The cat's mother?' Tempted though she was, Fran refrained. But it was nice to have a neutral memory of her mother pop up, when all her recent ones were of a woman whose quick tongue had been rendered vicious as her age weighed more heavily.

Dilly nodded, rewarding her fiancé with a quick sideways smile. But Fran could see something like resignation in eyes that should have been full of joyous anticipation.

'Will you carry on working for TVInvicta?' she asked, as much to fill a growing silence as anything.

The response cheered her. 'Of course. And Huw Venn's still got me down to do that feature on you when you leave the police force. That's definite. Nothing will stop me, not after what you and your team have done. Nothing.' Her jaw took on a welcome upwards jut.

McDine decided to step in. 'Can you tell me anything more about the man you've accused of stalking her? And why he did it?'

Did his phraseology suggest he still thought the whole thing a fantasy? Should she snarl at him? On the whole, she decided she couldn't be bothered. In any case, the sooner she'd got rid of them, the sooner she could look at the house details again and show them to Mark. 'He's Jim Holden from Dilly's William Murdock days: apparently he used to sit opposite her in class. He was off work after a car accident.'

Dilly nodded. 'It must have been very serious! He couldn't work.'

'That's right. But he can now, and makes a living fitting CCTV cameras — or failing to fit them, in the case of the one supposedly guarding your home. He fitted those in the Whitefriars Centre, so when he tailed you to and from TVInvicta he could make sure he was never picked up. Where he got the idea I don't know, but he was behind those jolly masks that peered through your windows. He wore the same ones when molesting young girls.'

Dilly shuddered.

'Paradoxically, the fact he fancied himself in love with you let you off lightly. We have evidence to suggest that he was involved in all sorts of sex crimes against women, all over the area, some minor, some much less so.'

'See! I was right!' Dilly exclaimed. 'I said I'd been tailed by someone with a Blair mask, and that it must be the same man!'

Daniel adopted the indulgent look of a man who knows he's in the wrong but would never accept the blame.

'It would have been helpful if you'd told us a little earlier. Think of the women who might have been spared horrible experiences,' Fran said, to Dilly but at McDine. 'It's a shame you don't see your writing as something to be proud of—'

'She's never going to make it on to the list of set texts,' McDine interrupted.

Bastard! Fran continued, '—because it is. And it took another woman to tell us about it. If she hadn't, your stalker might still be roaming the streets. Still, all's well that ends well, I suppose.'

'What sort of sentence will he get?' Dilly asked, suddenly reminding them all that she was an official crime correspondent.

'Hard to tell. Oh, he'll be put on the Sex Offenders' Register, no doubt about that. What he needs is not prison, but psychiatric treatment. I'm sure the judge will recommend that, in fact. Whether there are enough places in secure psychiatric units is another matter. He'll probably be sent to one prison after another, desperate for therapy but getting no continuity at all.'

'Poor man,' Dilly said.

After all, Fran did not anticipate a long and glittering career for her.

'Imagine trying to run a whole school full of people like him,' McDine huffed.

Dilly managed a cool sideways glance, but he took no notice. So she coughed. 'And how is your own case going, Fran? What'll happen to those kids who assaulted you?'

It took a lot to make Fran blush, and when she did this time it wasn't for a personal shortcoming. It was for her colleagues'. She had to save their face, though they would regret their sin of omission later. 'It's all in the hands of the Crown Prosecution Service,' she smiled.

* * *

She didn't smile when she heard her assailants had been let off with a caution. She smelt a spot of backstage legal bargaining here, playing off one injury against another. It wasn't just for herself she was angry. It was for all the other innocent victims who felt the law had dealt with their needs inadequately. The lack of information about how the case was progressing, the failure to check on the victim's health — and then a sense that with the miscreants walking free, that justice hadn't been done.

Well, she'd asked to be treated like Ms Average, and so she had. Maybe if a vacancy on an appropriate working party came up, she should take it after all.

* * *

The bar rang with triumphant voices. Although she was standing drinks for the whole team inevitably it was with the youngsters she'd worked with that she found herself sitting. The talk was about Rob.

'The question is, guv, will that kid ever be happy at that snotty school? Wouldn't he be happier at another school or maybe an FE college somewhere?' Tom looked genuinely worried. 'I know DCI Tanner would prefer him under her beady eyes, but look where that got him last time. He likes his gran, he's got a few mates up there in Yorkshire already and I'd have thought a clean start was just the answer.'

Sue, on the far side of the table, shook her head. 'That's letting the bullies win. You've got to face them down.' There was no doubting that she would have done.

Fran was careful not to look at Harbijan, lest she betray a confidence, but he put his glass down and said, 'Sometimes things are so bad you can't repair them. Never. Those teachers are going to be so pissed off their star pupil's going down for drug dealing and all his other little enterprises instead of heading for Oxbridge that they'll maybe pick on Rob.'

'Why? He was a victim, like!'

'And how many times have you heard people say rape victims have brought it on themselves? No, I reckon life'd be so intolerable he'd drop out.'

'He wouldn't have you to get him out of bed every morning, either, would he, guv?'

''Fraid not, Sue.' She had briefly toyed with inviting him into her home for a spot of respite care, but how could she inflict teenage angst on Mark, who'd been through it once with his own? Hell's bells, she didn't want it herself, or the effect it would have on their relationship in all its aspects. 'So it sounds as if Grandma's the best bet. Do you want me to drop a hint to Jill?'

'Rather you than us,' Tom said. 'Another, everyone?'

'My shout,' Fran said. 'And this is for your taxis home.' She fished some notes from her purse. 'Can't have any of you on drink-drive charges.' Her mobile rang. She was about to kill it, but saw who was at the other end. 'Hell. It's the Cornwall Police at long last. I'll take the call outside. Get the drinks in for me, Tom, would you?'

Outside the air was quite balmy, but her voice was icy. 'Fran Harman. What's the news?' One of her team would have heard further, implicit, words: *And why the hell has it taken so long to get back to me*? She listened without interruption, took contact details and returned to the youngsters. She could feel alert eyes trying to interpret her face. She sank half her wine in one go.

'How is he, that vicar, like?' Tom prompted her.

And the other half. 'He'll live, but he'll be paralysed, they say.'

Tom shook his head sadly. 'Trouble is, if Dilly marries that boring old fart he won't be the only one.'

Who was she to argue? In any case, there was Mark, ready to take her home.

CHAPTER TWENTY-FOUR

The full moon lit the vicarage as if it were about to feature in a ghost movie. Side by side, Fran and Mark leant on the front gate, contemplating it. Imagine having put in a firm offer, without all the preliminaries. And now, proud owners — they would certainly outbid any other offers that might come in, whatever they were — they had to see it again on their own, without the astonished estate agent.

'It needs a hell of a lot of work. Look at that roof.'

'There are probably grants available for a house that age.'

'What the brickwork will be like under that ivy, God knows.'

'Pointing's not all that hard a job. I could do some of it.'

'It's probably riddled with dry rot, wet rot and every other sort of rot.'

'They built to last in those days. The timber's probably as sound as that in your place or mine. But the gutters'll need replacing — and with a house this old you can't use your average B&Q plastic.'

'Who'd want to?'

'Listen!'

'I can't hear anything.'

'Exactly. No motorway, no barking dogs, no ghetto blasters, no factory.'

'Imagine trying to uncover that garden!'

'We'll pretend we've got a Roman villa underneath it all and get the Time Team in.'

'Yes. Or no. Once it's ours we can do anything. Anything we want.'

'Now we're together, there's nothing we can't do.'

They clasped hands.

THE END

THE JOFFE BOOKS STORY

We began in 2014 when Jasper agreed to publish his mum's much-rejected romance novel and it became a bestseller.

Since then we've grown into the largest independent publisher in the UK. We're extremely proud to publish some of the very best writers in the world, including Joy Ellis, Faith Martin, Caro Ramsay, Helen Forrester, Simon Brett and Robert Goddard. Everyone at Joffe Books loves reading and we never forget that it all begins with the magic of an author telling a story.

We are proud to publish talented first-time authors, as well as established writers whose books we love introducing to a new generation of readers.

We won Trade Publisher of the Year at the Independent Publishing Awards in 2023. We have been shortlisted for Independent Publisher of the Year at the British Book Awards for the last four years, and were shortlisted for the Diversity and Inclusivity Award at the 2022 Independent Publishing Awards. In 2023 we were shortlisted for Publisher of the Year at the RNA Industry Awards.

We built this company with your help, and we love to hear from you, so please email us about absolutely anything bookish at feedback@joffebooks.com

If you want to receive free books every Friday and hear about all our new releases, join our mailing list: www.joffebooks.com/contact

And when you tell your friends about us, just remember: it's pronounced Joffe as in coffee or toffee!

ALSO BY JUDITH CUTLER

FRAN HARMAN MYSTERIES
Book 1: COME TO HARM
Book 2: DO NO HARM

DETECTIVE KATE POWER MYSTERIES
Book 1: MURDER THE BOYS
Book 2: MURDER BY THE CANAL
Book 3: MURDER BY ARSON
Book 4: MURDER BY FRAUD
Book 5: MURDER IN DEVON
Book 6: MURDER ON THE JOB

Printed in Great Britain
by Amazon

42333985R00148